Cassidy's War

by

Susan Macatee

Cassidy's War

COPYRIGHT © 2012 by Susan Macatee

Cover Art by *Rae Monet, Inc. Design*

The Wild Rose Press
PO Box 708
Adams Basin, NY 14410-0708
Visit us at www.thewildrosepress.com

Publishing History
First American Rose Edition, 2012
Print ISBN 978-1-61217-011-4

Published in the United States of America

"I saw you at the tavern last night. With him."

She frowned.

He released his grip on her arm.

Taking a step away, she adjusted her felt hat. "Well, yes. I'm still trying to gather information, if you even care about the investigation anymore."

He caught the ire in her tone. "Did you?"

She shook her head. "Not anything that will help."

"I don't want you involved in the investigation any longer. It's too dangerous."

"But we can't just allow him to go free." Her fists clenched.

"I didn't say I'm abandoning the investigation, but there's more to it than you know."

Cassidy frowned. "What do you mean?"

He shook his head. "I can't tell you right now...but I don't want to see you anywhere near the man." He raised a finger. "I mean it, Cassie."

Her gaze darkened. He almost swore her eyes would spit fire. "I can't promise anything, George. You aren't being honest with me. How can I trust you? I'll do what it takes until he's brought down."

He grasped her arm. "You are being reckless. If your mother knew the risk you take by allowing Madison to court you, she wouldn't permit you to leave the house."

Praise for Susan Macatee

ERIN'S REBEL
Finalist, Ancient City Romance Authors
2010 Reader's Choice Award, paranormal category
~*~

"I love historical romances and Susan Macatee did a beautiful job with this one."

~Night Owl Reviews (4.5 Hearts)

"I loved the author's gentle hand with detail, her convincing touch with romance, and the twists and turns that she creates before a thoroughly satisfying ending…This book's well worth keeping on my shelf."

~WRDF Reviews

"Recommended read for paranormal and historical romance readers or if you simply enjoy a good love story."

~ParaNormal Romance

"*ERIN'S REBEL* is rich in history and mystery."

~TwoLips Reviews (4 Lips)

~~*~~

CONFEDERATE ROSE
1st place, First Coast Romance Writers
2010 Beacon Contest for Published Authors,
historical category
~*~

2nd place, 2010 New England Reader's
Choice Bean Pot Award, historical category
~*~

"If you like romance wrapped in the conflicts of the Civil War you will definitely enjoy this book."

~You Gotta Read Reviews

"*CONFEDERATE ROSE* is a magnificent work of fiction…I highly recommend this charming historical."

~Blue Ribbon Reviews at Romance Junkies
(4 Ribbons)

Dedication

To my nephew, Jason....

And in memory of my mom and dad,
Claire and Edward Xander.

Chapter One

Burkeville, Pennsylvania
April 11, 1870

"Help! Help me!"

The high-pitched, plaintive cry drew Cassidy Stuart's attention from the pots she washed in the basin on the table. She strode to the kitchen window, drying her hands on a towel, and scanned for the source. There, at the base of the oak tree beside the house, a tow-headed boy clutched his arm, the hand hanging limp.

Throwing down the dish towel, Cassidy grasped her skirts and swept out the door. Closer inspection revealed he was one of the Thompson twins. Just this past week, she'd examined both of them. Was this Joey or Bart...? She had trouble telling them apart.

"Joey?" she guessed.

The boy lifted his dirt-streaked face. "Yes, ma'am." He bit his lip, his face crumpling.

Cassidy's heart lurched. Such was the way of little boys, always getting hurt. "You were climbing the tree, I reckon."

He nodded.

Helping him cradle his thin arm, she gently lifted the injured limb he held against his chest.

"I'm right sorry, ma'am," he muttered. "I know I shouldn't have tried to climb all the way up."

She glanced toward the top of the majestic oak. "How far up were you anyway?"

"Almost clear to the top." A slight smile crossed

his face, quickly replaced by a grimace.

Gently, she probed and felt the break. *Clean, thank God.*

"Looks like it's broken. Stay right here, while I get it stabilized, then you can come into the office, and I'll make you a cast."

"Really?"

She smirked. "Sure. Now don't you move. I'll be right back." With a final glance to make sure he stayed, she rushed to her father's office.

Once there, a familiar pain washed over her as she remembered her father who had died in a carriage accident six months ago. She glanced around the room, which she still considered his office. Nothing had been changed since the day he had walked out the door to visit an ill patient. She shook her head to quash the image of her father, Dr. John Stuart. He'd been so proud when she'd decided to be a doctor after the war. But dreams were just that—dreams, some never coming true. Pushing her grief aside, she gathered a small splint and a roll of muslin bandages and raced back out.

After securing the limb, she lifted Joey to his feet, taking care not to jostle the boy, and guided him into the office. He clenched his jaw, obviously in a ton of pain.

"It's okay to cry," she told him.

"No, ma'am. Real men don't cry, especially in front of a lady."

Cassidy shook her head. *What fool had told him that?* "Once I get this set, I'll send someone for your ma."

He nodded and sat on the edge of the exam table. She wished someone else were home to hold him down while she set the limb. She brought out the container of *Plaster of Paris* and clean bandages and mixed the plaster to fashion the boy's cast.

Joey's gaze followed her. "What will it feel like

2

when you put that on?"

"A lot better than it does now. But you'll still have a lot of swelling, and your arm will hurt for a while as it heals. And you can't get this cast wet."

"Yes, ma'am."

She gently unwound the bandage securing the splint and examined the arm. Dipping a rag into the pan by his side, she wiped off a bit of dirt, then glanced at his face for any signs of distress. His jaw tightened, but he didn't cry out or flinch, although his face visibly paled. She placed a tongue depressor between his teeth. "Now you bite down on this. I've got to set the bone so it heals right. If you feel like crying, you go right ahead."

Joey bit down on the piece of wood, his eyes growing wide and his breathing strained. She hated like hell to hurt him, but the quicker she worked, the better.

After lifting the arm, she straightened it, then prepared to pull. "Okay, one, two, three..." She set the bone, stealing peeks at the boy's face for any undue distress. He bore down well.

"Good job. The worst is over. Now I'll wrap your arm in the bandage and smooth the plaster over it. Once it dries, I'll call on your ma."

An excellent patient, Joey nodded.

By the time she'd applied the plaster and allowed the cast to fully dry, the sound of the front door opening alerted her someone had arrived home. The office door creaked inward to reveal Cassidy's mother.

Arlene Stuart brushed a hand over her honey-colored bun to smooth it as she strode into the office. "I see we have an unexpected patient."

"Yes, ma'am, Mrs. Stuart," Joey replied.

"He fell from the oak tree outside the kitchen," Cassidy explained.

"Oh, I see." She inspected the cast.

"I'm finished in here," Cassidy said, "so now that you're home, I'll fetch his ma."

"I'd be more than happy to look after Joey." Her mother walked her to the office door. "I saw that fancy city doctor in town...Madison." She grimaced. "Folks don't have anything but praise for him. Think he's God's gift to the town now your father's gone."

"Doctor Madison," Cassidy spat. "He believes he can steal all our patients out from under us." She fisted her hands. "I just hope once Quinn finishes his internship in Harrisburg, we can rebuild the practice."

Arlene sucked on her lower lip. "What about the women you've been seeing as a midwife. They aren't abandoning you, are they?"

"I'm not sure. Mrs. Tasker mentioned Doctor Madison the other day. Wondered if he might be able to give her those newfangled pain relievers like ether or chloroform. And I'm not qualified to administer those."

"Oh, Cassie. I hope Quinn can help once he's back. Without payment from patients, we only have Matt's pay from the bank to keep us going." She glanced back at Joey who played with a tongue depressor. "Why don't you let his ma know he's here so she can fetch him? I'll keep him entertained in the meantime."

Cassidy nodded and left the office. She pinned her black felt hat on and threw a shawl over her shoulders, then sprinted to the Thompson home at the far end of town. Cassidy knocked on the door, but when no one answered, she discovered Mrs. Thompson behind the house hanging laundry. She stepped away from the clothesline at Cassidy's approach.

"Joey fell out of our tree and broke his arm. I've set it and put a cast on. My mother's with him now, if you'd like to come fetch him."

"I wondered where that boy had run off to. He's supposed to be cleaning out the chicken coop with his brother." With an exasperated sigh, the woman set the laundry basket aside and hurried after Cassidy.

Once Joey and his mother left, Cassidy decided to stroll through town. She pinned her reticule to the waistband of her skirt and tucked a small basket under her arm.

Across the street from the mercantile, she stopped. Bessie Mae Wilson and two other young women surrounded a tall, well-dressed man. Cassidy pursed her lips as Bessie Mae twirled her lace parasol and wiggled her bustle.

Was it Dr. Madison preening in front of more patients he aimed to steal? She'd only caught a few glimpses of the man since he'd arrived in town. He sported a thin mustache but was otherwise clean-shaven with chestnut hair on a handsome, though arrogant face, and appeared to be an outrageous flirt. She made it a point to steer clear of him whenever she could. Cassidy lifted her chin and straightened her hat. She'd seen enough of that charlatan.

She had stepped in the opposite direction when a familiar male laugh caused her to glance back. That voice had caused butterflies in her stomach many times. Bessie Mae giggled and turned in Cassidy's direction. Peering beyond the woman, Cassidy glimpsed the man she'd thought to be Madison. No, not the doctor. Getting a clear view, she gasped. The tall dark-haired man in gentlemen's clothing was none other than her former fiancé, George Masters.

Her urge was to turn and run as far as she could, but she froze in place. She hadn't seen George for five years, since he'd told her he couldn't marry her because she deserved much better than him.

After that, he'd left for lord knows where, leaving his ailing, alcoholic father behind. Not that she could blame him. Amos Masters had never been a father to his sons, and George's three older brothers had run off as soon as they were old enough. Amos had passed on several months ago, but no one could locate George, so the man was buried behind his shack without ceremony.

So, why was George here now?

****

George Masters peered beyond Bessie Mae's parasol. She'd only been a girl when he'd left town. Gawky and gangly as he recalled. But she'd filled out nicely, from her lush bosom to her perfectly rounded face. But frankly, he was perplexed by all the fuss. When he'd lived here, he'd been nothing but one of those no-account brats of Amos Masters. Even after returning from Confederate prison camp, he was looked on as nothing but his father's son, worthless in the townsfolk's eyes. He recalled all the stir he'd caused when Cassidy had accepted his marriage proposal. Gossip spread all over town at his audacity of daring to wed the respected physician's daughter. But now, after a five year absence, he'd returned to town wearing gentlemen's clothes.

Bessie Mae babbled on, drawing giggles from her friends, who crowded around him. She boldly rested a gloved hand on his coat sleeve.

"So, do tell, Mr. Masters. What have you been up to all these years since we last saw you?" She batted her ginger- colored lashes.

Glancing straight ahead, he gulped. He extracted Bessie's gloved hand from his arm. The woman he both longed and dreaded to see was in his sights. The woman he'd loved for years and planned to marry, Cassidy Stuart.

Her dark, shiny hair slicked smoothly back into

a bun at her nape and a jaunty black felt hat, adorned with a feather, perched on her head. Dressed head to toe in black, she would, of course, still be in full mourning for her father.

When she turned, she didn't appear to be wearing a bustle, a fashion many of the women in New York City now adopted. But then, Cassidy had never been a slave to fashion. He remembered how she swore to never wear a hoopskirt and even balked about wearing a crinoline.

She stood frozen to the spot on the planking across the road, her rounded lips forming a circle.

"Pardon me, Miss Bessie Mae, ladies." George eased his way through the women. "There's someone I must say hello to."

Bessie Mae's mouth gaped as her friends lifted handkerchiefs or gloved hands to their lips.

He ignored them and focused on the woman who'd been the love of his life since he was a lad. He'd followed her older brother around like a lost puppy and teased her mercilessly at every opportunity. Cassie, the only woman who'd kept his hopes up throughout the war, made his time in that hellish Rebel prison camp bearable, his one dream to escape and return to her.

Her green-eyed gaze drifted up and down his form as he drew close. He didn't have to turn his head to know Bessie Mae and her friends watched to see what would happen next.

"George...you look so...so..."

"You look real good, too, Cassie." He longed to wrap his arms around her but didn't dare. Not only because the whole town was watching, but knowing Cassie, she'd likely slap his face. Her all too familiar scent of lilac and her lush lips beckoned him nonetheless.

"What are you doing back in town? When your pa died, we couldn't locate you."

"I've been traveling these past five years. They weren't able to locate me...but when I finally got word, I thought..." He dropped his gaze.

"Of course. No matter what, you must show your respect."

"Cassie, I..." He poked his thumb over his shoulder. "...those ladies told me about your pa. I'm so sorry. He was like a father to me, too. You know that."

She nodded, biting her lip. He leaned forward. If he was going to hug her, now was the time. No one would fault him for comforting the woman he'd once planned to marry.

She allowed him to enclose her in his arms. Her warmth still enticed him even after all the years apart. Her face rested against his coat, and he sighed as her hands slid up his back. More fodder for the gossip mongers.

Abruptly, she yanked away, taking her softness and warmth with her. "George, I really have to go. I have an appointment with a patient."

"Patient?"

She nodded. "Quinn and I plan to take over Pa's practice...that is..."

He lifted her chin, forcing her to look into his eyes. "You're a doctor now?"

"Well, sort of. I never attended formal medical school, although I do plan to. But Pa taught me everything he knew."

"Glad to hear you're doing what you've always wanted."

She sighed. "I don't know. When Quinn comes back, maybe..."

"What's wrong?" George asked.

"Well, it's really not your concern, being you don't live in town anymore."

"Cassie, if something's troubling you, I want to know."

"I really don't think it's a good idea. I can fight my own battles, as you well know."

Pain burned his chest, but he backed off. What rights *did* he have after abandoning her?

"Goodbye, George." She abruptly turned away.

*****

Cassidy quickened her pace as she hurried home. Seeing George after so long had floored her. The sight of women fawning over him reminded her of when they were young. She'd spurned his attentions, thinking him nothing but a handsome flirt. At least until he'd gone off to war. After that everything changed.

But the emotions she'd buried deep inside after he'd left were still too close to the surface, threatening to send her racing back into his arms. She'd once felt safe there, but not anymore. When George left, she wondered how she'd ever recover. And with her father's death still so fresh, she had to take care of herself now...and not allow any man into her heart again.

Chapter Two

George gazed after Cassidy's retreating back. He couldn't blame her for shunning him. Hell, he was shocked she'd even spoken to him. Most women who'd been abandoned days before their wedding would be holding a shotgun to his chest.

No, he wouldn't force himself back into her life. She was trying to build a medical practice, a dream she'd had after the war. To be a doctor. He was not about to stand in her way. For all he knew, she'd married or had a beau.

George glanced around the town he used to call home. Not much had changed. The stable for visitors was exactly where he remembered. The scent of horseflesh, leather, hay, and manure mixed to fuel his memories. He'd lived on the wrong side of town and rarely ventured into mid-town. When he did, the merchants eyed him suspiciously.

He located the stable master and inquired about hiring a horse. He'd left his bags at the Golden Arms, the only hotel in this tiny town. For the past six months, he had called New York home. Before that, he'd moved from place to place, trying to forget Cassidy, his horrid childhood, and the war.

But at the Burkeville train station a memory of the day he'd gone off to training camp surfaced. After signing their enlistment papers, the new soldiers met at the station to leave for a camp in upstate Pennsylvania. Cassidy's entire family had come to see off her brothers, Quinn and Josh. No one saw him off. His father lay passed out drunk, and at that time, he hadn't seen or heard from any of his brothers for a number of years.

That day, he'd tried to steal a goodbye kiss from Cassidy. The memory made him grin. She'd taken a swing at him. Although he had ducked, he'd fallen flat on his back.

His father, the only member of his family left in town at the time, had railed when George joined the army. The old man drank himself into a stupor every day and depended on George to work odd jobs to earn money and tend the small field behind their shack. His father's sole income derived from selling those crops at a local market, as well as surplus eggs from their chickens.

But George had longed for escape from his tarnished upbringing, and his best friend, Josh Stuart, had convinced him joining the Union army would be exciting and glorious.

He shook his head. And now Josh lay six feet under in the National Cemetery in Gettysburg. Cut down in his prime. Just like many other men who had perished in that awful war. And sometimes when he thought how he'd treated Cassie, maybe he should have died, too.

After saddling his mount, George took a leisurely trot through town to the outskirts leading to his father's house. Although he'd lied—out of necessity—to Cassidy about his purpose in coming here, he still planned to see the spot where his father was interred.

The tidy streets and framed wood and brick homes spread out then completely disappeared as he rode through the countryside. When he found the building, he dismounted and stared at the shack he'd called home before the war. The one-room wooden structure looked even more ramshackle than he remembered. Of course, Pa would have completely neglected it. What else had he expected?

George strode around the side of the structure.

The corn patch Pa used to make spare cash to feed his liquor habit and buy a bit of food was cleared out, except for a mound of fresh dirt.

"Sorry, Pa," George intoned, "you gave me no choice but to leave."

When he'd proposed to Cassidy, he hadn't thought of the impact on his old man. Amos wanted George to take him in, but that was impossible. He would never have imposed the burden of his father on a new wife.

George walked back around the dilapidated structure and opened the door. He had to see it one last time. The interior of the shack was in worse shape than the outside. Stacks of dishes, pots, and cutlery lay on the table top and in wash pans, many still food-encrusted. Roaches crawled over the table top, and a rat scurried from beneath. George recoiled. One oil lantern sat on the table, the only other lighting fixtures seemed to be candles.

It's a wonder he didn't burn the place down years ago.

Memories of the years growing up in this place, feeling ostracized by the rest of the town, his mother's desertion, harsh punishments dealt out by his pa when he wasn't passed out drunk and the time he spent recuperating here after Gettysburg, crowded in and threatened to send him screaming out into the fresh air. Nothing but ghosts lived here now.

His only good memory...the care Cassidy had provided during his convalescence after he was wounded at Gettysburg. If not for her, he likely wouldn't have survived to return to his regiment.

Pushing the hurtful memories from his mind, he left the shack and breathed in the fresh air. For now, he had a real purpose in life, although he had to keep it from the town, and especially Cassie, for her protection as well as his.

****

Returning home, Cassidy pulled the pin from her hat and lifted it from her head, careful not to pull her bun out of place. She set the hat on the mahogany entry table and draped her shawl over the hook by the door. Her mother strode from the kitchen, wiping her hands on her apron.

Guilt niggled at her for lying to George, but she had to get away. His sudden appearance dredged up the hurt he'd caused her, even after five years. A pain she'd hoped never to surface again.

"Since I seem to have no patients, as usual..." She eyed her mother. "I'll do some gardening after I change into my work dress."

"That'll be fine, Cassie. With just you, me, and Matt here, I've got the baking well under control."

Cassidy bit her lip. "Thought you should know..."

Her mother turned back, a frown on her face. "Know what?"

"I saw George in town today."

"George Masters?" The frown turned into a scowl. "What's he doing here?"

"Nothing to do with me, Ma. He's here to pay respects to his father."

"Well, about time one of Amos's no-account sons showed up. If the undertaker didn't bury him, he'd still be rotting in that shack he called home."

"Ma!"

"Just be glad that man ran off before he married you instead of after."

Cassidy sighed. "I'd rather not discuss this right now. Just wanted to warn you in case you see him in town."

She turned from her mother's raised brows and climbed the stairs to her bedroom. After changing, she gathered her sun bonnet, apron, and a spade, then trudged to the small garden bordering the front porch.

Two days ago, she had promised her mother she'd attend to the weeds. New ones sprang up overnight after a few days of heavy rain. Maybe pulling weeds would get her mind off her worries about the practice and seeing George again after all these years.

A half hour later, Cassidy brushed her soiled hands over her apron and surveyed the garden, which now looked in fair shape to plant seeds. Rising, she glanced at the sun. Delicious warmth bathed her face. The past winter had been extremely cold with a lot of snow. If not for the work with her father's patients, hopelessness would have descended with nothing but endless chores to occupy her time.

Cassidy smiled as she remembered the day Ma had ordered Sarah to help Cassidy in the garden. Her sister had worn her best dress and bonnet in hopes Cassidy would send her on her way. When she threatened to smear Sarah's good dress with mud, she'd flown into the house in alarm.

Sarah had married a lieutenant she'd met during the war and now lived in York. Sarah and her husband, Wesley, weren't able to visit often, even though York wasn't much of a distance. They'd last been in town for Pa's funeral, then stayed for the Christmas holidays—not a very joyous occasion this year—but the family hadn't seen them since, only communicating through letters.

Her brother, Quinn, was serving an internship in a hospital in Harrisburg. Cassidy ached with jealousy. She wished she could follow in his footsteps by attending a real medical school like he had. His letters and frequent visits left her ravenous with longing. She wanted with all her heart to be a real doctor and set up her own practice. George thought she could. Her father had taught her well, but hadn't thought medical school practical for a woman. Her mother—while tolerating her daughter's work with patients, since her husband's death, as a way to earn extra money—thought Cassidy should set her sights on eligible men, especially once Quinn returned. But her brother would approve of her applying to a medical school. He was the only support she had.

"I miss you, Quinn," Cassidy muttered as she brushed off her apron in preparation for returning to the house.

"Who you talking to?"

The baritone voice startled her. She turned to find Matt pushing a hand through his dark hair. "I was commiserating the fact that Quinn isn't here."

Matt, a child during the war years, was too young to go off with their brothers and George to fight for the Union. But now, five years later, he'd grown into a strapping young man. At the local barn dances, the girls all vied to catch his eye.

Cassidy lifted a hand to brush an errant lock of hair from her younger brother's face.

"It's that medical school thing again, Cassie, isn't it?"

She sighed and gathered her skirts, settling on the porch steps. "I don't see why women can't go to medical school along with the men. What harm would it do?"

Matt scowled. "Reckon I don't know why any of you want to care for sick people. I prefer working at the bank. And I make good money."

Cassidy smiled and placed a hand on his arm. "You're like Josh. He wanted nothing to do with doctoring, either."

"I miss Josh." Matt laid his hand atop hers.

"We all do, Matt. I'd best go in and wash up."

She pulled away from him, gathered her skirts, and preceded her brother into the house. Talking of Josh, killed at Gettysburg, caused her mind to drift back to the time she'd found George seriously wounded days after that horrific battle.

He'd been gaunt, weak, and in turmoil over the loss of Josh. She'd felt so sorry for George that even though she'd just lost her oldest brother, George had stolen her heart.

His dark gaze raking over her, his familiar scent, and the feel of his arms around her evoked all the old memories. The sight of his sensual lips brought back the taste of his kiss. The drawn, almost skeletal man who'd returned from prison camp had filled out even better than before he'd left for the war. Five years had only enhanced the appearance of the man she'd loved so dearly.

He still wore the spade beard, covering only his chin, and a well-trimmed mustache. And despite the abusive upbringing at the hands of his alcoholic father, he'd always retained a fine sense of humor. Although she'd spurned him many a time before the war, thinking him nothing but a flirt, she wasn't able to keep herself from falling in love after he was wounded and nearly died.

She paused in the kitchen doorway, not sure she'd be able to resist his charms if he stayed in town too long. But she wouldn't allow George or any other man to turn her ordered life upside down.

Chapter Three

George cracked an eyelid and grimaced at the late morning sunshine streaming through cracks in the window shade. Today he planned to start his investigation of a doctor in town named Scott Madison.

He slid from beneath the bed covering, padded to the chamber set on the dresser, and splashed water on his face. Stepping to the window, he peered at the street below.

Ah, Cassidy. She'd been a rock for him to lean on at Gettysburg when he'd come so close to death. But they'd never had a moment alone, except for the months she had cared for him in his cabin. But then, he'd been too ill to act on his impulses, never having the chance to finger the strands of her silky hair loose around her shoulders, or share more than a cursory kiss.

And those long, harsh months in Libby Prison in Richmond, when he'd believed his time on earth at an end...his memories of Cassie the only thing keeping him alive... After the surrender, he *had* come back to her. And left.

He'd figured she must have married by now, but she'd said nothing to indicate that. Of course, she *had* been in an awful hurry to get away. And *his* life until six months ago had been a mess. On the advice of a gambling acquaintance, he'd applied for a job with the Pinkerton Agency as an investigator. His experience as an officer during the war helped secure him the job. Colonel Wellingham, who he'd served under during the war, had also given him a glowing recommendation.

Allen Pinkerton's son, William, had specially chosen him for this assignment, knowing he'd lived in Burkeville before the war. The colonel, whose daughter had been assaulted by the doctor when he still practiced at his father's prestigious Philadelphia office, learned Madison had gone to hide in the small town. The colonel contacted the Pinkerton Agency to hire an investigator to poke around and find any evidence he could against the physician.

The thought of the monster anywhere near Cassidy infuriated him. He'd kill any bastard who would take advantage of his position as a doctor to harm a woman. He'd make a point to keep abreast of her whereabouts, whether she liked it or not, but had to be careful his purpose in coming home wasn't revealed to her or anyone else.

****

By the time Cassidy finished washing the breakfast dishes, her mother stepped into the kitchen. "Cassie, you have a patient waiting in the office. You need to see her right quick."

"A patient?" Cassidy scowled. "I don't have any appointments scheduled until tomorrow."

"It's an emergency. It can't wait."

"Who is it, Ma?"

"Miss Baker, the new school teacher. She's cut her arm. It's bleeding a lot, I'm afraid. You may have to suture it."

Cassidy raced to the office.

The school marm peered up at her, her blue eyes smudged, face white. She held up her arm, draped in a bloodied towel. "I'm sorry, Miss Stuart, but I hoped you'd be in. Your mother cleaned and wrapped my arm and told me to wait here and hold it up to help staunch the bleeding."

"How did this happen?" Cassidy knelt beside the

woman, peering beneath the towel. Bright red blood oozed from the gaping wound. But at least the cut wasn't gushing. Her mother had done a fine job. "I'm afraid you'll need sutures, Miss Baker."

She nodded. "I thought I might. It wouldn't stop bleeding after I..." Her face flushed pink. "I was chopping wood for my classroom, and the axe slipped." She smiled wanly. "I didn't want to wait for the older boys to arrive. They usually do it. I briefly thought of going to that new doctor in town, but Mrs. Heller, one of my student's mothers, suggested you. She said you'd birthed her last baby and had been gentle and respectful." The teacher winced as Cassidy probed the wound.

"Sorry...I have to see how deep it is." She warmed inwardly at the words of her former patient. Mrs. Heller, a strong, sturdy woman and a model patient, practically delivered the baby herself only two months after Cassidy's father passed. At least she had a few loyal patients left.

The inch-long cut on Miss Baker's arm didn't appear to be too deep. Cassidy smiled. "I think a few well-placed stitches should do the job. I'm glad you didn't do yourself more serious damage. I'll send my mother in to bathe the wound again, while I get the sutures ready. It will hurt, but only a little. And after that, you'll heal up just fine."

"Thank you, Doctor." The teacher turned her cornflower blue gaze on Cassidy.

Her breath caught when she realized she'd called her "Doctor" instead of "Miss Stuart" or "Miss Cassie" like all her other patients did.

An hour later, Miss Baker was stitched up and ready to go home. "How much is the charge?"

"One dollar and you can bring it in ten days when you return. I'll remove the sutures then. Until then, keep it clean. We don't want any infection cropping up. If you notice any redness or puffiness come right back and see me."

"Yes, Doctor." Miss Baker beamed. "I surely will. Thank you for all your help."

Cassidy watched the teacher walk toward the school house. Would her treatment of Miss Baker and the few patients who'd remained loyal help turn the tide of desertion to Doc Madison? Maybe she could hold things together until her brother's return.

****

Scott Madison strolled through town square on his way to the mercantile. After living in Philadelphia all his life, this tiny town stifled him. Only a few stores and establishments graced the main thoroughfare and one hotel for the entire town. *How did one live like this? It's barbaric!*

But what better place to escape the press and rumor mongers? Obviously, his father had thought along the same lines, wanting his ostracized son someplace no one would ever find him. Unfortunately, when he arrived, the only doctor in town monopolized all the available patients. No one seemed willing to trust a virtual newcomer from the big city. But six months ago, Scott staged an apparent accident on a snow covered road, causing the untimely death of the good doctor. His intention had been to disable the man, but this worked out better. Now, Scott's practice grew by the day. The one person standing in his way, the late doctor's daughter, fancied herself a physician, even though she had no credentials other than assisting at her father's side.

Scott grimaced as he opened the door of the mercantile, but his gaze caught a delightful vision of beauty at the counter. On closer examination, he realized the dark-haired woman with vivid green eyes was the very one preventing his cornering the entire town's populace as his patients. His new adversary, the late Dr. Stuart's oldest daughter,

Cassidy.

His gaze drifted to her right. A man stood beside her. He wasn't either of her brothers, and she wasn't married. But he didn't recognize the man. *A potential beau from out of town?*

He sidled close enough to hear their conversation without being noticed.

"Where are you staying?" she asked the man.

"Over at the hotel."

"Well, my invitation stands. Come see us while you're in town." She nodded and maneuvered her skirts stepping toward the door.

Scott tipped his hat as she approached. "Ma'am?" She inclined her head but scowled at him with those lovely eyes. He held the door for her.

Lifting her chin, she slipped out and left without a word. He stared after her a moment, noting the sway of the posterior of her non-bustled gown.

He turned back, meeting the hostile gaze of the man, but decided to ignore him, maneuvering through the aisle to find his needed supplies.

The stranger walked through the aisles, choosing a few articles of clothing before paying the clerk. After the man left, Scott approached the counter with his items.

"How do, Doc." The rail-thin, balding clerk added up his purchase.

Scott handed him a few coins and stuffed the items in his pockets.

"How's business?" The clerk folded his arms, propping them on the counter.

Scott scowled. "It would be a mite better if I had more patients. But it seems the young lady who just left is practicing medicine, too. I'd thought after her father passed, she'd give up on it."

The clerk shook his head. "Cassie Stuart has had her heart set on being a doctor since she nursed soldiers during the war. Her pa was training her, and people around here say she has a knack."

"But she hasn't had any formal training. I'd think people would want to be treated by a real doctor."

The clerk leaned toward Scott. "Well, if you're really set on taking over Doc Stuart's practice, you'd best make your move before his son returns from Harrisburg. He *has* been to medical school. Reckon he'll take over when he returns, and Cassie can go back to being his assistant like she did for her pa."

"Her brother attended medical school?" Scott's blood heated.

Just what I need...more competition.

He'd have to quash this in the bud right now. In a town this small, he had no hope of making the kind of money he would have in Philadelphia, but right now, with half the populace going to Miss Stuart, he barely made enough to keep up his household.

After he bade the clerk farewell, a plan to discredit the dark-haired beauty started to form in his mind, but he had to do the deed before her brother returned.

Chapter Four

Cassidy woke from a vivid dream of a battlefield during the war. Although she'd gone to Gettysburg about a week after the bloodshed had ended, cannons boomed in her nightmare. Men fell, writhing in pain and the smell of blood rent the air. A soft voice called to her. She glanced down at the bodies littering the field for the source. A hand on her shoulder jolted her. She gasped as she gazed up into her mother's eyes, realizing she was in her own bed. What a vivid dream! Those horrific days as a battlefield nurse would never leave her.

Her mother lit the bedside lantern.

"What is it, Ma?"

"Ned Tasker was just here. His wife's about to give birth. They need you over there quick."

Cassidy shook off the dream and rose, gathering the clothing she'd taken off last night and left hanging on the back of a chair.

She swallowed hard. She'd hoped Mrs. Tasker's baby would've waited until Quinn had returned. The only other local doctor was Madison. She sensed Ned would have preferred the male physician, but Ellie insisted Cassidy deliver her baby. She'd assisted her father at a number of births before his death. She knew the procedures and should have no trouble.

Cassidy removed her nightgown and quickly dressed. "Reckon I'd best get going then."

Her mother nodded.

Cassidy gathered a bag full of supplies from her father's office, then lit a lantern to guide her in the dark, and walked to the Tasker home.

Ned met her at the door of the well-kept white with blue-trim house. Lanterns lit the interior.

"Where is she?" Cassidy asked.

"Upstairs in our bedroom."

She nodded and followed the stocky man up the stairs into a narrow hall and slant ceiling room. His wife, Ellie, lay in the bed, her face pale, brow beaded with sweat.

"Oh, Cassie, I'm so glad you're here. I think the baby's coming quick."

Cassidy stepped to the bed and placed her hand on the woman's protruding stomach, trying to feel for the position of the baby. The head was down, so this should be an easy, uncomplicated birth.

She smiled at Ellie. "I'll examine you to see if you're ready." Glancing at Ned, who hovered in the doorway, she added, "I'll need a pan of water and some sheets or towels."

"Yes, ma'am." Ned disappeared.

Ellie reached up and clasped Cassidy's hand. "If anything happens, please tell Ned I'll always love him."

"Shh." She patted Ellie's hand. "Nothing will go wrong. I promise."

"But just in case." The woman's face contorted as a contraction caused her to spasm. She sank into the mattress, gasping, her gaze focused on Cassidy. "You swear you'll tell him."

"Of course I will," she assured Ellie.

After a brief examination under the covers, Cassidy warned her patient, "You're almost ready to push, but not yet. I'll tell you when."

Ellie nodded. "It hurts so much. I don't reckon you can give me anything for it."

Cassidy shook her head. Many physicians now gave their childbirth patients chloroform to draw patients away from midwives.

Ned arrived with water and towels, and Cassidy

instructed him to dab his wife's brow. "It's best I don't give you anything for the pain, Mrs. Tasker. You'll recover much sooner."

As the contractions and Ellie's moans continued, Cassidy watched the clock. A first baby should take a while. She'd attended many first births, and some of them had lasted a whole day.

Toward dawn, Cassidy's body quivered with exhaustion. With Ellie finally in position to push, Ned clasped her hand, while Cassidy pressed on her stomach trying to help the baby into the world. But the longer nothing happened, the more worried she grew.

Ellie shrank against the bedsheets, her face ghastly white.

Ned's brow knitted into an intense frown, and he kept glancing at Cassidy. "Why isn't the baby coming?"

She shook her head, feeling helpless. "She needs to push harder. Encourage her."

Ned glanced at his wife and smoothed her brow. "Come on, Ellie. Miss Cassie says you have to push."

"I can't," Ellie moaned. "I'm too tired."

Ned glanced at Cassidy, his gaze boring into her. She swallowed hard but tried to compose her features. She didn't want him to lose faith in her abilities to see this birth through.

"Miss Cassie," he whispered.

She rose to look Ellie in the eye. "Come on, Mrs. Tasker. Don't you want to see your baby?"

Ellie shook her head. "I can't do this."

"You can and you will. Hold Ned's hand. Just breathe and do as I say."

Ellie clutched her husband's hand. Cassidy gave him a nod and resumed her place at the foot of the bed. A spasm overtook the woman.

"Take a deep breath and push as hard as you can," Cassidy said.

Ned patted his wife's hand and nodded. "Come on, Ellie. You can do this."

"Now push," Cassidy ordered.

Ellie moaned, keeping her gaze locked with her husband, who called encouragement.

After two more long pushes, a downy head emerged. "The baby's coming," Cassidy said. "One more push should do it."

Ellie screamed and a torrent of blood gushed over Cassidy's hands as she tried to maneuver the baby out. A chill raced down her spine. *Too much blood.*

"Ellie." Ned's voice warbled. "Miss Cassie, something's wrong."

Cassidy lifted the baby. A bluish cast tinged the tiny face. She concentrated her efforts on encouraging his first breath.

"Ellie, darlin'," Ned said, "don't go to sleep now. Our baby's here."

Prickles of fear shot through Cassidy's body. The baby wouldn't breathe. She massaged the tiny chest, trying to draw a gasp. Her body chilled and her heart thudded.

"Ellie, please!" Ned groaned. "She won't wake up." He grasped Cassidy's arm. She still held the baby, but her efforts weren't bringing him around.

"I'm sorry." A feeling of unreality swept over her. This couldn't be happening. "Take the baby." She thrust the child into Ned's hands, then moved to Ellie.

Examining the woman, she realized nothing would save her. She'd lost too much blood, her face pale as marble. Turning to Ned, Cassidy's lips trembled as she tried to form words.

"She's gone, isn't she?" He laid the still form of his child on the bed by her side. "And so is my son."

"Ned, I'm so sorry."

A knock at the door revived the man. He

trudged down the stairs. A few minutes later, he reappeared, followed by another man.

"It's Doc Madison," Ned intoned.

Cassidy glanced up. Madison strode into the room, scowling. She didn't have the strength to ask why he'd arrived now. Ned couldn't have summoned him.

"One of my neighbors told me your wife's child was due any time and thought I could be of help..." His words trailed off as he took in the scene.

Cassidy dropped her head. She wanted to scream, she wanted to hide.

What have I done?

****

Scott examined both mother and child, pronouncing them dead. He stole glances at Miss Stuart, huddled in a chair by the door, her apron and hands covered in blood.

When he'd learned of the impending birth and that the mother wanted Miss Stuart to attend, he'd kept his ears peeled. One instance of medical incompetence would discredit her as a physician, and then he'd have the town of Burkeville in his pocket. He thanked his good fortune this had occurred before her brother's return.

"There's nothing can be done for them, I'm afraid," Scott told Ned. "I'll stay until you summon your family to take care of the bodies." Keeping an eye on Miss Stuart, Scott leaned toward Ned.

"You should have called me before this. I could have saved them both."

The young husband nodded, stealing a glance at Miss Stuart. "Ellie wanted her." His face twisted with grief.

Scott patted his shoulder. "Go wash up and fetch one of your relations. I'll take care of Miss Stuart."

As Ned descended the stairs, Scott bit his lip to hold back a grin of triumph.

****

Cassidy sat like a stone, unable to move, think, or feel. After what seemed an eternity, she lifted her face to view the horrific scene. Although Ned had left the room, the image of his pale, drawn face, and Madison's accusatory glare were etched in her memory. The doctor blamed *her* for the deaths. She longed for her father's presence, or Quinn's.

"You'd best go home, young lady," Madison suggested. "This is no place for you." He took her arm, urging her to wash the blood from her hands, then escorted her to the door. She hadn't even noticed the blood, in her numbed state.

Dazed, Cassidy arrived home where her mother quizzed her on what happened, but she couldn't explain without bursting into tears. With an offer to make tea, her mother sent Cassidy to her room to rest.

She climbed the stairs, as if her legs were made of lead, and collapsed across the bed. She'd killed two people—a mother and an innocent baby. The sight of the tiny blue face would haunt her forever. She lifted an arm to cover her eyes in an effort to erase the horrid vision.

A light tap on the door was followed by her mother entering the room with a cup of hot tea. "Drink this, Cassie."

Cassidy shook her head.

"It will make you feel better," she urged.

"Nothing will make me feel better."

Her mother sat beside her and placed the tea on a nightstand. "Tell me what happened."

"They're dead! And I killed them!"

Her mother gasped. "Mrs. Tasker?"

"And her baby." Cassidy scrubbed her hand across her face. "I'm not fit to be a doctor."

"Cassie, don't say that. It wasn't your fault."

Cassidy's eyes stung. "I should've been able to

save them. It was a routine birth." She rose and paced, her hands crossed over her chest. "You were right all along."

Her mother hugged her, but Cassidy didn't want comfort right now.

"Ma, I really need to be by myself to think a bit."

Her mother bit her lip but nodded and left the room, closing the door softly behind her.

Alone again, Cassidy broke into a sob. No patients would want to come to her for treatment ever again, especially after Dr. Madison told them all of her guilt.

Chapter Five

When George entered the hotel lobby, patrons and staff were abuzz about the happenings of the previous night.

"If only Ned had called Dr. Madison instead of that poor girl. Just because she assisted her father, doesn't make her a doctor, or even a skilled midwife." The thin clerk shook his head.

"But Miss Stuart assisted at many births," an amply bosomed woman protested. "Her father had every confidence in her skills."

The names Madison and Miss Stuart in the same conversation sent a shock through George.

"Pardon me." He approached the clerk. "I know the Stuarts. Are you by any chance talking about Cassidy Stuart?"

"Yes, sir." The clerk nodded. "She was assisting at the Tasker's birth last night. Sad story."

George's blood chilled. "Why? What happened?"

The woman shook her head. "Both mother and baby have passed on. If only her brother had been there. She shouldn't have tried to birth the baby alone."

"Or if Dr. Madison had arrived earlier. He heard of the impending birth from one of his neighbors and rushed over there, but it was too late."

"I see." George turned away and raced out the door. His business with Madison would have to wait.

He rushed to the familiar house, ignoring the stares of people passing by. He didn't care what anyone thought of him now, or then, he needed to see Cassidy.

He gulped as he ascended the porch steps. How many times had he spent here as a boy with Josh? And the day he paid a visit to Cassidy to see if she still cared for him lingered in his mind. That day he'd decided to return to his regiment.

His hand lifted, but he paused. After taking a deep breath, he rapped on the door.

A moment had passed before the door swung inward. Mrs. Stuart's mouth gaped, but she recovered. He always remembered Cassidy's mother as a gracious lady. No matter what she thought of anyone, he'd never heard a harsh word pass her lips.

"How do you do, ma'am," he said. "I've come to pay a call on Cassie."

Mrs. Stuart gazed at his shoes, her tongue grazing her lower lip. "I'm afraid Cassie isn't feeling well today."

"Ma'am." He tipped his hat. "I've heard about the incident at the Tasker's. I thought I could be of some help."

Her face crumpled. "It's horrible what happened. If only Quinn had been here last night..."

George shook his head. "I know Cassie. She's dedicated and knows how to care for patients. If it had been possible to save them, she would've."

Mrs. Stuart's throat worked. He hoped he'd convinced her to allow him entrance. After glancing over her shoulder, she flung the door open. "If you can help Cassie, please do. I can't stand seeing her suffer like this."

George removed his hat as he passed her. "Ma'am, I hope she'll allow me to talk to her. I wouldn't be surprised if she tossed me out bodily."

He ascended the stairs, Mrs. Stuart on his heels. "I'll stand outside the door for propriety...that is, if she even allows you in."

"Of course, ma'am." He rapped on the door.

"Who's there?" A muffled call answered.

"Cassie, it's George. I'd like to talk to you. Will you allow me in?"

Silence followed his question. He pressed his ear to the door and heard footsteps. The door opened, and Cassidy glared at him, eyes swollen, face streaked and puffy. Dark hair had pulled loose from her bun, hanging in tendrils around her pale face.

"If you would allow me in, maybe I can help." He gestured toward Mrs. Stuart. "Your mother will be right outside, keeping watch."

Cassidy glanced around him, frowning. When she spotted her mother, she nodded and stood back, allowing him entrance.

He traced his finger down Cassidy's arm and gazed into her eyes. Sweet, familiar sensations he'd missed all these years. "I want you to tell me everything that happened last night."

She bit her lip, then nodded. Once the story started, she seemed unable to stop. She ended with the blood all over her hands. "There was just so much blood. And the baby wouldn't breathe, and Mrs. Tasker was so white..."

She collapsed against him, her warm, soft body inviting his embrace. Careful not to alarm her mother, he brushed his hands over Cassidy's back as she sobbed against his coat, her familiar warmth and scent increased his yearning to have her back in his life again. He turned back to catch Mrs. Stuart's glance. She mouthed, *Thank you*, then turned away.

"There, there," he said to Cassidy. "You can't blame yourself for what happened."

"But I thought I could be a doctor. I'm nothing but a failure." Her arms tightened around him as if she clung for her life.

"I heard in town the new doc—Madison, I think his name is—arrived afterward."

She didn't speak but didn't release her hold. After a long moment, she lifted her tear streaked face. "Yes, he was there. Too late to help...and he blamed me for all of it."

"The bastard!" George gripped her tightly wanting to protect her. "Pardon my language, Cassie, but I can't abide the man." He wouldn't let Madison allow her to take the blame for something not her fault. "What did he say?"

She frowned as if trying to remember his exact words. "Something about...Ned should have called him. He could have saved them both." She tightened her grip around his waist. "Oh, George! I've never felt this horrible in my whole life. Even during the war..."

"I know..." He kissed her forehead. "Life or death...it's all in God's hands. You didn't do anything wrong. All you did was try to help a patient."

"And I failed." Her face scrunched up. In all the years he'd known Cassidy, he'd never seen her cry like this. Even when he had left her. But once he was gone for parts unknown, she might have fallen into grief. And of course, it had been less than six months since her father's death.

He glanced toward the doorway. Although it was open, her mother no longer hovered there. Had she left to allow them privacy? Lifting Cassidy's chin between his fingers, he tilted her face forcing her to look at him. "Cassie, I know I didn't do right by you all those years ago, but if you'll allow me to help...?"

She frowned. "Help? Help how?"

He leaned down and pressed his lips against her soft, warm ones, tasting her sweetness and the salt of her tears. He moved slow, keeping his gaze on the door.

After a moment, she softened in his arms and responded to his kiss, shooting delightful sensations to his groin. But he had to take this easy. He released her and gazed into her eyes.

He wanted to warn her about Madison but

couldn't chance revealing his knowledge about the doctor, even to her. He glanced back at the doorway in case Mrs. Stuart or someone else lingered.

Cassidy drew in a deep breath and wiped her eyes.

Movement outside the doorway drew George's gaze to Mrs. Stuart. "Cassie, I'd like you to come to the kitchen and eat something."

"Oh, ma." She ran a hand over her mussed hair. "I must look a fright."

"You look beautiful, as always," George said.

Mrs. Stuart smiled but eyed George warily. "You and George come downstairs and eat something. You've been moping up here far too long. And we can catch up on what George has been up to."

George winked, relieved her mother didn't send him on his way. "I do miss your ma's fine cooking, Cassie."

"All right," Cassidy said, "but I'd like to freshen up a bit first."

Her mother nodded. "Come down when you're ready." To George, she said, "Come with me so we can get acquainted again, while we wait on Cassie."

"My pleasure, ma'am." After a final glance at Cassidy, George followed her mother down the stairs, delighted he wasn't being thrown out on his ear.

****

Cassidy washed her face and changed into a fresh gown. Although she'd dreamed of George returning to her after all these years, she was sure he wouldn't stay. She had to keep her emotions under control. He'd only hurt her again. But the thrill of his hard body against her and the press of his lips on hers set her pulse racing and her body heating. But he was here to pay respects to his father and would be on his way again.

Before she'd finished redoing her hair, her

mother appeared to check on her and told her George would be staying for dinner. Despite mixed feelings concerning George, Cassidy wanted to look her best. Since the botched birth, she'd cloistered herself in her room, too ashamed to show her face to anyone. And the thought of what poor Ned Tasker had to endure set her teeth on edge and threatened to send warm tears coursing down her cheeks all over again. How would she ever face the man or the town again?

By the time she finished pinning up her hair, a knock at the door sounded.

"Yes?" she called.

"Cassie." George's deep voice sent her heart fluttering. "I've come to escort you downstairs to dinner."

"I'll be right there." She fastened earrings to her lobes, then checked herself in the mirror. Despite the hours she'd spent crying, her face showed just a hint of puffiness around the eyes.

She opened the door. George smiled at her. He raised his arm, and she grasped the wool sleeve of his coat. His warmth enveloped her, and she wondered how her life would've been different if he'd stayed and married her after the war. Would they have a house and a brood of children?

Throughout the meal, he was charming and solicitous. Disapproval for George melted away. Her mother sat enthralled with his stories of life in New York City and California. Her younger brother, Matt, seemed impressed as well. So much so, he pushed his fork through the chicken and dumplings he usually downed with abandon.

Cassidy set down her fork and studied George. "Now, you are making me so jealous."

His dark brows rose. "How's that?"

She spread her hands. "You've been so many faraway places. The farthest I've ever been was

Washington City during the war."

George shook his head. "It wasn't an easy way to live, being alone on the road." His gaze dropped.

She cleared her throat and glanced around the table. "If everyone's finished, I'll start clearing the table."

Her mother pinned her with a narrowed gaze but waved an arm for Cassidy to proceed. Matt polished off his plate and handed it to her.

George frowned but said nothing more.

Once the dishes were cleaned, George stepped into the kitchen and asked Cassidy if she'd accompany him to the porch so they could talk alone. The light shawl she'd thrown over her shoulders chased away the slight chill of the evening air.

After settling her on the wicker settee, he sat beside her, enveloping her hand and rubbing it between his large, warm ones. His sandalwood and male scent invited her to lean into his warmth, but she held herself rigid, her emotions on guard.

She had so many questions she wanted answered, like where he'd been all these years and how he made his living.

"Cassie, I know you must hate me for leaving you."

She narrowed her gaze. "It's hard to think kindly on someone who leaves you, no matter what the reason. I know you were hurting, but we could have made a life together. Healed each other."

He shook his head. "I would've held you back."

"From what?"

"Well...you're a doctor. That was your dream when I returned from prison camp."

"And look what a fine mess I've made of that." She bowed her head, studying his hand wrapped around hers. His warm touch sent tingles straight to her core. But what was he doing here? Did he really come back for her, or had something or someone else drawn him to Burkeville?

"George, what's the real reason you're here?" She held her breath, hoping for the answer she wanted to hear.

He withdrew his hand from hers, taking his warmth with it. "I thought I should come back and check on Pa." His dark gaze settled on her. "I didn't reckon you'd ever want to see me again, especially after the disaster I made of my life—and yours."

She leaned back. "George, you're wearing fine clothing, telling us about your adventures in New York and California." She shook her head. "Doesn't sound to me like your life's a mess."

He chewed his lower lip. "I haven't told you all of it. After I left you, I wandered for a long time. I'm not really clear on all of it, because half the time I was so drunk I didn't know who or where I was."

Cassidy stood. "Well, I have to say, you look none the worse for wear after all you've been through."

"Cassie, I..." George grinned, lifting his thumbs to the lapels of his coat. "I always had a knack for poker. Cleaned out many fellow soldiers during the war."

"Are you telling me you're a professional gambler?"

He grimaced, dropping his gaze. "I'm not the type of man a physician should associate with. To tell the truth, I figured you'd already forgotten me. I expected to find you with a husband and children by now."

"There's no one else, George, if that's what you're getting at. Since you left, I haven't exactly had a slew of suitors at my door." She eyed him, not sure why she'd told him.

"What about that new doc in town?" He looked toward the road.

"Madison? I despise the man. All he does is try

to discredit me. He's taking all the patients from Pa's practice. I only hope we have a few left when Quinn returns."

George audibly exhaled, a small smile playing on his full lips. "Quinn? Where is he?"

"He's interning at a hospital in Harrisburg but should be finished in a day or two. He plans to try to salvage what's left of Pa's practice over the summer, but I fear I've just complicated things." The sting of tears threatened once more, but she must stay strong. Crying and hiding wouldn't help her situation.

George studied her as if considering something. "Cassie, I have absolutely no right, but...I'd like to spend time with you while I'm here, if I may?"

She scowled. "So you can work yourself back into my heart and then leave?"

"No, I..." He lowered his gaze. "Reckon I deserve that."

"I think you should take your leave. Now."

He nodded, then stood, but paused on the top porch step, before he turned toward the road and lifted his hat to his head.

She sat and watched him descend the steps without looking back. But she couldn't take her gaze off his broad back. Now he was back in town, she had to sort out her feelings regarding George. She still cared for him but couldn't stand to be hurt again.

Chapter Six

Scott Madison examined the medical instruments lined up on his desk. Since the Tasker deaths, the whole town seemed to rally around him. Ned's parents thanked him for seeing to Ellie and the baby, even though it had been too late. As long as Miss Stuart had no allies, he didn't think he'd have any problem destroying her practice. And if that didn't work, maybe he could plan another accident, for both the Stuarts.

As he toyed with a metal probe, his mind drifted back to his days as an apprentice in his father's prestigious practice in Philadelphia. After his stint in medical school at the University of Pennsylvania, he thought he'd settle in, taking on more of his father's patients as his own, and when his father retired, the practice would be his.

But the young woman, Miss Audrey Wellingham who claimed he assaulted her, had closed the door on his future. As if the little whore hadn't wanted his attentions. His father had been so afraid of the aftermath he'd banished Scott, not only from the practice, but his home and the city itself. Now he was left with no other choice but to live in this nowhere town and try to reestablish himself as a trusted physician while his father hushed up all accusations against him back home.

He studied his appointment book. The first one penciled in was Miss Baker. He smiled. The young schoolteacher was fairly new in town. She lived at the boardinghouse where he'd stayed before purchasing this house with the money his father had sent him. She seemed reserved and quite respectable but was a real beauty with large cornflower blue eyes and honey-colored hair he imagined felt like pure silk. He'd longed to lay his hands on her the first time he'd seen her. And now, she was to be his first patient. The door chime drew him from an erotic vision of what he'd like to do with the lovely Miss Baker.

A moment later a rap sounded at his office door. "Yes?"

The dark-haired maid, Tillie, poked her head into the open doorway. She was a middle-aged widow, a local he'd hired on a part-time basis, until he acquired enough patients to pay her wages full time. Tillie always seemed to wear a perpetual scowl, but as long as she did her job, he had no problems with the sour disposition.

"Sir, your first patient has arrived." She shook out the rag in her hand. Apparently, the caller had interrupted her dusting.

"Thank you; could you please show her into the examining room? I'll be there after she disrobes."

Tillie's eyebrows shot up. "She's to completely disrobe, sir?"

Scott waved a hand. "If I'm to examine her, it's necessary. Have her put on one of the examination gowns."

"Yes, sir." The maid scowled but closed the door, a blush coloring her usual pallid face.

Scott smirked. He planned to have some sport with Miss Baker. His pulse raced as he anticipated examining the smooth, lovely skin of his patient.

Another rap on the door was followed by, "Sir? Miss Baker is ready."

"Thank you, I'll be right there."

Scott tapped on the door before entering and found, to his delight, a half-naked Miss Baker clutching the flimsy gown around her pale shoulders to cover her bosom. She turned, eyes wide, and swallowed. Scott's blood warmed as he closed the door behind him. As he edged close to the table, the scent of rose and something both spicy and sweet enticed him. He was more than ready to rub his hands all over her smooth flesh.

"Good morning Miss Baker. What seems to be the problem today?"

She glanced away. "I...Miss Stuart stitched up my arm yesterday and told me to keep it clean and watch it for infection. While I was at school today, I noticed it seemed to be a bit red and puffy, so I thought I should have it looked at."

"Ah, yes. You're the local school marm."

She nodded but dropped her gaze. "I'd planned to go back to Miss Stuart, but after I heard about the Taskers, I thought..."

"Rest assured, Miss Baker, I'm a quite competent physician. I attended the University of Pennsylvania and practiced in Philadelphia before coming here." He smiled, hoping to assuage any fears and relax her for the exam.

She sighed. "I suppose I've come to the right doctor, then."

"Very well. Shall we start?" He stepped closer and examined her eyes, then brushed his hands along her face to her throat. Her pulse was rapid, breathing shallow. "Aside from the redness around the stitches, do you have any other symptoms, Miss Baker?"

She swallowed. "I do feel a bit warm." She lifted her arm. "Is it infected?"

Scott examined the wound, brushing his fingers up to her upper arm, and noted her slight shiver. "I'll clean it with antiseptic. You can come back to me when it's time for the stitches to be removed. Lie down and I'll complete the exam."

She pulled the gown tighter around her and lay

back on the table. He feasted his gaze on her lush bosom and curvaceous hips arranged in such a vulnerable position. He strained against his trousers as his hands descended to cup her breasts.

"Is—is this really necessary, Doctor?" Her chest heaved in his hands.

"If I'm to perform a complete examination, it is. Isn't that what you're here for, Miss Baker?"

Her throat worked. "I suppose so, but shouldn't the maid be in here with us?"

"Whatever for?"

"For propriety, sir."

"It's not necessary, Miss Baker. I'm a man of medicine." He brushed his hands over her narrow waist and lush, feminine hips, then trailed his fingers down her thighs. Her sharp intake of breath drew his gaze back to her face.

He longed to take her full lips. How sweet they would taste. But he had to be careful. The teacher would have to come back, since she'd likely not trust Miss Stuart to treat her again. He'd bide his time.

Once Miss Baker dressed, he placed his hand against the small of her back. "Tillie will make an appointment for you next week. I want to keep an eye on your wound to be sure you don't develop an infection."

"Thank you, Doctor." She turned toward the front room where Tillie waited with the appointment book.

Ah, yes. Scott would be counting the days until he could be alone again with the luscious school teacher.

****

Early Thursday morning, Cassidy rose, dressed, and descended the stairs. George's visit yesterday had mollified her somewhat. Maybe the deaths hadn't been her fault.

At the bottom of the stairs, she caught sight of

her mother swirling through the hall with a feather duster. "Isn't it a bit early to be housecleaning, Ma?"

"I got a letter from your sister. She and Wesley are coming for a visit."

"Sarah's coming here? When?"

"Today." Her mother turned her back and continued dusting the table.

"Today," Cassidy sputtered. "Why is this the first I'm hearing of her visit?"

"She sent the post as they were leaving. It arrived today."

That explains it. Typical Sarah, always impulsive.

"Did she tell you why she's coming?"

"She says it's a surprise. I can't wait to find out what it could be." Her mother scurried into the parlor, her feather duster almost flying through the air.

Cassidy sighed. While she did miss her sister, she could be a whirlwind, disrupting the whole house. "Where's Matt?"

"He took the carriage to collect them. They're arriving by train." Mrs. Stuart called from another room.

Before Cassidy could utter another word, the door opened to peals of laughter. Matt strode through first, his arms loaded with luggage. Sarah bustled in behind, followed by her husband, Wesley Tynan. The tall, lean, fair-haired man was still as handsome as the day they'd married five years ago after the war ended. Wesley was a Union army lieutenant Sarah had met at a local dance during the war years.

Cassidy hurried forward to embrace her sister. She wore a fashionable feathered hat perched on her chestnut curls and a stylish black gown pushed out in back by a bustle.

"You look wonderful, Sarah," Cassidy said.

43

"You too, Cassie. I'm sorry it's been so long between visits, but Wesley's been very busy at the finance office."

Cassidy stepped toward Wesley, who gave her a peck on the cheek. "It's good to see you too, Wes."

"And you, Cassie. You're looking well."

Their mother strode into the room and embraced the couple. She leaned back eyeing Sarah. "And what is this surprise you have for us? I'm just bursting to hear."

Sarah beamed. Wesley nudged his wife's arm. "Are you gonna tell them or should I?"

"Wesley and I...are going to have a baby!"

"Oh, Sarah," her mother said. "What wonderful news!"

Cassidy smiled but backed away as Sarah babbled on about the impending birth. The image of Mrs. Tasker and her child, both covered in blood, threatened to send her screaming from the room.

A few hours later, after Sarah and Wesley had been set up in the guest room, Sarah approached Cassidy and asked if they could talk in private.

Cassidy led her to the small room they'd shared before Sarah had married and moved to York. After they'd settled on Cassidy's narrow bed, she asked her sister, "How are you feeling, really?"

"Elated. And scared of course. I'd feel more comfortable if I was living here and you could attend the birth."

"Me?"

"Sure. You've worked alongside Papa for the past few years delivering babies. I'd love to have you attend the birth. Is there any chance you could come to York and stay with us for a while?"

Cassidy bit her lip. "I don't think I'm the person you want."

"Why?" Her sister frowned. "You're the perfect choice."

Cassidy sighed. "You haven't been home long enough to hear..." She swallowed, finding the words difficult to say. "I attended a birth the night before last and it ended badly."

Sarah wrapped her arms around Cassidy, her rounded belly brushing up against her. "I'm so sorry, Cassie, but I know whatever happened wasn't your fault."

Cassidy rested her hand on Sarah's stomach. "Has he been kicking yet?"

"Not yet, but I *have* felt some fluttering."

"That's good. You've been to a doctor in York?"

"Yes." Sarah grimaced. "A gnarled old man. I reckon I could find a midwife, but I'd much rather have you. I love you, Cassie."

"I love you too, Sarah. Give me some time to think on it."

Sarah smiled and patted Cassidy's hand. "And how has it been going with you since I've been gone? Any beaus?"

Cassidy scowled. "No."

"No one since George?" Sarah frowned, her words revealing the contempt she had for Cassie's former fiancé.

"I haven't had the time. I've been busy helping Ma with the house. And since Papa passed, I ended up with all his patients, at least until Quinn finishes his internship." She glanced at her sister who probably didn't hear a word she'd said.

"You need to go to dances, Cassie, be escorted to dinner and taken on picnics."

Cassidy spread her hands. "It's not like there's a gaggle of men sniffing around me. We *are* still in full mourning, after all, plus the town has been deserted since..."

Sarah sighed, half reclining on the bed. "I know. Since the war. There just aren't enough men to go around."

Cassidy recalled the available men in Burkeville. Half were old enough to be her father, and the other half weren't out of school. But George was back. *Don't you dare let him invade your thoughts. He's not the courting or marrying type.*

"...And I can't help thinking about Josh." Sarah continued. "Do you think about him often, Cassie? I've always wondered if he hadn't died at Gettysburg, would he be married, have children?"

"As much as we loved our brother, it doesn't help matters to dwell on what might have been. The war's in the past. We've got to move on. It's what Josh would want. Papa too." Cassidy brushed a tear from the corner of her eye. She'd tried hard to keep her mind off both their deaths. The family seemed cut in half.

"And Quinn's still in Harrisburg working at the hospital?"

"Yes, but his internship is just about up. He'll be returning for good. We expect him home any day now."

"Reckon he'll take over Pa's practice?"

Cassidy shrugged. "I suppose that's his plan."

"Then you'll be free to pursue a husband." Sarah straightened to face Cassidy.

A slight smile tipped her lips. *Sarah will never quit trying to find her a husband.* "Well, what I really want to do when Quinn comes back..." She trailed off.

"Is what?"

"I'd like to attend medical school."

Sarah frowned. "With all those men? Whatever for?"

"Although I do the work of a physician, no one in town calls me doctor. I'm just *Doc Stuart's daughter.* And I need to attend school to have a chance at performing surgery. Right now, I feel like all I am is a nurse."

"Well, there's nothing wrong with that, Cassie. Since the war, lots of women are going into the nursing field."

"But that's not what I want." Cassidy rose from the bed and paced. "I want to be a doctor. It's what I'm good at. I want to feel legitimized. Respected."

Sarah sighed. "You *need* to find a man. Start thinking of having a home. Children."

Cassidy clenched her fists. "Everyone says that, except for Quinn. He's my only ally since George left."

"I'm sorry." Sarah twirled a finger through one of her curls. "But George just wasn't the marrying kind, I reckon. Wonder where he is now?"

"If you must know, he's back in town. He was here yesterday."

"Oh, no, Cassie..." Sarah shook her head, sending her curls dancing. "Don't get involved with George Masters again. He's nothing but a bad seed and will never amount to anything. He'll drag you down with him."

Cassidy clenched her teeth. Her desire to defend him warred with the reality of what he had done. She fisted her hands on her hips. "Believe me; I don't intend to get involved with him ever again."

Chapter Seven

Friday, Cassidy stood at the sink peeling carrots and potatoes. Banging at the door and voices caught her attention. Drying her hands on her apron, she rushed to the foyer.

Wesley stood with his back to her, conversing with someone on the threshold. When he stood back, she caught the sight of rust colored hair on a handsome clean-shaven face. She rushed forward. "Quinn!"

Quinn caught her gaze and broke into a broad smile. "Cassie."

She wrapped her arms around his back as he held her close. Her older brother hadn't been home for months and had many tales of his times at the hospital.

She pulled him toward the parlor. "What have you been up to? Tell me all of it!"

Quinn smirked in Wesley's direction. He waved the two siblings off and retreated.

Cassidy settled on the settee before the fireplace, while Quinn took one of the upholstered chairs. "So, come on, tell me."

Quinn grinned, running a hand through his hair. "Well, it's been a lot of work. I've been on call for a week straight. No time for sleep and forget about any social calls."

Cassidy sighed. "It was like that for me before Pa died. But now...we're losing patients by spades, since Dr. Madison set up his practice."

Quinn grimaced. "Now that my internship's up, we'll work on getting those patients back."

"I don't know, Quinn. When you hear what happened the other day, there may be no practice for you to return to." She twisted her hands in the folds of her skirt.

"What happened?" He leaned back and studied her.

"I attended a birth. Mrs. Tasker."

He nodded.

"Both mother and child died." She licked her lips. "I don't know what happened. And then Dr. Madison appeared and blamed the whole thing on me."

"Cassie..." Quinn reached for her hand. "Women die in childbirth and so do babies. It happens more than I'd like to admit."

She shook her head. "But what if I was the cause...what if I killed them?"

"You didn't *kill* anyone. I can assure you of that." He scowled. "This Dr. Madison is just trying to make you look bad. Maybe I should pay him a visit and see what he's all about."

"You'd do that?" Cassidy's anxiety lifted knowing her brother would rally for her. Help her.

"Of course I will."

She bit her lip. "George paid us a visit yesterday."

"George?" Quinn's rust colored brows rose. "You don't mean George Masters?"

"One and the same."

"He's back in town?"

She nodded. "Just a few days ago."

"Well..." Quinn furrowed his brows and crossed his arms over his chest. "Wonder why he's here?"

"He's here to pay respects to his pa. Now he has, I suspect he'll go back to wherever he came from. He never really said."

"Where's he staying?"

"At the hotel."

Quinn grinned. "Maybe I'll just pay him a visit, too, before he leaves. And don't you worry about Madison, Cassie. If he's trying to ruin Pa's practice, I'll see if I can find a way to discredit him in the town's eyes."

"I surely hope you can." She shivered. "I really don't know what to do anymore. I wish Pa were still here."

Quinn covered her hand with his. "I know. We all do."

****

George rose to answer a rap on his hotel room door. Expecting the maid or a hotel clerk, he drew in a breath as he gazed at a young woman with wide blue eyes, dark lashes, chestnut colored hair, and a stylish hat perched on her head.

"Morning, ma'am." He glanced down the hall but saw no one else. "To what do I owe this visit?"

She smiled. "I'm your contact from the agency."

"My contact?" He'd expected a man. "I'd invite you in, but under the circumstances..."

"I understand." She held out a small piece of paper. "I'm staying at the boardinghouse across town under the name of Mrs. Sadie Claymore. I'll be available to take messages back and forth. If you need me, contact me at the boardinghouse, but be discreet."

George grinned. "I always am, ma'am."

She smiled again and turned to leave.

George's gaze never left her as she stepped toward the back stairwell, her fashionable bustle swaying. Had she come in this way? But of course, she'd never have taken the chance of leaving the message at the front desk.

Once she'd retreated from his sight, he closed the door and read the post.

Mr. Masters,

Please send all correspondence on Madison case

50

*via courier. Only emergency correspondences are to
be sent by telegraph.*

*Mrs. Claymore is very reliable. She'll wait in
town until you have information then relay it to us in
New York.*

Sincerely,

William Pinkerton

George grimaced. He'd been so concentrated on
Cassidy, he hadn't had the chance to get anything on
the doctor yet, but he did know where he lived and
practiced.

Talking to people in town hadn't gotten him
anywhere. The townsfolk had nothing but praise for
the new doctor. He feared Cassidy would lose any
patients she had left, especially after the Tasker
deaths. His heart broke for her. What had she done
to deserve this twist of fate?

He had to find something he could use against
Madison. If the townsfolk wouldn't give him
information, maybe he'd pay the good doctor a visit.
He'd pose as a patient and try to wrench as much as
he could from the man himself. Tapping his lower
lip, he reconsidered. Maybe he could pretend to be
interested in information about Cassidy, since
Madison seemed so eager to discredit her, and throw
the doctor off the scent. As a boy, he'd developed the
ability to talk his way out of anything and get others
to reveal things they wouldn't ordinarily. If the
doctor had anything to hide, he'd try to wriggle the
truth out of him. The hard part would be finding
proof of anything he learned.

He slipped into his vest and coat, patting his
bowler into place on his head. He had to get the
goods on the man before he caused Cassidy any more
grief.

****

Cassidy spent the next few days quizzing Quinn
on all the medical procedures and cases he'd

witnessed in the Harrisburg hospital. She sighed with envy at the stories of post war veterans he'd treated and the arcane medications some of the doctors prescribed.

"One of them was actually giving calomel to a patient," Quinn told her. "Can you believe it? Pa would be spinning in his grave."

"He surely would." She gazed at her brother as they strolled toward home, after a short stop at the mercantile. She glanced at the leaden, overcast sky, the scent of rain in the air. "What did you do?"

"Well...what could I do? I couldn't allow the man to poison a patient, no matter how many years he'd been practicing medicine." Quinn grinned. "So, I confronted him."

"You didn't?" Cassidy's pulse raced with delight imagining her brother questioning an older doctor's orders.

"I did."

"And then what happened?"

"He threatened to have me dismissed."

"Oh, Quinn, I'm so proud you stood up for that poor patient. I wish I could've been there to see it."

"Well...in the end it didn't matter much. The man died."

"I'm sorry." She wrapped her arms around her brother's neck, inhaling his spicy warmth and comforting strength. "You stood up for a patient; that's what matters."

He shook his head. "I don't know, Sis. Doctors have to change their way of thinking, if anything is going to improve. A lot of men who served as stewards and doctors during the war are now working in hospitals and private practices all over the country. I hope it's enough to start us on the road to advancing medicine and saving lives."

Cassidy nodded.

Quinn's head swiveled toward the right. "Who's

that?" he breathed.

She followed his gaze. The new schoolteacher emerged from one of the shops, a basket slung over her arm. Glancing back at her brother, she noted the widening of his eyes as he followed the young, blonde-haired woman.

"Oh." Cassidy shrugged. "She's the new school marm. Miss Baker."

"Miss?"

She gulped to avoid laughing. "Reckon you'd like an introduction."

Quinn scowled but continued to follow Miss Baker's progress until she strolled beyond the building out of sight. "She lives in town?"

Cassidy nodded. "She's staying at the boardinghouse for now. But I do believe she's looking for a permanent residence. She cut her arm a few days ago, and I had to suture it. I told her to see me in ten days to have them removed. Since you're back to stay, you'll have a chance to be formally introduced."

Quinn licked his lips. "Reckon so."

"Well, sir." She reached for her brother's arm. "We really should hurry back. Ma's prepared a light supper in your honor, and I made a peach pie."

"Peach?" He smiled. "My favorite. Don't want to miss peach pie. Let's go." He crooked his arm.

****

Late Monday morning, George stood on the threshold of Dr. Madison's residence as the maid, a middle-age, dark haired woman appraised him.

"Do you have an appointment with the doctor, sir?"

"Ah...no, ma'am. I'm new in town, and my illness came on right quick. The only other doc in town is a woman and I..."

The woman scowled. "I can quite understand your qualms about seeing Miss Stuart, sir." She leaned forward. "She's not really a doctor, you know, though she pretends to be. Her father was the town doctor before Dr. Madison arrived, but he met with an unfortunate accident."

George smiled, nodding. "So you can see why I'd prefer to see Doc Madison."

"Of course, sir. Come right inside." She led him through a foyer with patterned wallpaper, blue trim, and two large portrait renderings of a man and woman. He wondered if they were the doctor's esteemed parents. A maple table sat by the rail at the bottom of the staircase with a potted plant and upholstered chair on either side of the table.

He followed the woman into another room down the hall. "You can wait here, while I summon the doctor." She closed the door behind him.

George scanned the room. A typical examining room with a desk. Papers and a file sat on top. He leaned casually against the desk, in case someone opened the door, and lifted the file. A paper bearing the name "Miss Elizabeth Baker" lay inside. He scanned the form quickly. Seemed to be just a routine exam. She was single, twenty-two years old. The exam seemed to be for treatment of a minor infection on her arm.

Maybe he'd just find this Elizabeth Baker and see if anything improper happened during the exam. She was the same age as Colonel Wellingham's daughter.

By the time the door opened, George had left the desk and lounged in a straight back chair across from it. The doctor entered, scanning George as if trying to place him.

"My maid tells me you're new in town Mr...."

"Masters." George suddenly recollected the brief encounter at the mercantile. They hadn't spoken, so he hadn't realized at the time the man was Madison. Had he seen George speak to Cassidy? He'd have to play his hand differently than planned.

The doctor held out his hand. "A pleasure to meet you, sir. I'm Dr. Madison."

After shaking the doctor's hand, George sat back waiting for him to take a seat behind the desk.

"And now, Mr. Masters, what seems to be the problem?"

George leaned forward. "It's not a physical problem I have, Doctor."

Madison's brows rose. "Go on?"

"I'm actually here to gather information on a Miss Cassidy Stuart." George settled back waiting for Madison's reaction.

Madison sputtered. "Why she's not even a competent midwife! If you've been in town long enough, I'm sure you heard of the Tasker deaths." The doctor frowned. "Just a minute, I saw you in the mercantile. You were speaking to the lady in question, and if I recall correctly, she invited you to visit her home."

George laced his fingers together. "I'd contacted her previously by post, so I could speak to her in person."

"She seemed to know you, sir. It's hard for me to believe you've never been here before or made acquaintance with the lady."

George sighed. "This is irrelevant. The point is, I'm investigating her."

"On the Tasker's behalf? Are you a lawyer?"

"No, sir, I'm just conducting an investigation, as I said." He raised his hand, palm up. "If we could get back to the night in question? I've learned you were in attendance."

"After the fact, sir. If I'd gotten there sooner, believe me, this all could have been avoided."

"What would you have done different, Doctor?"

Madison waved a hand. "Why, I would have given Mrs. Tasker something for the pain. It would have eased her suffering and the birth would have been an easy one."

George frowned. "Not sure I understand how it would have made a difference."

"Are you with the town paper, sir?" Madison scowled.

"No, Doctor, I assure you I'm here on my own."

"You say you're new in town. You're not here for a physical ailment...but you're gathering information on Miss Stuart..." His gaze drifted over the file on his desk.

George held his breath, praying he'd left the file in the same spot and condition the doc had.

"Well, Mr. Masters, I have no more information to give you on Miss Stuart, and I've pressing matters to attend to, so if you aren't ill as my maid had indicated, I'm afraid I'll have to ask you to leave." Madison stood, forcing George to do the same.

"If you ever are ill, feel free to make an appointment." Madison's gaze narrowed.

"I sure will, Doc." George strode through the door.

Once outside, he scanned the placid, tree lined street. Next, he planned to pay a call on Miss Elizabeth Baker.

Chapter Eight

Tuesday afternoon, Quinn escorted Cassidy to town square for supplies. She strode through the mercantile to the druggist, extracting the list of items she needed from her reticule.

"How do, Miss Cassie." The druggist, Mr. Henson took her list. After scanning, he nodded. "Be just a few minutes, ma'am."

She smiled, then approached Quinn, who examined items on the shelves. He picked up a porcelain shaving mug and rubbed his clean-shaved jaw. "Reckon I could use one of these. Mine's chipped."

The bells above the entry door jingled, drawing her gaze. Miss Baker entered, fiddling with the strap of her reticule. Quinn's head jerked up, and Cassidy tried to hide a grin. His eyes widened, his mouth gaped. Her older brother seemed enchanted by the blonde-haired woman.

Miss Baker maneuvered her bustle through the narrow aisle and nodded to Cassidy. The teacher's smile wavered as her gaze settled on Quinn. Her delicate brows rose.

Cassidy cleared her throat. "I hope you're well today, Miss Baker."

"And you as well, Miss Stuart."

"How's your arm?"

The teacher glanced downward. "It's fine."

Turning to Quinn, Cassidy gestured. "Quinn, allow me to introduce Miss Baker. She's the new school marm. And Miss Baker, this is my older brother, Quinn."

Miss Baker's gaze rose to meet Quinn's.

Cassidy glanced at Quinn, then back to the teacher. Although she didn't know the woman well, she appeared nervous about something. Cassidy cleared her throat. "He's been interning at the hospital in Harrisburg."

"Oh, I see." Miss Baker bit her lip.

Quinn frowned. "Yes, ma'am. Mighty pleased to meet you."

She blushed. "Will you be in town long, Mr. Stuart, or should I say, Doctor?"

"Either is fine, ma'am. I've just finished my internship and plan to stay in town for good."

Miss Baker cleared her throat. "Well, I surely hope to see you again soon." She turned to the druggist as he returned with Cassidy's items.

"How may I help you, ma'am?" he asked.

The teacher produced a small piece of paper. "If you have these items on hand, sir, I'd be most grateful."

The druggist scanned the list. "I believe I do, ma'am. If you'll allow me to take care of Miss Stuart, I'll be right happy to look."

"Thank you, sir." Miss Baker stepped back to allow Cassidy access to the counter.

As she paid for the supplies, she couldn't help but steal a glance back at Miss Baker. Something seemed to be bothering the teacher. Unless she was just shy around new men. Of course, Cassidy would never pry into another's business.

****

George entered the mercantile and glanced around. He needed some tooth powder and a new toothbrush, as well as information on a woman named Miss Baker. As he surveyed the shelves for the items he needed, he caught sight of Cassidy standing at the counter.

He stepped toward her, the familiar lilac scent

wafting to him. She didn't notice he stood behind her as she picked up a packet of scented soaps from her basket, lifting each under her pert nose, she closed her eyes and sniffed.

He stepped closer.

She turned and gasped. "George, what are you doing? You nearly scared me to death." Her lush lips parted, stirring his body to react to old, but delightful memories.

"I'm here for supplies," George said. "Ran out of soap and shaving cream."

She adjusted her hat. "I reckoned you'd be leaving town now you've seen to your pa."

He shrugged. "I'm not ready to go quite yet."

She swallowed. The slender curve of her ivory throat enticed him. He had a sudden urge to lean over and kiss the pulse point, then work his way up to her full lips. In a haze, he realized she'd said something and eyed him with a raised brow.

"Uh, pardon me?"

She quirked her luscious lips. He could almost recall the taste but longed to refresh his memory.

"You said you've been to California and New York, but never told me where you've living now?"

He cleared his throat. "New York City."

"You've a home there?"

He shrugged. "Can't really call it a home. I'm living in a hotel."

"Oh." She glanced away. "Well. Be sure to stop by the house before you leave. Quinn and Sarah are home. Reckon they'd like to say hello. Quinn was here with me earlier today, but I had to stop back again because Sarah coerced me to purchase her favorite soaps."

"Well, I would enjoy seeing your brother again, but Sarah...if you recall, she didn't much like me. And I can imagine she hates me since I left you. And Quinn's likely none too happy with me either. I wouldn't be surprised if he punched me in the jaw." He glanced around the store, glad Cassidy's brother wasn't with her.

"Well, I don't want you to leave again without at least saying goodbye." She gazed at him, then turned toward the counter and engaged in conversation with the clerk.

George stood frozen to the spot, not registering their chatter as she paid for her purchases. Was she serious about him paying another visit to the house, or being polite?

****

After first checking at the boardinghouse and finding she wasn't in, George discovered the elusive Miss Elizabeth Baker at the one room school house. The only one in town. He stood outside the school, as eight children of varying ages raced past him on their way home. A few of them shot him curious glances, but most seemed intent on escaping their studies for another day.

Through the glass paned windows, he glimpsed the school teacher moving about. She must be tidying up the classroom before leaving. George had no intention of going to the door. He didn't want to frighten or corner her. He'd wait until she left for home, no matter how long it took.

He passed the time eyeing a flock of sparrows chattering in the trees overhead, beating their tiny wings against the branches. And he thought of Cassidy. Regret washed over him. Why had he left? Had he been afraid to try to make a life with a woman who truly loved him? He sighed. Likely, he'd returned much too late to do anything to change her opinion of him. She'd never trust him again. And he couldn't blame her.

When Miss Baker finally opened the door, she halted, her eyes widening. He didn't move from the spot on the grass, his back against a massive oak.

She backed away, hand still on the doorknob, light brows drawn.

"Ma'am." George stood but didn't approach. "I'm sorry if I frightened you. I just wanted to ask a few questions."

Her gaze darkened and her throat worked, but she didn't close the door or move from the doorway. Used to charming information out of people, George couldn't afford to frighten the teacher. He stood his ground, not daring to draw closer.

"I wanted to ask you about Dr. Madison."

A white hand rose to her throat, and her gaze narrowed. "Why ask me about him?" She glanced about as if searching for help.

George raised his hand. "Please, ma'am, I mean you no harm, I swear. All I want to do is ask you a few questions about your visit with the doctor."

She bit her lip.

"If you'd allow me to come a bit closer, we wouldn't have to shout."

Her gaze darted about, and she tightened the blue plaid shawl around her shoulders. He should have brought Mrs. Claymore with him. She would have had a calming effect on this timid, young woman. Or maybe, if the children hadn't rushed off after school, she would have been less scared.

She stepped toward him, but halted. He held his breath, afraid any move would send her scurrying in the other direction. Like a wild rabbit who had been chased by a wolf. Or worse, screaming her lungs out for help. A few feet from his position, she stopped again, her brow knitting into a scowl.

"Why do you want to know about my doctor visit?" She worried her bottom lip with her teeth.

"I'm investigating Dr. Madison."

"Why?" She scanned the school grounds, like she expected someone to jump out and grab her.

George sighed. He didn't want to reveal himself

as a Pinkerton agent, but he had to gain her trust. "Because he harmed a patient in his former practice...in Philadelphia."

Miss Baker frowned. "Harmed a patient? How?"

"My client..." He spread his hands. "He told me the doctor assaulted his daughter."

The schoolteacher's eyes widened and her mouth gaped. "I... all he did was examine me and apply antiseptic to my arm. Nothing else..." She blushed a bright pink.

"Are you sure that's all he did, ma'am? If he hurt you..."

"No... Of course, he didn't..." She turned and raced back to the schoolhouse, slamming the door behind her.

George stared after her. Her demeanor told him more than her words. But he didn't dare approach her. Maybe in a few days. He didn't reckon she'd spill anything to a man, anyway. He needed someone who could draw her out.

****

Scott leaned back in his chair nursing a glass of bourbon. At midafternoon, empty tables and stools at the bar signaled an off time for the local tavern. The solitude allowed his thoughts to drift to the lovely school teacher. At her next visit, he'd go a bit further, and if his actions didn't scare her away...well... A smile flitted across his lips as he raised his glass. So long as he could control her, he wouldn't have to fear repercussions, like with the bitch in Philadelphia, who went running to her father.

He frowned. But now he had Mr. Masters poking around in his business. Who was he anyway? If not with the paper, perhaps he was with law enforcement. Had the bitch's father sent Masters to find some new evidence to discredit him? If so, and he connected with Miss Baker, they could disgrace him with more vicious gossip and accusations. And that did not fit into his plans, not one bit.

After Miss Stuart had botched the Tasker birth, he'd thought his fortune was turning around. Scott planned to rake in the townsfolk as the only reliable doctor left in town. He wouldn't allow *anyone* to ruin his chances of starting over, no matter what he had to do to stop them.

The bartender sauntered toward him, but Scott waved him away, dropping a bill onto the counter.

"Leaving already, Doc?" the burly man asked.

"I have some pressing business to attend." Scott stood and straightened his coat, lifting his hat to his head. Maybe he'd just pay a call on Miss Baker to be sure she hadn't talked to the man. And then, he'd find out just who this Mr. Masters really was and what he should do about him.

Chapter Nine

"George!"

George glanced up from his usual corner table in the tavern where he'd been taking most of his meals. He recognized the familiar voice: Cassidy's brother.

Quinn stepped over to the table, his grin widening. "Ma and Cassie told me you were back in town. I've been hoping to run into you."

George fingered his jaw, trying to assess Quinn's mood. "Have a seat, unless you've come to sock me in the mouth."

Quinn laughed. "Don't think I didn't want to five years ago, but time heals...at least I hope Cassie's gotten over you." He pulled out a chair and sat. "She told me you were in town to pay respect to your pa."

George nodded. "There's a bit more to it than that." Quinn had been a great ally when they served together during the war. George might have to reveal some part of his purpose here in order to recruit Quinn's help and gain his confidence. "I can't say too much, but I'm concerned about what a doctor named Madison is spewing about Cassidy."

Quinn glanced around the tavern. "I've been in Harrisburg, but she told me he's been trying to take our patients. If he has his way, the whole town will belong to him, and our practice will be ruined."

"I hear tell he had problems with his former practice in Philadelphia. A patient complaint."

Quinn straightened. "That so? Now I'm extremely interested, George. If I could meet you somewhere private..." He glanced around at the few patrons and the serving woman. "... away from prying eyes and ears."

"Come by my hotel room in a few hours." George drew a few bills from his coat pocket and placed them on the table. "I'm trying to gather evidence from one of his patients here in town. A young woman."

Quinn nodded. "I'll be there."

****

Cassidy cornered Quinn as soon as he arrived home. She wanted to let him know what she had planned now that he was home for good.

As they settled at the kitchen table, she set a slice of pie before him. "I have some ideas for the practice...at least I had, before Dr. Madison had to come and ruin it all."

Quinn raised a brow. "What did you have in mind, Sis?" He lifted his fork and dug in.

Cassidy leaned her elbows on the tabletop and folded her arms. "Well, with you back and the few patients I've been able to hold on to, I thought, you wouldn't really need me all that much."

"Just where is this going?" He set his fork down. "Of course, I'll need you."

"Well, once we rebuild the practice, if that's even possible now. But I thought, with you here, I could apply to medical school."

"What school?" He frowned.

"The one you attended in Philadelphia." She glanced at him, daring him to utter a protest.

He pushed a hand through his hair. "Well, Cassie, I think that's an admirable idea."

"You do?"

"But...it's hard for a woman to get accepted to that school."

"I've heard of women attending medical schools," she protested.

"Well..." He swallowed. "How about we discuss this after dinner? I have an appointment in town

65

right now."

"All right," she agreed. But she had to wonder if Quinn would betray her by using the same arguments Papa had to keep her at home as his assistant.

****

George glanced out the window, catching sight of Quinn strolling toward the hotel. Although he had to tell the man something, he'd avoid revealing his true identity. At least for now. He waited for the rap at the door, then opened it to Cassie's brother.

"C'mon in." George motioned him into the room, then closed the door.

Quinn settled on the one chair in the room. George sat across from him on the bed.

"So, George, what do you know about Madison?"

"Reckon I should start at the beginning." George leaned forward. "I was living in New York City with no money but gambling earnings, when who did I meet but Colonel Wellingham. Remember him?"

"Do I!" Quinn grinned. "How's the old man doing?"

"Well..." George spread his hands. "It seems he had a run in with Doc Madison in Philadelphia. His daughter had catarrh, and the doc examined her."

Quinn leaned over on his elbows. "And?"

"Let's say, the doc got a bit personal with the young lady. He took liberties and she slapped him, then ran out of the office half naked. When she told her father, he confronted Madison, but he denied the whole thing, blaming Wellingham's daughter. Accused her of being a strumpet who accosted *him*."

Quinn whistled. "What did Wellingham do?"

"He believed his daughter's story, of course, and threatened to call in the authorities."

Quinn nodded.

"But Madison's father, Dr. Horace Madison, is a very wealthy and prestigious physician in

Philadelphia. He apparently has a lot of politicians in his pocket, so the colonel wasn't able to press charges against Scott Madison. He later learned the doc had left his father's practice and disappeared. Wellingham wondered if he'd gone somewhere else until the gossip about the incident cooled down."

"What happened to his daughter?" Quinn asked.

"She was disgraced. She quietly married a man who'd served under the colonel. They moved out west to avoid ostracism. But Wellingham heard a rumor about Scott setting up practice in a small town in Pennsylvania. He investigated and found out he was in Burkeville. Knowing I was from here, he asked for my help."

"So, you're here to investigate and get some new dirt on Madison."

"I surely hope so." George rose from the bed and paced. "I respect the colonel and want to make things right for him and his daughter, as well as getting a dangerous man out of this town, so he can't prey on any more young women."

Quinn grimaced. "I'd like to see him out of here, too. Cassie's had a hard time keeping up the practice with him in town and now the Tasker deaths have added to the fire. He's accused her of being incompetent."

"I know. I hate to see her blamed for something not her fault. I want to see this bastard not only run out of town, but if I catch him harming a patient, the colonel could bring the law into it as well. I just need proof."

Quinn looked up. "You mentioned a young woman in town..."

"I went to his office, pretending to be a patient. I saw a file on his last patient. A Miss Elizabeth Baker."

Quinn's rust-colored brows rose. "The schoolteacher?"

"You know her?"

"Cassie just introduced me to her. She's young and very pretty."

George nodded. "Just the type of patient Madison likes to prey on, I reckon."

"You mean he...?"

"That's what I'm trying to find out. I interviewed Miss Baker, but all she'd say was that he'd treated her arm and nothing improper happened."

"Wait a minute." Quinn's gaze narrowed. "Cassie said the teacher cut her arm, and Cassie had to suture it. What was she doing seeing Doc Madison?"

"That's interesting." George stroked his beard. "She said he'd applied antiseptic to her arm. Wouldn't she have gone to your sister if she had an infection?"

Quinn nodded. "Something's not right...but if Miss Baker heard about the Taskers, she may have been wary of seeing Cassie again."

George sighed. "Reckon I'll have to have another talk with the teacher. Of course, I'm a stranger and a man. If something improper *did* happen, I'm the last person she'd tell. She's likely humiliated and fears ruining her own reputation."

Quinn shrugged. "So, what can we do?"

"I thought..." George threaded his fingers together. "...I thought maybe we should tell Cassie. She's a woman and a doctor, and she's already treated Miss Baker, maybe she could coax the information out."

"Why don't you just ask Cassie yourself?"

George shook his head. "I'm not sure she trusts me. But this is to go no further, Quinn. The last thing I need is for Madison to find out I'm investigating him."

Quinn nodded. "I'll talk to Cassie."

****

After dinner, Quinn kept his promise and escorted Cassidy to town square. She gathered her wool shawl around her shoulders to ward off the April chill. As they stopped outside the mercantile, Quinn shook his head.

"You know, even though I've only been away a few months, it's still startling to recall just how tiny this town is."

Cassidy giggled. "Can you blame me for wanting to go to Philadelphia?"

"No, ma'am." He grinned.

"I've heard medical schools are very picky about the women they allow in, at least that's what Pa used to tell me. He said, even if they did accept me, they'd be very hard on me." She glanced at her brother. "He didn't think I'd make it."

"I don't agree, Cass. You've had tons of experience nursing during the war and assisting Pa. If you'd like I could send a recommendation."

"You'd do that for me?"

"Sure. Don't know how much it would help, though. I've just completed my internship."

"You don't know how happy you've made me, Quinn."

He led her to a bench at the end of the street. "Cassie, sit down. I have a favor to ask."

After settling on the bench in front of the closed shoemaker's shop, she frowned up at her brother. "What is it? Is something wrong?"

"Not with me, Cassie. The favor I'm asking for concerns George."

"George? Why should I do *him* a favor?"

Quinn sighed. "Well, this favor would help not only George, but our practice and others in town."

"How?"

"Well, it concerns the reason George is here."

"He's here to pay respects to his father."

Quinn shook his head. "That's not the real

reason he's here."

Cassidy's pulse quickened. "Then why *is* he here?"

"He's investigating Dr. Madison."

"So that explains why he hasn't left yet! But why? George isn't in law enforcement or working for a newspaper, is he?" His story about living as a professional gambler might just be a front.

Quinn cleared his throat and leaned toward her so they almost touched. "He told me Madison took liberties with one of his patients in Philadelphia. The patient in question is the daughter of a colonel we served under during the war."

Cassidy's pulse quickened. "So George is doing the man a favor...or is the colonel paying him?"

"I can't really say, but if Madison's as unscrupulous as George claims..."

Cassidy's face heated. "I'd do anything to see the weasel discredited."

"Colonel Wellingham is the one who allowed you to bring George home after he was wounded at Gettysburg."

Cassidy recalled an image of a kind, dark-haired officer. He'd made sure she had the means to bring George home to recover.

"I remember Colonel Wellingham," she said. "But how is George supposed to prove Madison harmed the colonel's daughter?"

"He can't. That's why he has to watch him, to see if he harms another patient here in town."

"And how can I help?"

"Well, George visited the doc, pretending to be a patient and saw a file on Miss Baker. She was the doc's last patient. George tried to talk to her, but all she'd tell him was that the doc treated her arm for an infection. He thought..." Quinn gazed across the square. "...he thought if you could try to talk to her, maybe she'd open up about her visit with Madison."

Cassidy's blood warmed. "She went to Madison after I'd stitched up her arm? I told her to see me if she had any sign of infection. She's also supposed to come back in a few days to have the stitches removed."

"I told George you treated her. Maybe she'd heard about the...um..."

"You can say it." Cassidy's face burned. "The Taskers. She heard about the Taskers and ran to Madison." She sighed. "Can't say as I blame her. She wasn't a regular patient, being new in town."

Quinn draped his arm over her shoulder. "Don't dwell on it, Cassie. We need to know if the doc acted improperly. George couldn't get anything out of her, but maybe you could."

"Maybe she's just nervous talking to a strange man. George can be charming, but he can also..." She closed her eyes. "He can set a woman's heart racing." She eyed her brother. "And it could turn out to be nothing, just like she said."

"But at least he'll know. And if Madison *did* harm her in any way, you'll be doing Miss Baker and the town a favor, as well as George."

Cassidy bit her lip. What harm to have a conversation with the teacher? Her mind drifted to an image of the attractive, charming, but arrogant physician. The way he'd blamed her, discredited her as a doctor. If he was using his position and looks to take advantage of young women, she'd do all she could to disgrace him.

"All right." She nodded. "I'll do it. When will you see George again?"

"As soon as I have your answer, which I already do. Thanks, Sis." He leaned over and kissed her cheek. "You won't regret this."

Chapter Ten

Wednesday afternoon, Cassidy piled plates and cups in the sink, then wiped down the table. Movement in the kitchen doorway caught her gaze. Matt approached waving a paper.

"Cassie, a post came for you."

"For me?" She strode toward her brother. "Who's it from?"

He scanned the envelope. "The University of Pennsylvania, in Philadelphia."

Her pulse raced. "Give it here." She snatched the post from her brother's hand and held it against her chest, taking a deep breath. In anticipation of Quinn's return to the practice, she'd applied to the school, hoping to be accepted for the September class, so she'd be around through the summer to help Quinn. This had to be her medical school acceptance or rejection. Her hands trembled as she considered the possibilities.

"Well, aren't you gonna open it?" Matt frowned.

"I—why yes." She pried the seal and opened the parchment trying to keep her gaze focused. Dizziness swept over her. She plopped into a chair.

Matt shook his head. "If it's bad news, you should just read it and get it over with."

"Reckon you're right." She took a deep breath and read the post.

Dearest Miss Stuart,

We regret to inform you...

Cassidy's face heated. They weren't going to accept her. She refocused to read the rest of the post.

...unfortunately, your qualifications aren't up to

our standards.

Sincerely,

Dean of Students, Mr. Emory Braun

Cassidy set the post on the table and bit her bottom lip. Her vision blurred.

"Bad news, Sis?" Matt asked.

She jerked, then recovered, smoothing her skirts. She cleared her throat. "I'm afraid so. Looks like I won't be going to medical school anytime soon."

Her brother stepped to her side and squeezed her shoulder. "I'd miss you too much anyway if you went off to Philadelphia."

She reached up and grasped his hand, willing herself not to cry. A lump rose in her throat. She swallowed hard.

"Thanks, Matt. Guess I'll just have to figure out what else I can do with my life."

"You can stay here and help Quinn, like you did for Pa."

Cassidy nodded but said nothing. Her throat thickened, and she feared her voice would betray her feelings.

"You all right, Cassie?" Her brother seemed hesitant to leave her side.

"Sure, Matt. You go on now; I'll be fine."

After he left the kitchen, she buried her face in her hands. Her dream of going to Philadelphia and attending a real medical school shattered. She took a deep breath, hoping to compose herself before any other family member saw her. She'd allow herself to cry in her room.

Rising, she grasped the post. Burning it would be for the best. Then she'd never have to look at those hateful words again. A sound in the doorway startled her. Had Matt returned?

The man in the door wasn't Matt, but George. Had her mother let him in? He eyed her and frowned, his gaze drifting to the post in her hand.

Oh, Lord, just the man I don't want to speak to right now.

"Cassie, Matt tells me you got a post."

Drat, Matt! She chewed on her lower lip. *Might as well tell him, he'll find out anyhow.*

She swallowed. "It's from the medical school in Philadelphia, the University of Pennsylvania." She dropped her gaze.

"And?" George prompted.

"They won't accept me as a student." She gazed into his eyes and shrugged. "I shouldn't have tried."

"I'm sorry, Cassie." He stepped to her side and settled his arm over her shoulder. "I know how much this meant to you."

She longed to collapse in the comfort of George's arms. She'd found solace there years ago, when she thought him the man for her. But instead, she stiffened her spine.

"It's all right," she said. "It was foolish of me to try."

George enveloped her in his strong arms. She bit her lip hoping to stave off the torrent of tears threatening to course down her cheeks. She yearned to bawl and scream at the injustice. She had the same credentials as Quinn, except for his experience as a steward during the war. But she'd served as a nurse, basically the same thing. Why wouldn't they allow her to try?

George rubbed her back in an all too familiar gesture. The men in her life always felt the need to soothe her hurt away. Her father would've done the same.

She glanced up, frowning. "What are you doing here, anyway?"

He grimaced. "Not happy to see me? Reckon I deserve that. I spoke to Quinn. He told me he'll be rebuilding your father's practice."

She nodded. "Now, he'll be able to see patients

over the summer and I'd hoped..." She swallowed, crumpling the post.

"It'll all work out, Cassie." He spun her to face him, and she buried her face against his rock hard chest. He'd filled out since she'd seen him five years ago.

She raised her face to his, losing herself in his dark gaze. He brushed her cheek with his fingers, then lifted her chin, sending delightful shivers through her body. Her lips parted in anticipation as he lowered his face to hers. His mouth brushed hers, gently at first, then pressed against her, shooting hot sparks to her core. His comforting scent of sandalwood, leather, and male enveloped her.

She sighed into the kiss, her tongue swirling inside his mouth. Her insides coiled with spiraling heat. She'd never been with a man and often imagined what it would feel like to have limbs intertwined, bodies pressed tightly with the one who set your soul aflame.

"Oh, George," she gasped as he released his hold. Her skin moistened, body growing hotter by the minute. As a physician she knew what went on between a man and woman, but George sent her analytical thoughts spinning as want and need threw everything to the wind. She didn't want the kiss to ever end.

"I know exactly how you feel, Cassie, but we have to stop now."

"I know." She nodded, not wanting to leave the warmth of his strong arms, but knowing she must. She gestured to one of the chairs.

"Sit, I'll make tea. Then you can tell me why you're here."

****

George sat across the table from Cassidy and sipped the sweetened tea. His blood raced and his shaft hardened, making concentration difficult. An image of Cassie sprawled on her bed as they made love caused his breathing to quicken. But he couldn't entertain the thought. Not in her home.

"Quinn told me about Miss Baker." Cassidy sipped her tea and flicked her tongue out to lick her lower lip.

George took in a deep breath, trying to regain his concentration. Cassidy eyed him with a tilt of her chin.

"He also told me about Colonel Wellingham's daughter. How horrible, if it's true!" She set her cup in the saucer.

"I can assure you, it is. The colonel's convinced his daughter didn't make up this story. It happened."

Cassidy sighed. "We have to prove Madison is the monster you believe he is, before he harms anyone in town."

"Unfortunately, I need proof; otherwise, Madison goes on as he has." George leaned on his folded arms. "If you could get it out of her, I know I could find some way to prove it."

"But what if he only examined her, as she claims?"

He shrugged. "Then I'll have to stick around town a little longer. He's bound to slip up sometime."

Cassidy's lips curved into a slight smile. Was she happy at the prospect of him staying in town? He hoped so. She drew her cup to her lips again and sipped, her delicate tongue swirling over the cup rim.

George drew in a deep breath. How much longer could he stay without taking her in his arms and running his tongue over her lips and cheeks, down her ivory throat?

"George?" Cassidy's gaze narrowed. "Are you all right?"

He cleared his throat. "Fine." He swallowed the

rest of his tea, now cooled.

"What do I have to do?"

"See Miss Baker. Maybe you could pay her a friendly visit at the boardinghouse. Tell her you're concerned about her arm. Anything. Then get her talking. Maybe she'll confide in you."

"I don't know. She seems to be a very private woman. I don't know if she'd tell me if Madison assaulted her or even kissed her."

George sighed. "Well...it's worth a try. Otherwise, we'll have to start over. I'd have to visit and interview all his patients, but I suspect he preys on young, beautiful women who have no one else in town. Exactly like Miss Baker."

Cassidy leaned forward. "You're right, of course. Who else would that weasel prey on? I'll pay her a visit first thing tomorrow."

****

Scott spent Thursday morning treating patients for cuts, scrapes, fevers, and other minor ailments. But his mind never strayed from the liberties he'd taken yesterday with Miss Baker. His mistake...acting too soon on his impulses. He should have taken his time, perhaps courted her. But now, if his threats didn't keep her quiet, he might just find himself in a heap of trouble as he had in Philadelphia. Maybe he should forget the vixen and move on. But with the Stuart practice in shambles, he'd never have a better opportunity to embed himself in a new town.

He lanced a boil on his patient, Mr. Jenkins. The elderly man cried out.

"Sorry, sir," Scott apologized. "My mind's a bit befuddled today."

The old man winced. "Well, can't blame a man for getting overwhelmed. See you got a house full of patients waiting on you out there." He poked his thumb over his shoulder toward the office door.

"Have I?" Scott smirked.

"Seems you've gotten to be the popular doc in town."

"The only doc in town," Scott emphasized.

Mr. Jenkins nodded, as he slid off the exam table.

After finishing with his last patient and eating the lunch Tillie had prepared, Scott decided a walk through town would be in order. Maybe he'd just take a stroll by the boardinghouse.

Scott stepped down the lane, adjusting his coat. He greeted all passersby and shop owners who were outside on this fine spring day. While browsing in the mercantile, he learned a bit about the man, George Masters, who'd visited his office.

He'd lived in town years before and returned a Civil War veteran but had left after standing Miss Stuart up two days before their wedding. His most recent homecoming to pay respects to his late father, buried behind a shack on the outskirts of Burkeville.

So, if this were true, why hadn't Masters left? Did he hope to rekindle his romance with Miss Stuart? Scott tipped his hat to a passing pair of middle-aged women, then gazed across the street.

Ah, the lady in question.

Miss Stuart stood outside the mercantile conversing with an elderly woman. As the woman took her leave, he decided to make his move. Making sure Miss Stuart didn't catch him watching her, he eased his way across the street out of her line of vision. As he grew close, he caught her scent. She turned abruptly toward him as if she'd sensed his presence. He bumped against her, as if by accident, then took a step back.

She gasped, then stared at him.

"I'm so sorry, ma'am." He grasped her arm to steady her. "You must excuse my clumsiness."

She adjusted her hat. "I'm quite all right, sir.

Would you care to unhand me?"

"Of course, I'm so sorry." Scott dropped his hand from her arm. Her scent, lilac and something very sweet and all woman, enveloped him. She looked much better than she had the last time he'd seen her covered in blood.

She eyed him, her gaze narrowing. "Are you here to gloat?"

Scott frowned. "Of course not, Miss Stuart. In fact, I may have a proposition for you."

Her eyes widened a bit. She seemed to be appraising him. "Doctor?"

"My practice is growing rapidly, and I could use a skilled assistant. Since your practice seems to be shrinking, perhaps I could hire you."

She cringed. "Sir, my brother has returned to take over, and I'll be assisting him. We plan to rebuild our father's practice, you see."

"Ah, yes, your brother. He's home to stay, you say?"

"Yes, he's completed his internship and is now a licensed physician." She wrinkled her pert nose. "So, as you can see, I wouldn't have time to work as your assistant. Nor would I want to even if it was the last position on earth."

Scott tipped his hat. "I'll give you the summer, but when the town turns to me, you'll both have to look elsewhere for employment, I'm afraid."

"So you say, sir. May the best physician win." She nodded and turned on her heel.

Scott eyed her posterior as she angled across the street. She headed in the direction of the boardinghouse.

He'd learned Masters had a room at the hotel, so who in the boardinghouse was Miss Stuart going to see?

****

Cassidy adjusted the basket she carried, then

yanked on the string of her reticule, pinned to the waistline of her skirt.

Her face flamed at the doctor's audacity. How dare he threaten to take away her patients? Then offer her a job? She'd die of hunger before she'd work for him!

As she stomped up onto the boardinghouse porch, she cleared her throat and adjusted her hat. What an arrogant ass!

Although the women in town all fawned over him, thinking him an eligible gentleman, Madison was nothing but a fake! His frock coat, cut of the finest cloth, his chestnut hair and thin mustache perfectly groomed and his dark eyes magnetic, almost hypnotic, might have small town women swooning, but daughters of families in Burkeville, he'd likely not touch for fear of repercussions. She hoped Miss Baker would have something she could give George to bring the haughty doctor to his knees and drive him from this town forever.

****

When George emerged from the hotel lobby, he narrowed his gaze as a man and woman faced each other on the opposite side of the street. Cassidy and Madison.

He backed into the doorway, staying out of their line of sight. If Madison as much as touched Cassidy, he'd be over there in a shot. But for now, he'd wait to see what happened.

Cassidy turned on her heel and strode toward the boardinghouse. The doctor watched her but didn't follow.

George held his breath until Madison turned and walked in the opposite direction. Cassidy was obviously on her way to speak to Miss Baker. He'd best stick around to make sure Madison didn't interfere.

Chapter Eleven

At the boardinghouse, Cassidy rapped on the door, which opened to the plump, doughy-faced proprietress, Mrs. Peadmont, peering out.

"Good morning, Miss Stuart." The woman squinted. "What brings you here so early this morning?"

"I wonder if I could speak to Miss Baker. It's rather urgent."

The landlady's wispy brows rose. "She hasn't left for school yet, I don't think. I'll see if she's in."

"Please do. And thank you."

The woman opened the door wide. "You can wait in the parlor. If she's in, I can have her meet you downstairs or you can go up to her room."

"I'd prefer to speak to her in private, if that's all right."

Mrs. Peadmont scowled, but nodded. "Of course, if that's what you want." She waved Cassidy toward the parlor.

"Thank you, ma'am." She lifted her skirts and stepped into the cozy room. Two men, seated near the windows, halted their conversation and eyed her.

"This is Miss Stuart," Mrs. Peadmont explained. "She's here to see one of our guests. Miss Stuart, this is Mr. Engels and Mr. Walters. They've been staying with me for the past few weeks."

"How do you do?" Cassidy said.

"Ma'am." They spoke in unison, both rising.

"Please, have a seat." Mr. Engels waved her into the chair he'd vacated.

Cassidy edged her way into the room as the

landlady retreated. After taking the proffered seat, she gestured to the men. "Please, sit. Don't allow me to interrupt your conversation."

"Of course not, ma'am." Mr. Walters sat. "My friend and I were discussing business. Nothing a young lady would be interested in, I'm sure."

Cassidy smiled. "Oh, you're wrong. What kind of business are you in?"

Mr. Walters leaned forward. "We're looking to build here in Burkeville."

"Build here?" Cassidy frowned. "This town is so small; it isn't even on the map. Who on earth would want to come here?"

"You'd be surprised, ma'am," Mr. Engels put in, settling into the settee. "People are looking to build homes anywhere, and many want to get out of the big cities."

"Is that so? Why, I'd love to live in a big city."

"Have you ever been to the city, ma'am?"

"I've been to Washington City during the war. I worked in one of the military hospitals as a nurse."

Mr. Walters' heavy brows rose. "Why, you don't look old enough to have been more than a child during the war."

"I can assure you I did serve as a nurse in the hospital and battlefield as well."

"Well, I'll be..." Mr. Engels smiled. "No wonder you're not satisfied living here. You want a taste of excitement, I reckon."

Cassidy nodded. Before she could answer, a woman appeared in the doorway. She looked like she'd just arrived from someplace like New York City, dressed stylishly in a green gown and bustle, with shiny chestnut hair pulled off her face in an elaborate upsweep.

"Pardon me." She eyed Cassidy and the two men.

"Do come in, Mrs. Claymore." Mr. Engels

extended a hand. "This is Miss Stuart, a resident here in town."

Mrs. Claymore inclined her head. "How do you do?"

Cassidy inclined her head. "Are you visiting like the two gentlemen here?"

Mrs. Claymore settled on the seat Mr. Engels vacated for her. "Just for a short while. I've business in New York City."

"New York?" Cassidy's face heated. "Do you know George Masters?" she asked on an impulse.

"Don't believe I do, Miss Stuart."

The landlady appeared at the parlor door. "Miss Stuart, Miss Baker will see you now."

"Thank you, Mrs. Peadmont." She smiled at the two men. "Gentlemen, it's been a pleasure conversing with you." She glanced at Mrs. Claymore. "A pleasure meeting you, too."

"And you as well, ma'am," Mr. Walters said as he and Mr. Engels rose.

She followed the landlady to the top of the stairs, where she pointed to the door on the left. "That's her room."

"Thank you." Cassidy nodded and waited until the woman descended to the bottom of the stairs before raising her hand to knock.

Her light rap met silence. She raised her hand to knock again, but the door swung inward. Miss Baker peered out, then motioned Cassidy inside.

"I must apologize, Doctor Stuart." Her face flushed. "I should have come back to you to see to my arm."

Cassidy motioned for her to sit on the bed. "It's quite all right, Miss Baker, considering..." Her throat closed, and she let the statement die.

Miss Baker grimaced. "Everyone was saying such horrible things about you. I'm new here and wasn't sure what to do."

Cassidy bit her lip. "It's quite understandable."

The teacher rolled up the sleeve of her wrapper. "If you'd like to take a look..."

Cassidy peered at the blackened stitches against Miss Baker's pale skin. "The wound looks fine. In a few days, you can have those stitches removed."

"Doc Madison told me he'd take them out, but I'd rather you..." The teacher gazed around the room as if searching for something to focus on, ashamed to meet Cassidy's gaze.

She cleared her throat. "I'd like to talk to you about Doc Madison."

Miss Baker shrugged, her gaze dropping. "What about him?"

"Well...to put this delicately...did he harm you or do anything improper during the exam?"

The teacher's face colored. "Whatever do you mean?"

"Did he touch you anywhere he shouldn't, try to kiss you or say anything improper?"

Miss Baker's throat worked. Cassidy clenched her hands. The urge to move closer, draw her out, shake sense into her, caused her teeth to grind, and palms to itch, but she held back. She must be careful.

"No...no, Doctor Stuart. All he did was look at my arm and apply an antiseptic. He said an infection was starting."

"And that was the last time you saw him?"

"No, he came to see me at the schoolhouse."

"The schoolhouse?" Cassidy leaned forward. "Why?"

"To check on my arm to be sure the antiseptic had worked." The teacher gulped. "That's all it was."

"You're sure?" Cassidy met her gaze.

Miss Baker glanced away again. "He did nothing else."

"But you don't want him treating you anymore?"

"I...I'd feel more comfortable coming to you, Doctor Stuart. I made a great mistake in doubting your abilities."

Cassidy nodded. "Well, I'll be happy to remove your stitches and would love to take you on as a patient, but..."

Miss Baker rose from the bed. "I really *do* have to get ready for school. The children will be there ahead of me otherwise. I'm sure you understand."

"Of course, Miss Baker." Cassidy stood and opened the door. "Just be sure to come see me in a week." She pointed to the teacher's arm.

"I will." Her smile wavered as Cassidy stepped into the hall and closed the door behind her.

She leaned against the wall, heaving a heavy sigh.

What am I going to tell George?

****

George blew out a breath of relief when he spotted Cassidy emerge from the hotel. Madison could still be lurking around but for now, wasn't anywhere in sight. When Cassidy stepped off the bottom porch step, George raced forward grasping her arm.

"Did she tell you anything?" He steered her to the opposite side of the street.

She glanced over her shoulder. "Mrs. Peadmont may be eavesdropping. She seemed real interested in why I'd come."

"What about Miss Baker?" He pulled Cassidy up alongside the bakery and propped her against the wall.

"She wouldn't tell me anything." Cassidy glanced around. "Should we be talking about this here?"

George sighed. "I hoped you'd draw her out...unless he really *did* just examine her."

"I don't know. That's what she says, but I

85

suspect there's more."

George shrugged. "But if she won't talk, I have nothing to go on."

Mrs. Armstrong exited the baker's shop and frowned. Cassidy smiled and nodded. George tipped his hat.

"Ma'am?"

The woman inclined her head and turned away but glanced back once, her dark brows arching.

"I fear we're drawing too much attention here," George said. "I'd ask you to meet in my room, but..." He grinned.

"We don't need to give my neighbors more fodder for gossip. And if it got back to my mother, well, I wouldn't want to be *you*."

"No, ma'am," George agreed. "Reckon we'll have to talk at your house."

Cassidy bit her lip. "Come over in an hour. I don't have any patients scheduled today. Maybe I'll urge Ma to spend the rest of the morning shopping."

George nodded. "I'll see you then."

****

An hour later, George strolled down the tidy, tree-lined lane leading to the Stuart home. Memories abounded of his childhood years when he'd all but lived there in an effort to escape his own father and home. He barely remembered his ma. She'd left when he was small. Likely his mother wasn't able to handle Amos's imbibing, while trying to raise four robust sons.

In the weeks preceding his wedding, he'd imagined living in a house like the Stuart home, he and Cassie raising a gaggle of happy children. But the townsfolk had looked down on him, and even though Cassidy's parents seemed accepting, George had the feeling they'd always thought their oldest daughter could have done much better.

Even now, telling the truth about his purpose

would raise his esteem in the town's estimation, as well as with Cassie's family. He had to wonder if his position as a Pinkerton agent would matter to her.

He glanced up at the well-kept red-brick house with green and white trim, a long wraparound porch and a flower garden on each side of the porch steps. Green leaved oak trees flanked the house on each side. A shingle amidst the flowers, proclaimed, *Dr. Stuart, Physician.*

George breathed in a long, full breath. *This could have been my home, if only...*

He climbed the steps. Wide railings along the edge of the structure held colorful flower boxes on each side.

At the door, he hesitated, then rapped a few times.

A moment later, Cassidy opened the door. "Come on in. Ma's already left."

"What about Matt?"

She smirked. "He's at the bank. Won't be home for a few more hours."

George removed his hat, then followed her down the entry hall. On the right, a steep stairway with a polished mahogany rail led to an upper floor. Straight ahead, a short, narrow hall with a small table and chair, set along the edge of the stairs, flanked on the left by a closed door. At the end of the hall, an open door led to another room. The dining room.

Cassidy gestured toward the door on the left. "Have a seat in the parlor. It'll allow us more privacy in case Ma returns early." She opened the parlor door and waved an arm for him to go inside. "I'll be with you in a few minutes."

He watched her tread down the hall, then retreated into the formal parlor. Two chairs and a settee set around an ivory trimmed fireplace, upholstered in a combination of blue and gold. The wool carpet beneath his feet was a red, blue, and black blend. Burgundy drapes covered the windows, but gold tasseled sashes held them open to the sunshine.

As he moved through the room, he studied family photos. One of Cassidy's father seated in a chair, with her mother's hand resting on his broad shoulder. Two other photos, Quinn and Josh, both standing tall and proud in their army uniforms. Another photo contained all the Stuart children. Cassidy and Sarah sat while their brothers, Quinn, Josh and Matt, a small boy at the time, stood around the girls.

He lifted the photo of Josh in uniform. The day his best friend had died on the battlefield at Gettysburg flooded back. The last time George had ever cried. Josh had meant everything to him. So much so, he'd followed him into the army. And then lost him forever.

Movement in the hall startled him. He turned, the photo still clutched in his hand. Cassidy stood in the open doorway watching him.

He flushed and cleared his throat, as he placed the photo on the table. "I sure do miss old Josh."

Cassidy nodded, gazing at the photo. "We all do, but I know how much he meant to you."

George blew out a breath. "Josh was the one real friend I had in town. Well, so much for old memories."

He motioned her to take a seat.

She gathered her skirts and settled onto the chair. George sat across on the settee, not wanting to be too close right now. He might not be able to keep his hands, lips, tongue off her, and if her mother returned, there'd be hell to pay.

"George, I was thinking..." She leaned forward, elbows on her knees, her brow furrowed.

"Thinking what?"

"Well, if Miss Baker won't tell us anything, there may be another way we can get the goods on Madison."

"And what might that be?"

She ran her tongue over her lip, enticing him to move close, but he steeled himself to concentrate on what she said. "In town just now as I was on my way to see Miss Baker, Madison offered me a position as his assistant."

"He what?" George's bile rose.

"He told me since my practice was practically non-existent, I could work alongside him as I did with Pa."

George's blood chilled. "You told him no, I hope."

"Of course. Why would I want to work for that arrogant ass? But now..." She clasped her hands as if in prayer. "...if I did take the position, I could get close to him. Bait him."

"Absolutely not!" George rose to his feet. "You are not to go anywhere near him. That's an order."

She scowled. "You must know by now how well I follow orders." She stood and faced him, hands on hips.

"He assaulted a young woman. I will *not* take the chance that he'd harm you. I won't."

"You're not my father, George. Or my husband."

Her words stung like a physical blow. "Cassie, I'm sorry, but I worry about you."

"If you'd worried about me five years ago, we'd be married by now. You were the one who left me here alone." She folded her arms across her chest and turned away.

"Please, Cassie, I know you're angry, but if Madison harmed you, I'd never forgive myself. Just promise me you won't go anywhere near him. Especially if no one else is around."

She turned back and sighed. "All right. For now I promise, but if you can't get the information out of

Miss Baker, what's to stop him from hurting her or any other woman in town?"

"I don't know, but I'll figure something out that doesn't involve you working for him."

Chapter Twelve

By the time Cassidy's mother returned from town, George had left. Cassidy still bristled over his reaction to her plan. She'd thought it a good way to get to Madison. And she wasn't frightened of a sniveling coward who preyed on women. She could defend herself quite well. In fact, the intrigue George had involved her in, thrilled her. Living in a small town didn't afford much in the way of excitement.

While she helped her mother prepare dinner, though, warmth crept up her face at how protective George had been. But if he cared so much about her, why had he left her in the first place?

She stirred the pot of beef stew, her mind on what to do about Madison. When she glanced up, she found her mother frowning.

"Is something wrong, Cassie?"

She shrugged. "Why do you think something's wrong?"

"You're distracted. I'd swear you were miles away." Her mother pursed her lips. "You're thinking about George, aren't you?"

Cassidy scowled. "Why do you say that?"

"Mrs. Armstrong told me she saw the two of you together today, at the bakery."

"Well...I was in town to look in on Miss Baker. You know, her stitches? And George *is* staying at the hotel. We ran into each other outside the bakery and stopped to talk. That's all."

She pinned her mother with a glare.

Her mother shrugged. "She just wondered if the two of you had reconciled."

Cassidy propped her hands on her hips. "Is that what the whole town thinks?"

"It's only natural, Cassie." Her mother picked up two oven mitts and lifted one of the pots, draining the excess fluid in the wash pan. "You were planning to marry and after he left, you never allowed anyone else to court you." She scowled. "For five years."

Cassidy dropped her gaze. "What's between George and me is our business. No one else's."

"You've lived in a small town all your life. You must know by now everything that happens here will spread around town like wildfire." Her mother eyed her. "And she also told me she saw George speaking to another woman. One she didn't recognize."

Cassidy shrugged, but an uneasy prickle crept up her spine. "Must be someone new in town or someone staying at the boardinghouse. I met two men and a woman when I went to look in on Miss Baker." The memory of the attractive woman caused her face to heat. She may have been the one George talked to. Memories of his flirtatious ways before the war added to her unease.

"She's seen this woman around town for the past week. After George first arrived here."

Cassidy's shoulders drooped. "But they didn't come together, I'm sure."

"I only wanted to caution you. You know first-hand how fickle he can be."

Cassidy scowled. "I don't plan to reconcile with George anyway. I'm still not sure how I feel about him yet."

Her mother brushed her arm. "Is he staying in town, or will he be leaving for the city again?"

Cassidy sighed. "I honestly don't know, Ma."

"Well, then, you'd best guard you heart." She sucked on her lower lip. "Maybe you should find out his intentions and what he does for a living. He hasn't married, has he?"

"No, Ma. He surely would've told me if he had."

Maybe she should find out more about the woman at the boardinghouse.

****

George sat at the bar in the local tavern and sipped his bourbon. His teeth clenched at the idea of Cassidy working for Madison. She'd promised she wouldn't, at least for now. But he had to find another way to flush the doctor out. He wouldn't allow her to put herself in harm's way.

After he'd downed his drink, the bartender approached. "Looks like you could use another."

George shrugged. "Reckon I'll have one more."

"Very well, sir." The thin man turned back to pour George another drink. After placing the beverage in front of him, he asked, "You plan to stay in town long?"

George wrapped his fingers around the glass and shook his head. "Not real sure."

"I remember you. You left town just after the war." The bartender leaned an elbow on the bar. "Where you been all these years?"

"Been living in New York City."

The man whistled. "Must be exciting living in a big city like that. Nothing ever happens in a dive like this." He glanced around the tavern.

"Sometimes a body longs for peace and quiet."

"Maybe when I'm an old man, but I keep talking about getting out of this town. Ever since the war, I realized there's more out there I'd like to experience. We were so starry eyed and full of dreams of glory back then."

George took a sip of his drink, allowing the warmth to seep down his throat. "Reckon we were. Sure didn't turn out like I thought, though."

The bartender shook his head. "None of us expected what we went through. And a lot of us

93

didn't survive." He turned away as another customer slid onto a stool at the other end of the bar.

Thoughts of the war, of Josh, of Cassidy and the hellish Reb prison camp left George longing for escape from his memories. Coming home had dredged up so much he'd tried for the past five years to forget.

****

Although Cassidy had promised George she wouldn't be alone with Madison, it couldn't do any harm to speak to him.

She had extended an invitation for him to visit her home Sunday afternoon on the pretext of reconsidering his offer.

Her mother was home when he arrived, and she found Quinn still in the process of unpacking after his extended stay in Harrisburg. She told him what she intended to do, although he didn't like her plan any better than George.

"I don't intend to actually work for him, Quinn. I just want to find out more about him. Promise me you'll help and won't give anything away."

Quinn scowled but agreed to stay quiet on the subject. His main purpose in staying would be to keep Madison's hands off her.

While her mother settled Madison in the parlor, Cassidy prepared a fresh batch of lemonade, then fixed a tray with a pitcher, four glasses and a stack of peanut butter cookies her mother had baked early in the afternoon, and carried them to the parlor. As she eased through the doorway, Madison rose and stepped to her side.

"Please, allow me to take that for you, Miss Stuart." He reached for the tray. She allowed him to take it but avoided touching his hands. He inclined his head, and she preceded him in. She stopped in front of the settee and turned back to him.

He set the tray on the table in reach of everyone

and gestured for her to take a seat. Her gaze rose to his and he smiled. The last thing she wanted was to sit beside him, but her mother and brother had taken the two chairs and made no move, so she gathered her skirts and sat. He settled beside her. She made a conscious effort not to shirk away.

She leaned forward to serve the lemonade. After everyone had a full glass, she sat back. "Well, I hope you've all been getting acquainted."

"Yes, Miss Stuart," Madison said. "Your family is very cordial." His gaze traveled over her mother, then settled on Quinn.

Quinn raised his brow. "I was just telling Dr. Madison about my internship."

"Yes," Madison put in. "Your brother is building quite a diverse medical background. He also told me he served as a steward during the war."

"Where were you during the war, Doctor?" Cassidy pinned him with a glare.

"I...I served in a hospital. In Washington."

"So you were never in the field?"

"Cassie," her mother reprimanded. "You're being rude to your guest."

Madison raised a hand. "It's quite all right, ma'am. I can understand your daughter's ire. After all, your two sons served with the infantry, and I saw first-hand the suffering of the brave soldiers who passed through our doors."

"Cassie served as a nurse during the war," Quinn put in. "In the hospitals with Pa and on the battlefield."

"Ah, a woman after my own heart, courageous and caring." Madison wriggled closer. Cassidy fought the urge to slide away. When the doctor's hand rested on her arm, she noted her brother's narrowed gaze.

Please don't do anything to alert him.

But Quinn didn't say a word, and her mother

hadn't caught the gesture.

"That's why I've asked your sister to take on the position as my assistant," Madison said. "But she told me *no*."

Her mother raised her brows, but to her credit, didn't comment.

"Perhaps we could talk about the possibility," Cassidy said. "After all, Quinn's back for good now, and we don't have that many patients. The experience of working alongside a schooled physician might be beneficial to me."

Quinn cleared his throat.

"You object to your sister working for me?" Madison asked.

"No, sir. I think it might be a good match. She can learn from you while I reacquaint myself with our situation and we could share her..." He glanced at Cassidy. "If it's all right with you, Sis."

She spread her hands. "Give me a few more days, Doctor. I'll give you an answer then."

****

Monday afternoon, Cassidy stood at the kitchen counter slicing carrots and potatoes for stew. Her mind drifted to thoughts of George. He wouldn't be happy about this turn of events, but how else could they get anything on Madison, if Miss Baker refused to talk?

The doctor was handsome and charming, but knowing his background, she shuddered at the memory of his proximity to her yesterday. When he'd settled his hand on her arm, she'd had the urge to slap his face and bolt from the room. How could she go through with this? Maybe George and Quinn were right, and she should just stay away from the man.

Her mother strode into the room, humming a dance tune. "Oh, Cassie, I didn't know you'd already started." She pulled out an apron and tied it around her waist.

"I thought I'd get the vegetables cut up, since I've finished cleaning the examining room."

"Well, I was planning to do this as soon as I returned from town, but Mrs. Bigsley, she's such a gossip, held me up asking about Dr. Madison."

Cassidy glanced up, the knife suspended in her hand. "What did she ask about him?"

Her mother placed a pot on top of the stove. "Well, like everyone else in town, she's considered going to him, instead of you. She wanted to know if you'd be folding up your father's practice."

Cassidy pursed her lips. "And what did you tell her?"

"Well, I told her Quinn is back and plans to take over, and you'd go back to assisting like you did for your father. She also asked me about George. Wanted to know if the two of you would get back together, or is he involved with that new woman staying at the boardinghouse."

"I can't believe this town." Cassidy cut up another carrot and scooped vegetables into the pot, her blood heating. "Maybe he was just being polite and talking to her, as he did when he saw me in town."

"Well..." Her mother looked sidelong at her. "You two have a history, no matter how badly it ended. And George does have a reputation with the ladies."

Cassidy sputtered. "That was a long time ago, and they were girls then, not ladies. And I don't even know how long George will stay in town. Why would I want to get involved with him, knowing he might leave again?" *Or still flirted with other women.*

Her mother sighed. "You're right of course. You shouldn't get involved with him again. You should set your sights on someone new."

"Who, Ma?" Cassidy shook her head. "The one new eligible man in town besides George is Dr. Madison."

"Well, he's a handsome man, and he's asked you to work as his assistant." Her mother's eyes narrowed as she struck a match and lit the stove. "Something may come of it."

"I don't know." Cassidy shrugged. "Something about him just doesn't sit right with me." As the water started to heat, she lifted a long wooden spoon and stirred the vegetables.

Her mother wiped her hands on her apron. "I know how you felt about George, but it would be wise of you not to stir up that pot again. The man's a born drifter. He'll never be content to hold down an honest job and raise a family."

Cassidy turned away. She didn't want to hash all this up with her mother *again*.

"Cassie," her mother said, "you know I'm right. He left you two days before your wedding."

"He had a hard time during the war, Ma. And the time in that prison camp..."

"He's not marrying material and don't you forget it."

"I already told you; I haven't." Cassidy moved away from the stove and glanced out the window to avoid her mother's gaze. She couldn't help but allow her thoughts to drift back to George. He'd grown more handsome than when he'd left her five years ago, and he wanted to protect her. But after his business with Madison finished would he leave again?

She had to control her emotions around him. She and George had no future.

Chapter Thirteen

Tuesday afternoon, Cassidy sat in the parlor reading one of Quinn's medical texts. The sound of female squeals alerted her that Sarah had returned.

Wesley had to travel to California on a business trip and didn't want to leave his pregnant wife home alone. So, Sarah would be staying with the family until he returned. While Cassidy loved to see her sister on occasion, the idea of her living here again, with all the disruptions she caused, left her uneasy.

Sighing, she closed the text, placed the book on the table, then strolled out to the hall. Her mother enfolded Sarah in her arms. Wesley stood behind them, a suitcase in each hand.

"Please, Wesley," her mother said. "Put them down here. I'll have Matt take them to the guest room."

Wesley set the cases aside and pecked her mother's cheek. "Ah, Cassie." Wesley turned toward her, and she allowed him to kiss her as well.

Sarah ran into her arms. "Oh, Cassie, I look so forward to staying here. It'll be like before the war."

Cassidy hugged her sister. "Yes, it will."

"In fact," Sarah said, breaking away from her and looking at their mother. "I'd like to stay here when the baby's due. Cassie has agreed to deliver my child."

"I—ah." Cassidy's face burned. "I said I'd attend the birth...if you needed me, that is."

"Oh, but I do. I've already discussed this with Wes." She glanced at her husband. "He said it would be all right if I stay here in my last trimester and

99

have the baby here."

"That's wonderful news," her mother said. "We'd be more than glad to have you stay here to have the baby."

"Yes," Cassidy agreed, although she felt like bolting from the room. "You *do* have a few more months to go yet, though."

"About a month and a half, so the doctor says. Isn't that right, Wes?"

Wesley nodded. "I can bring her back here the first of June. We'll both stay if that's all right, Mother Stuart."

"Of course, Wesley. I'd be thrilled to have you both. And we have more than enough room for you and the baby."

Although Cassidy nodded, she wasn't sure she liked this idea at all.

****

Wednesday morning, Cassidy had her arms up to her elbows covered in dough. She planned to get the loaves kneaded and in the oven before setting up for her first patient. A moan alerted her she wasn't alone. Glancing toward the kitchen doorway, she spotted Sarah, clothed in her wrapper, her chestnut hair loose around her shoulders.

"Where's Ma?" she asked.

"I told her to sleep in for a bit. She'll be down shortly to get breakfast started." Cassidy glanced at the doughy loaves. "I wanted to get the bread in the oven early. I'm seeing a patient today."

Sarah waddled into the kitchen, pulled out a chair, and thumped down into the seat. She set her elbows on the table and settled her head between her hands.

Cassidy peered at her. "Are you feeling poorly?"

"It's my stomach." She pressed her hands against her growing abdomen. "I'm feeling sick. Don't know if I can eat anything."

"Why don't you go on back to bed for a while?"

"I wanted to talk to Ma."

"Well, just sit there, until she comes down."

Sarah groaned again. Cassidy finished shaping the loaves and shoved them into the oven. She stirred the embers then turned to her sister. "Can I make you a cup of tea?"

Sarah raised her head, her blue eyes bleary. "Would you, please?"

"Of course." Irritated at her altered plans to finish up and get to the office, she gritted her teeth and filled the kettle, using the jug she'd topped off with fresh water earlier from the pump outside.

"I hope I'm not causing you too much trouble," Sarah said.

"No. Don't be silly. This will only take a few minutes." She set the pot on the stove to heat.

"That new doctor in town is very charming, don't you think?"

Cassidy glanced at her sister. "You've met Dr. Madison?"

A smirk replaced her sour expression. "Not exactly. Bessie Mae heard I was in town and invited me to the ice cream parlor to catch up on things. It was after Wes left, and you were busy with patients. She told me all about him. She's been to see him several times."

Cassidy narrowed her gaze. "She has?"

Sarah lowered her lashes. "Well...she thinks he's very handsome. On the way back she pointed him out to me. He was leaving the mercantile. She took me over and introduced me to him. He *is* a dashing and well-dressed man and is obviously doing quite well."

Cassidy scowled. "I reckon so."

"He's one of the most eligible men I've seen here in town for quite a while, and Ma told me he paid a visit on Sunday and seems to have taken an instant liking to you. He's also very handsome. You should set your cap for him."

Cassidy scooped crushed tea leaves into a tea ball and inserted it in a cup. "I don't plan to set my cap for anyone. At least not right now. I've the practice to think of."

"But if you wait, it might be too late." Sarah's brows rose, her morning sickness apparently forgotten.

"I'm not going to flirt with the man. And you should stay away from him, too."

Sarah scowled. "I'm a happily married woman. Whatever would I want with him?"

"That's not what I meant. Just don't go anywhere near him."

Sarah wagged a finger. "I know why you're not pursuing any beaus. It's because of George, isn't it? You still love him." The statement sounded like an accusation.

"George and I are history." Cassidy poured boiling water from the teapot into Sarah's cup and set it before her. "I don't quite know what my feelings for him are now."

"From what I've seen of him, he must be doing very well for himself." Her sister's gaze narrowed. "Just what *does* he do now?"

Cassidy shrugged, not wanting to reveal too much. "I wouldn't know. I just spoke to him briefly at the mercantile."

Sarah shook her head. "That's not what I heard. Bessie Mae told me all about the intimate conversation the two of you had outside the bakery." She shook her head. "Don't allow George to ruin your one chance for happiness."

"Are you saying Dr. Madison is my one chance at happiness?" Cassidy huffed out a breath. "Bessie Mae should mind her own business and stop filling your head with gossip."

Sarah folded her hands in her lap. "I'm saying unless you leave Burkeville, your choice of eligible men will be limited. You don't want to end up a spinster, do you?"

"I want to be a practicing physician. That's my one and only ambition right now."

"But surely you want a home—" Sarah patted her stomach. "—and children? You need a husband. One who can give you a comfortable life, like my Wes."

Cassidy sighed. "Whether or not I allow Dr. Madison or any man to court me is entirely up to me. As for George, I'm sure he'll soon be gone. Likely, we'll never see him again."

Sarah lifted her cup and took a sip. "It's for the best, dear sister. George has always been bad news, even when he was a boy."

****

Later in the day after her chores were complete and supper simmered on the stove under the watchful eye of her mother, Cassidy stepped onto the front porch to savor the sparkling spring day. Leaning her arms on the railing, she inhaled the scent of the colorful blooms spread around the porch.

The door opened behind her. She turned to find Quinn edging through the doorway. "Going somewhere?" she asked.

Her brother shook his head. "Just thought I'd come outside for a little fresh air."

"Are you finally unpacked?"

Quinn stepped forward and leaned on the rail beside her. "Yes, ma'am." His brow furrowed.

"Is something wrong?" Cassidy asked.

"If you must know, I'm concerned about your recent contact with Madison. I'm afraid he could come after you."

She turned to face him. "Why would he do that?"

Quinn raised a brow. "I don't know, but I didn't

like the way he looked at you Sunday afternoon."

"I can take care of myself."

He huffed out a breath. "Makes me doubly glad I'm back to stay. With George staying all the way across town, you'd only have Matt around to protect you women."

"Believe me..." Cassidy pinned her older brother with a meaningful glance. "If I need George, he'll be here."

"I do believe that, Sis. Despite his past shortcomings, he seems to be a changed man."

Cassidy smirked, not willing to voice her unease regarding George. "Everyone keeps telling me I should stay away from him before he hurts me again."

"What do you think?"

She shook her head. "I'm still not sure. But I do believe he wants me to stay out of harm's way."

"As do I, Sis, and I've been thinking of your future."

She straightened and stared at her brother. "What about it? Don't tell me you want me to find a good man, too?"

He laughed. "No, I was thinking of the new medical school in Philadelphia. It's a school just for women, called *Female Medical*. I think you should apply, Cassie. You'd have a great chance of getting accepted."

Her heart raced as she considered the possibilities. She backed away from the railing and took a few steps across the porch. "I don't know if I should right now."

"Give it a try. The worst can happen is, they'll say no."

Cassidy bit her lip and grinned at her brother. "You really think I should?"

"Absolutely. And I'll help you every step of the way."

She threw her arms around him in a fierce hug. "How can a girl be so lucky as to have a wonderful big brother like you?"

"You should know by now, Cassie, I'll always be here for you."

****

A rap at his hotel room door drew George from the depths of a dream about Gettysburg, the day Josh died. He slid off the bed, grabbed his shirt, and slipped it over his head.

"Be right there," he called.

He'd expected the maid, who always seemed to awaken him from a sound sleep, wanting to clean his room. His scowl withered as he opened the door to Cassidy's brother, Quinn.

"May I come in, George?" Quinn's expression didn't brook any argument.

George waved him in and shut the door. "What's wrong? Is it Cassie?"

"No...well, maybe." Quinn settled on the chair and ruffled his hair. "Frankly, I'm worried."

George sat on the bed opposite Quinn. "Damn it, man. Tell me what's bothering you."

"Cassie has been cozying up to Madison. She invited him to the house for lemonade on Sunday."

"She what?" George's bile rose. "I told her to stay away from him."

"Well, she has this idea that if she pretends she wants to work for him, she can get information out of him."

"Oh, I know just what she plans to do." George jumped from the bed and paced the room. "She wants him to attack her, so I'll have the proof I need."

Quinn shook his head. "My sister may be daring, but I can't believe she'd go that far."

"I do. And that's exactly what she plans to do."

Quinn's rusty-colored brows rose.

"Don't worry." He patted Quinn on the shoulder. "I'll get right over to your house and nip this whole scheme of hers in the bud."

****

By the time George strode through town toward the Stuart home, his heart pumped like thunder. If Cassidy wouldn't listen to him and stuck to this foolhardy plan, he'd just have to take Madison on himself. He wasn't about to let the man's scurvy hands touch *his* Cassie.

When he arrived, no sound emerged from the house, but someone must be home. Quinn indicated Cassie had a patient to see this morning.

Sarah answered his rap. Her chestnut brows rose on her round face.

"Oh, George. Cassie's with a patient right now, but you're more than welcome to come in and wait."

He tipped his hat. "Mighty pleased to see you again, Sarah. Been a while."

He didn't miss her answering scowl. "You didn't exactly leave on the best note, George." She turned and waddled, leading him to the kitchen.

The cozy room smelled of the last meal, coffee, bacon, butter, and maple syrup. He inhaled deeply.

"Would you care for a cup of tea?" Sarah asked.

"No, ma'am, I'll be just fine."

Her smile wavered. "I'll be in my room if you need anything then."

After she retreated, George rose and surveyed the room. Memories of the hours he'd spent here with Josh and meals he'd shared with the family were eclipsed by his memory of his first leave from the army. He'd come home for Christmas with Josh and Quinn, the one time they'd been granted leave for the holidays during the four year ordeal. Cassie and Matt were the only ones home. Everyone else had gone to a Christmas Eve party across town.

She'd made them hot chocolate as snow drifted

down, blanketing the town. Before her parents returned, he cornered her in the kitchen, where he kissed her for the first time. Granted, his lips just grazed her forehead, but the kiss got him through a year and a half of battles, before he saw her again at Gettysburg. He remembered awakening on the floor of a home in town to the face of an angel. His wounds grave enough she'd taken him home, at least for a while, and helped him heal.

Voices outside the kitchen alerted him. Cassie spoke to a man. Perhaps he was the patient Sarah spoke of. He listened as the front door opened and closed and sat back, waiting.

Cassie strode into the kitchen and halted.

"George? How long have you been here?" She fisted her hands on his hips.

"Not long. Sarah let me in and told me to wait." He pulled out the chair beside him. "I have to speak to you."

She bit her lip but stepped over and sat. "What about?"

"I spoke to Quinn this morning."

"And?" Her light eyes narrowed.

"He told me you invited Madison here on Sunday. What the hell are you trying to do?"

She fisted her hands on the table top, her fingers intertwined. "I'm trying to help you."

George blew out an exasperated sigh. "I don't need your help. Not if you'll be alone with him. I won't have it."

"So you've told me. But I think this could work. I could draw him out."

"What if he attacks you?"

She spread her hands. "All the better. Then we'd have proof."

"Cassie, you are not thinking this through." He pounded his fist on the table. She flinched.

"You are not my husband and even if you were, I

wouldn't permit you to run my life."

"I'm not trying to run your life; I'm trying to protect you."

She leaned back, folding her arms across her chest. "I can do whatever I want."

He pointed a finger at her. "If you go near the bastard, I can't guarantee what I might be forced to do."

"What do you mean?"

Before he could form an answer, Mrs. Stuart stepped into the kitchen forcing a halt to the confrontation.

"I heard raised voices." She pinned George with a glare. "Is something wrong?"

"It's nothing, Ma." Cassidy waved her hand, dismissing her mother's concern. "George was just leaving." She pursed her lips and crossed her arms over her chest.

George glanced at Mrs. Stuart and then Cassidy. Best not to upset the Stuart household by continuing this conversation. He excused himself and bade them goodbye but swore he'd do whatever it took to keep Cassidy safe.

Chapter Fourteen

Miss Baker arrived Thursday afternoon to have her stitches removed.

"They do itch so," she told Cassidy.

"Then I reckon you'll be glad to be rid of them." Cassidy examined the healed skin.

The school teacher nodded.

As Cassidy worked the stitches out, she thought she'd try querying the woman about Madison. "I assume you don't plan to see Dr. Madison again."

Miss Baker shook her head. "No."

Cassidy slid out the final stitch. "There. All done."

When the teacher stepped down from the exam table, Cassidy tried again. "A lot of the town's people like Dr. Madison."

"I...I didn't care for him." She turned up her nose as she rolled her sleeve down and fastened the button.

"Did he do something specific?"

Miss Baker glanced away.

"I'm just asking because I'd like to know what I'm doing right. I'd like to keep seeing patients, even though Quinn is returning to the practice."

"Oh, yes your brother." Miss Baker blushed. "He seems like a very nice man."

"He is." Cassidy smiled. "And he's not married, nor is he courting."

The school teacher's blush deepened.

Cassidy motioned Miss Baker to the door. "Since he's taking over the practice, Quinn would be most grateful if you continue as a patient."

Miss Baker's smile widened. After she left Cassidy realized, even though she hadn't gotten any information on Dr. Madison, she might have found the perfect match for her bachelor brother.

****

Late Saturday morning George arrived in a carriage to take Cassidy on a picnic. If she allowed Madison to call on her, he'd be damned if he couldn't too. He'd paid a worker in the hotel kitchen to prepare a sumptuous meal of fried chicken, coleslaw, potato salad, biscuits, jam, fresh apples, and oatmeal cookies. He even had a decanter of fresh lemonade.

He hoped he and Cassidy could spend some time relaxing and having fun. They'd had so little time to enjoy being together, even when he'd lived in town before the war. Back then, she'd always rejected his advances and when they'd finally gotten together, he'd been wounded. Although he planned to wait until he resolved the issue with Madison, he wouldn't allow the doctor to be her one suitor, even if her only interest in him was milking damning information.

What he wouldn't give to have her in his arms, in his bed. But he had to be careful. For now, he planned to court her properly. She deserved that.

He stopped the carriage on the road in front of the flower garden leading to the house. The door opened and she emerged, mouth gaping.

"George, what are you doing here?"

He waved his arm. "Get your hat. We're going on a picnic."

She frowned. "You could have told me in advance. I have chores to do."

"That can wait until after lunch. I'm sure your ma will understand."

As if on cue, Mrs. Stuart stepped from the side of the house, her arms wrapped around a basket filled with laundry. "What on earth?"

"I've come to take your daughter on a picnic." He tipped his hat. "If it's all right with you, ma'am?"

Cassidy shrugged. "I knew nothing about this."

Her mother smirked. "Oh, go ahead. I'll take care of lunch. Sarah can help." She shifted the basket to one arm and waved with her freed hand. "Shoo."

Cassidy smiled, waving to George. "I'll be right back."

George grinned as she and her mother disappeared inside. When she returned, over her best black gown, she wore a matching shawl and a straw hat, with wide black ribbon. Even clothed drably in black, she set his blood warming. She carried a small satchel.

Alighting from the carriage, George strode up the short path and steps to take her hand. He glanced at the satchel. "You don't have to bring anything. I've brought plenty to eat."

"Oh." She smirked and shrugged. "This is nothing. Just some raspberry tarts I made."

He smiled. "I do remember your raspberry tarts. Let's get going."

She laughed. "You're in such a hurry, sir." She raised her gaze to the clear, blue sky.

"It's a beautiful day. Don't want to waste a minute." He crooked his elbow. "Shall we?"

She nodded and slid her hand around his arm. He assisted her up the carriage step, then circled the conveyance, settling on the opposite side.

"Where did you get a carriage?"

He shrugged. "Rented one at the stables."

"How much is Colonel Wellingham paying you?" She frowned.

"Not all that much." His face heated. "I won a few rounds of poker last night."

"I see." She straightened her shoulders, her lips curving up a bit.

As they headed for the pond, her warm presence and sweet scent intoxicated him. He hoped there wouldn't be too many curious eyes at the pond today. He planned to steal as many kisses as he could get away with.

Once they settled on a spot away from families with young children racing about, George spread the checkered table cloth and unpacked the basket. Cassidy added her tarts to the luncheon.

George swiped one from the basket. "Mmmm, Cassie, delicious." He took her hand and helped her to sit on the ground.

"They're for dessert, you sneak." She spread her skirts and sighed, surveying the pastoral scene. Two children, a boy and a girl, stood at the pond's edge, enticing a goose with a crust of bread. Cassidy smiled.

"I can just picture you with a brood of dark haired children, frolicking with the geese," George said.

She frowned, eyeing the children. "It won't bite them, will it?"

He laughed. "I'm sure they'll be just fine." Opening the crock of jam, he spread a dollop over a biscuit and lifted it toward her. "Bessie at the tavern assured me the jam's delicious." He grimaced. "I'm afraid it's also raspberry. That all right?"

She raised her brows. "Bessie?"

"Ah, Cassie. You don't have to be jealous of Bessie. She's old enough to be my grandma."

She smirked. "Just don't like the idea of sharing you with anyone, I reckon."

He focused on her lush pink lips, just inches away, the biscuit between his finger and thumb. She took a delicate bite, her lips grazing his fingertips, sending a jolt through him.

He bit into the sweet treat, then set the biscuit down. Leaning toward her, he stroked his thumb over her cheek. Noticing a small speck of jam on her lip, he brushed his lips over hers. Sweet and warm. His senses tingled.

"George," she warned. "We're hardly away from prying eyes. This is a small town. Folks will gossip."

He glanced around. "Reckon I'll have to sneak you back to my hotel room later on."

A slight smile and shiver answered for him. "We have to be careful, George. It's more than gossip we have to fear."

"I know. I won't risk your reputation. Someday soon I plan to propose and marry you proper."

Her dark brows rose. "Oh, George! Do you mean it?"

He shrugged. "After finding you again after all these years, how could I not?"

Her gaze dropped as her hands crumpled the folds of her gown. "I wish this business with Madison was finished. Until then, we can't go on with our lives as we wish."

"We'll get him, Cassie, I swear." His gaze bore into hers.

"Well, we might just have an advantage now." She smirked, reaching for a chicken leg. "It seems Miss Baker likes my brother."

George raised his brows. "And Quinn..."

"He's entirely besotted." She grinned. "I thought maybe if he courted her, she'd eventually open up."

"If Madison *did* do anything improper, and she talks, he might come after her, or anyone she might tell."

She nodded, biting into the chicken. She swallowed and dabbed her chin with a napkin, before she spoke. "I hate having to draw Quinn into this, but I see no other way." Her gaze rose to meet his. "If we can't discredit Madison, our practice may be ruined and Quinn's returned to town for nothing."

George reached for her hand. "I'll do everything

in my power to protect you and your family. In New York City, I lived the life of a gambler and learned how to protect myself. And you know I'm no stranger to firearms."

She bit her lip. The gesture sent his pulse racing. He longed to lean over and steal another kiss, but the presence of others held him in check.

"You don't reckon Madison knows his way around a gun, do you?"

George sighed. "I surely hope not, but I can't take any chances concerning your safety."

She shook her head, reaching for the glass of lemonade. "He doesn't seem the sort to resort to firearms, but I do sense a streak of cruelty and violence under his false charm."

George scowled, reaching for a chicken leg. "If he so much as touches you, I want to know." He poked the leg at her for emphasis. After taking a bite, he leaned forward, reaching for her hand.

He stroked his thumb against her palm. Her eyes closed part way. He continued the motion, his breath catching as he realized how much he cared for this woman. "I promise you, I won't rest until Madison is finished as a physician in this town."

"I don't know how..."

He brushed his thumb over her velvety lower lip. "We'll prove what he is and the town will drive him out on a rail, if the authorities don't get to him first."

****

Cassidy sighed. The motion of George's callused thumb on the back of her hand sent swirling sensations to her core. She longed to lie on the tablecloth and allow him to undress her, take her, in front of the whole town. In all the years since he'd left, she'd never entertained such thoughts with other men. But George made her feel like a wanton.

He leaned in, his sensuous lips a breath away

from her mouth. She pulled back.

"As much as I'd love for you to kiss me, George..." She glanced around at the children racing along the edge of the water and brushed off her skirt.

He gestured to the spread before them. "But we haven't finished our lunch."

She smiled. "I'd love to spend the entire day here, but I've got those chores."

"Ah, Cassie, you have a knack for spoiling the perfect opportunity." He frowned but gathered the leftovers, packing them into the basket. His gaze rested on the tarts. "Would you like to take them home with you?"

"No, I made them for you."

His brows rose. "But how did you know I had this planned?"

She smirked. "I was going to bring them over to your room today. As a sort of peace offering."

He quirked his lips, and she fought the urge to wrap her arms around him and devour him whole.

He bowed his head and packed everything, then stood, reaching for her hand. She allowed him to help her to her feet. She shook out and smoothed her skirts, while he retrieved the checkered cloth and folded it into the basket.

She settled in the carriage, but her gaze never left him. He jumped in beside her, and she leaned toward him, her lips close to his ear.

"We'll have another chance to be together soon," she whispered.

His answering smile sent a shot of pure desire pulsing down her spine.

****

Later in the day, Cassidy decided to stroll through town, her purpose to pay a surprise visit to Dr. Madison. If George could, why not her? Although, she wouldn't pose as a patient, but a potential employee.

Tillie answered the door and escorted her to the parlor.

"The doctor is seeing his last patient for the day. He'll be with you shortly."

After the maid left the room, Cassidy peered through the open doorway. A door opened and closed, and she caught the sound of muted male voices. Madison and who? She stood and sidled to the door. Old Mr. Jenkins, from across town, stood in the hall shaking hands with the doctor.

Madison glanced toward the parlor and caught her gaze. His chestnut brows rose.

"Miss Stuart! What a pleasant surprise."

She stepped into the hall, but he waved her back.

"Sit. I'll speak to you in the parlor." She resumed her seat and waited. A few moments later, he stepped into the room and slid into the chair across from her. "Tell me; to what do I owe this surprise visit?"

She folded her hands in her lap. "I've thought about your kind offer. Quinn will begin seeing patients again, and I only have a few I'm still treating, so I thought..." She let her sentence die.

"Yes?" He leaned toward her.

"I thought I could assist you part time, so I'll still be available to help Quinn."

"Just how many patients do you have left?"

She ticked them off on her fingers. "I have three...no, four. Miss Baker came in today to have her stitches removed."

His gaze darkened. "Oh, yes, Miss Baker. She indicated that she was more comfortable with a female doctor."

Cassidy nodded, hoping to draw him out. "You saw her, I understand."

"Yes, once or twice." He waved his hand. "She

had an infection, you see."

"She told me."

"Told you what?" He frowned.

"That you'd treated her for an infection." She leaned back. "She's a very congenial patient, don't you agree?"

"Oh, yes." His smile wavered for a moment, but then he brightened. "If you'd like, I'll show you my office and exam room before Tillie cleans up."

Cassidy smiled. "I'd like that very much, Doctor."

The brief tour of the office and exam room included numerous pats on the hand and arm. Madison brushed against her every chance he could and on one occasion, Cassidy feared he'd go too far, but the threat of Tillie stepping into the room or overhearing anything may have kept him in check.

After the tour, Cassidy breathed a sigh of relief and settled her hand in the crook of his proffered arm for the stroll to the front door. "Would you consent to join me for a meal at the tavern, unless you need to be home for dinner?"

Things were going exactly as planned. "I'd love to, Doctor."

Chapter Fifteen

Saturday evening, George strolled from the hotel to the tavern. Realizing Cassidy wouldn't heed his advice in staying away from Madison, he'd paced his room trying to come up with a solution that wouldn't reveal his identity to the doctor. His stomach started to protest. The last thing he'd eaten had been at the picnic that afternoon. He smiled at the memory. Since staying at the hotel, he'd taken most of his meals in the tavern. As he entered, a couple seated in the center of the room caught his gaze. Cassidy and Madison sat across from each other.

Not wanting to draw attention to himself, George slinked to a two seat table in the corner.

After the barmaid took his order, he focused on their conversation, jaw clenched as the urge to grab Cassidy away from the man, overwhelmed him.

"Since setting up my practice here in town, Miss Stuart, I thought of you as a threat to my livelihood, but I've come to grow quite fond of you. While I'm thrilled you're considering working as my assistant, I hope you'll allow me to court you properly." He reached a hand across the table and covered hers.

George slunk lower in his chair, his gaze fixed on Cassidy. She didn't yank her hand away.

What the hell is she doing?

Lifting her tea cup to her lips, she sipped. Madison's thumb traced intimate circles over the back of her free hand. When she jerked her hand away, George blew out a relieved sigh. "Dr. Madison, I don't believe we should be holding hands like this in a public place."

He glanced around the room and smirked. "Of course not, Miss Stuart. If you're finished with your tea, I'll be happy to escort you home."

George turned away and gritted his teeth. The thought of the bastard touching her made his skin crawl. How could she allow him to court her?

He hid his face behind a menu as they left the tavern, then sat for a time trying to decide what he should do.

****

Since sunset, the evening air had taken on a chill. Cassidy shivered.

"Are you cold, my dear?" Madison asked.

"A little," she admitted. He placed an arm around her shoulder and drew her close. Prickles of unease shot up her spine.

When they drew abreast of the hotel, he pulled her aside. "I'd like to show you something."

She wanted nothing more than for him to take her home, but she acquiesced and followed his lead. Maybe he'd do something to help George prove his guilt. The alley he led her down dead-ended. The prickles returned and her breath caught. "What do you want to show me here?"

He propped her against the wall, removed his hat, and lowered his mouth to hers. Before she could utter a protest, his tongue pressed against her lips, trying to push them apart.

She shoved with all her strength. "Dr. Madison! I must insist you take me home. Now!" She struggled to keep her breath even as she watched his smoldering expression grow cold.

He leaned away from her, pushing his hand through his hair, then settled his bowler back on his head. "You must forgive me, Miss Stuart. I should never have taken such liberties. But your beauty has mesmerized me."

"Please take me home. Now."

Madison tightened his grip on her wrist. Movement outside the alley drew her startled gasp.

George raced to her side and yanked Madison's hand from her arm. "Take your hands off her, you filthy scum!"

Madison's eyes widened. "See here!"

Before he could utter another word, George raised his fist and slammed it into the doctor's face.

"George, don't!" Cassidy cried.

George paid no attention. Madison growled and swung at George. He ducked and the doctor swung again, this time connecting with George's jaw and knocking them both to the ground.

The two wrestled and grunted, rolling around in the dirt.

Cassidy stepped to the edge of the alley, her heart thudding. No pedestrians strolled by. Wringing her hands, she turned back. She had to stop this herself.

"Will you please stop acting like school boys or common ruffians?" She glared at them, hands fisted on her hips.

"I won't let you hurt Cassie, you pompous ass," George ground out.

"Looks to me like *you* already have," Madison spat.

George swung and connected with the doctor's nose.

A loud crunch drew a gasp from Cassidy.

George glanced up, his lip curled upward. He rose to his feet, breathing hard.

Dr. Madison lay flat on his back, cradling his bloodied nose in both hands.

"George Masters!" Cassidy glared into his dark eyes. "Just what are you doing?"

"He—I..." George arched a brow. "He had you alone in a dark alley. What am I supposed to think?"

She lifted her fisted hands to rest on her hips. "So you punched him?"

"Well...he hit me, too." He rubbed his jaw.

She sank to the ground beside the doctor. "Are you all right?"

He grimaced. "Did the son-of-a-bitch break it?" he ground out.

She leaned over to examine Madison's nose. "It doesn't look broken, but just to be sure you'd best come over to my office. I can take a better look there."

He nodded, retrieved a handkerchief from his vest pocket, and pressed the cloth against the free flowing blood.

"Here." Cassidy reached for his hand. "Allow me to help you up." He placed his hand in hers, and she helped pull him to his feet, then braced her arm around his waist. "I'll take you to my house."

George's mouth gaped.

"Out of my way."

"Cassie, you are not taking him home. Not unless I come too—"

"I said out of my way," she repeated.

"You have to listen to me." His dark gaze pinned her, but she wouldn't allow him to ruin this chance to gain Madison's full confidence.

"George, I always knew you were nothing but a common ruffian and this proves it."

He took a step back and sighed.

Dr. Madison scowled. "Leave the lady alone, or I will have you arrested for assault. I'm sure you'd prefer not to spend the night in jail."

"That won't be necessary, sir." George's posture stiffened.

Cassidy caught his gaze, hoping he would understand her intent to shield his true purpose in town from Madison. If he thought of George only as a jealous ex-beau, this incident might work in their favor. But she couldn't say a word in front of the doctor.

George snatched his bowler from where the hat had rolled to the ground during the fight. "I'll be on my way, then. If that's what you want." He scowled.

She nodded. "Yes, George, that's what I want."

He dusted off his hat and placed in on his head. He tipped the brim and, with a final glare at Madison, turned away.

Biting her lip, Cassidy glanced at the doctor. "I'm so sorry. He's always been this way. I can't believe he actually hit you." She turned back, but George was no longer in sight.

"Shall we go, Doctor?"

"Of course." Holding his handkerchief to his nose to staunch the flow of blood, he leaned on her as they exited the alley. Thank God, no spectators hovered around.

In silence, they walked to her house. At the door, he turned to her and sighed. "I'd like to thank you for coming to my aid. I didn't deserve it after what I did back there. I would very much like to formally court you, if you'll still allow me." His hang dog expression seemed earnest, but Cassidy knew his intentions were far from honorable.

"Let's get inside so I can take a look at your nose and get the bleeding stopped."

Once she'd treated his nose, which fortunately wasn't broken, she saw him to the door. "Do you feel well enough to make it home? I can have my brother, Matt—"

He halted her with a raised hand. "You needn't bother your brother." He reached for her hand and brushed his thumb over the sensitive skin on her palm. "Please, Miss Stuart. I do hope my actions won't dissuade you from allowing me to court you. It would surely kill me if I couldn't see you again."

She smirked. "I don't believe being away from

me would be fatal to any man, but I'll consider your proposal."

"Thank you, Miss Stuart." He released her hand and tipped his hat. He left her standing inside the door. She watched him descend the porch steps, then shut the door and leaned her back against it.

Dr. Madison's kiss had been forceful, plundering, not like the gentle, playful kisses she'd shared with George. Had he done this to Miss Baker, or worse? If only she could get the schoolteacher to tell her.

She had to find George and explain what she planned to do to draw the doctor out.

****

Late Sunday morning after church services, Cassidy scrubbed pots, left over from breakfast. Light footsteps on the stairs drew her attention to the kitchen stairwell door. Sarah emerged, her hair loose, still clothed in her wrapper. Her growing belly protruded as she settled her hands on the rounded swell.

"Are you feeling poorly again, Sarah?"

Her sister groaned and settled into a chair. "The baby kept me up half the night with all his kicking. I told Ma I couldn't bring myself to attend services today."

Cassidy smirked. "Well, it's bound to happen. Means you've got a healthy little boy or girl."

Sarah's face brightened. "You really think my baby could be a girl?"

"There's a fifty-fifty chance." Cassidy shrugged.

Sarah clasped her hands together. "I so want a little girl, but Wes wants a boy."

"Don't all fathers?" Cassidy turned back to the sink.

"I miss Wes. When he used to go on business trips, he always took me with him."

Eyeing her sister, Cassidy said, "Your life will

have to be different now you're having a child."

"I know." Sarah scowled. "But I don't want things to change. I like wearing all the latest styles." She rubbed her stomach. "Now, I can't even wear my new bustle."

Finished with the pots, Cassidy turned back to her sister and wiped her hands on her apron. "We often have no choice in the matter. Life goes on, whether we want to go along or not."

"Reckon so. I heard Dr. Madison last night. How did he break his nose?"

"He didn't break his nose; he just got into a little scuffle is all."

Sarah's eyes widened. "With who?"

Cassidy sighed. "Must we discuss this? The doctor wants the whole matter kept private." She hoped to staunch Sarah's questions. The whole town didn't need to know George had hit Madison.

"He's such a handsome man, Cassie." Her sister batted her lashes. "Has he asked permission to court you yet?"

"Sarah..." Cassidy scolded. "He did, but I'm not sure I want to."

"Oh, Cassie, why not? He'd be perfect for you."

"Why do you think so?"

"Well, he's so good looking, and a doctor, and he seems to be well-off." Her sister leaned forward, her eyes bright. "You need to get married and start a family soon, Cassie, otherwise..." She trailed off.

Cassidy glanced up. "Otherwise what?"

"You know..." Sarah glanced around the kitchen as if trying to avoid Cassidy's glare. "...what they call women your age who aren't married."

"Are you trying to say I'm a spinster?" Cassidy crossed her arms over her chest.

"Well..." Sarah stammered. "Not yet, at least. But you have to start allowing eligible men to court you. I know George hurt you, but all men aren't like him."

"George had been through so much. He couldn't come to grips with Josh's death, the war, the prison camp. And his life even before all that happened was harsh."

Sarah scowled. "Are you saying it's not his fault for leaving you?"

"Not entirely."

"Oh, Cassie. You've a lot to learn about men. You need a man who will treat you well and put you above his own selfish needs. Besides, as far as I can tell, George doesn't have a job. How can he compete with a doctor?" Sarah sighed.

Cassidy bristled. What *did* George do for a living besides his claim of gambling winnings? He said he was investigating Madison for the colonel, but she'd thought it just a temporary job. She wondered how much the colonel paid him. "I need time to think about what I want."

"Just don't take too much time, you hear?"

Cassidy shook her head as she wiped her hands on her apron. *Why did I defend George?* The memory of his dark gaze, male scent, and tender kisses set her pulse racing. She'd explain to him her attention to Madison last night was a ploy. George had to understand she'd not only put herself in peril for him, but for the good of the entire town.

Chapter Sixteen

George strode from the hotel. The first order of the day, to get hold of Cassidy and demand to know what the hell kind of game she'd been playing last night. How could he protect her, if she insisted on taking such risks?

Halfway down the block, he caught sight of a familiar dark-haired woman striding toward him. *Perfect.*

Halting in his tracks, he waited for Cassidy to approach.

"George." Her rasping voice clued him she'd raced over here. "I have to tell you—"

He cut her off with a raised hand. Pulling her close, he whispered. "We can't talk here."

"Then where?" She glanced down the street.

"My room."

"George?" She raised her brows. "Not a good idea."

"It's the only place we can talk in private. Are you coming or not?" He pinned her with a glare, hoping she'd agree.

She nodded, heaving a sigh.

He led her around the back entrance to the hotel. He'd not ruin her reputation by taking her through the lobby, although someone could see them anyway.

He pressed his hand against the small of her back.

"George," she whispered, "are you sure we should do this?" Her breath against his ear sent tingles shooting down his spine.

"I need to talk to you, Cassie. This is the one place we can."

She nodded, allowing him to guide her through the back entrance to the stairs off the kitchen. Fortunately, the cook was nowhere around. At the top of the stairs on the third floor, he glanced down the hall to be sure no one watched them enter his room. Producing his key, he hustled her to the door, opened it, and guided her in, while again scanning the hall.

So far, so good. But he still had to get her out later.

After securing the door, he turned to find her brushing her hand over the one upholstered chair in the room. Good thing he'd hung up his extra pair of trousers so she had a place to sit. He motioned to the chair.

"This is a very nice room, George." She smoothed her skirts, pulled the pin from her hat, and placed it on his bed before sitting.

"For a hotel room." He pushed the hat aside and sat on the bed facing her.

She cleared her throat and glanced around the Spartan room. "No. It's very nice." She caught his gaze. "Not so nice as your room in New York City, I reckon."

"No, but it'll do for now." He reached for her hand and eased the kid glove off. "Now, I want you to tell me what you were doing in an alley with that bastard. Did he hurt you?"

"If you must know, I was trying to get close to him."

George folded his arms across his chest and scowled.

"To get information, of course." She lifted her chin. "To see if he'd..."

"If he'd try to accost you?" George stood and paced the small room. "Cassie, I can't believe you put yourself in such a position."

"I'm trying to help." She gazed about the room. "If Miss Baker won't tell us what happened, we have to find out some other way."

"Do you really believe Madison would tell you?"

She shrugged. "Well, no..."

George approached her and brushed a finger along her cheek. Her scent and softness sent his pulse racing. "Because if anything were to happen to you, darlin', and I had the power to stop it, I'd never forgive myself. I know how brave you are and how much you want to help, but I can't risk it."

She glanced down at her hands in her lap. "I've been leading him on, pretending I want to work as his assistant. Then he seemed interested in courting me. I thought, if I played into his hands, he'd relax and say or do something that would help you, help us."

George grimaced. "What did he do in the alley before I showed up?"

"He kissed me." She glared at him. "That's all, nothing else."

He blew out a sigh of relief, but his blood heated at the thought of Madison touching her in such an intimate way. He stepped over to the window to cool his face. "I'm afraid if you allow him to get closer; he'll try something else..."

She shook her head. "If he's courting me, he wouldn't do anything improper. He wouldn't want to scare me off." She looked off into space.

He scowled. "You can't be sure."

"He only asked to court me, not to marry him." She gazed up at him candidly. "I need to draw him out. Gain his confidence."

He glanced out the window at the people strolling along the street, his emotions warring. "There has to be another way, Cassie. This is *my* investigation, not yours." George moved across the room to kneel by her side. "If Madison hurts you..."

She rubbed her arm. "I promise I'll stay in the public view. To be truthful, I'm afraid to be alone with him again."

"Cassie, I fear for your safety."

She reached up to stroke his cheek. His face heated at her touch.

His teeth clenched at the thought of Madison manhandling her. Once the man's indiscretions were out in the open, he wouldn't wait for Wellingham to mete out justice; he'd kill the scum himself. He brushed his thumb over Cassidy's dewy cheek.

"Come on, I'll walk you home."

"No, George." She shook her head. "I want to stay here...with you."

He swallowed hard. "Do you know what you're saying? If you stay here much longer, I won't be able to keep my hands off you."

She smiled. "I know. I feel the same way." She rose and led him to stand by the bed. "So many years have passed since the war ended. I dreamed of marrying you, being with you as your wife. In all the years that passed, I never stopped loving you. It's the reason I couldn't even feign interest in the other men who courted me afterward. They weren't you."

"I can't believe you're saying this. I've loved you all these years, too, but hoped you'd found happiness with another man...a better man than me."

"George..." She took his hands and gazed up at him. "You're the best man I've ever met in my life. You're the one I want to spend my future with."

He reached behind her head and pulled the pins from her hair, allowing the dark, silken strands to flow in waves over her shoulders. "Cassie, you're even more beautiful than my memory of you. I've never stopped dreaming of being with you all these years."

"Then why didn't you stay?" Her breath hot

against his face, she nuzzled him and kissed her way along his cheek, her lush lips sliding to his mouth. He instantly grew hard.

"I wanted you to be happy," he breathed as his lips slid over hers. "I thought you'd find a good man to marry and have a life with."

"Oh, George..." She wrapped her arms around his neck and slid her tongue against his mouth. He opened, sliding his tongue out to meet hers.

The room grew hot. He reached for the buttons of his coat. She grasped his hands, soft, warm fingers gliding over his and helped him unbutton. Together, they slid the coat from his shoulders to the floor. Next she undid his vest. The garment joined the coat at his feet.

When she reached for his shirt buttons, he covered her hands with his. Although she knew about his chest wound from Gettysburg, she hadn't seen him shirtless since she'd treated him before he left to rejoin his regiment. He feared the scar would repulse her. "Cassie, if we go much further, I'm afraid I won't be able to stop."

"You won't have to," she breathed into his ear. "I want to be with you, George, in every way." Her heated gaze convinced him to allow her to open his shirt and pull the fabric over his head.

She gazed at his bared chest, gliding the tip of her tongue over her bottom lip. No disgust existed in her expression. She reached up and slid her fingers along the scar, then her lips followed.

His pulse raced. He longed to undress her, too, but hesitated. Had she been with a man before?

Fingering the brooch at the neckline of her gown, she unfastened it and opened the top clasp of her bodice. She leaned against him, pressing hot kisses over his chest.

How much more can I take?

Emboldened, he stepped back and fingered the

clasps of her bodice, loosening it. She shrugged out of the garment, exposing the lace trimmings of her chemise and corset.

Lowering his lips to the edge of the chemise, where her ivory skin lay exposed, he licked his way across, savoring the sweet taste. He fingered the button on her skirt, unhooking it.

She smiled and allowed the skirt to slip to the floor at her feet.

Next, he pulled the strings of her petticoats, and they joined the skirt and bodice in a pool on the floor. His pulse raced as he gazed at her. Even days before their wedding five years ago, he'd never seen her this way but had always imagined what their wedding night might have been like.

"Darlin', you're beautiful."

Her gaze dipped, as she unhooked the top clasp of the corset. Her fingers slid down the garment, until the fabric fell away, exposing the natural swell of her breasts.

"Oh, Cassie...you heat my blood."

"I want you to see me, as I long to see all of you."

He grasped the hem of her chemise and lifted it over her head. Her midnight dark hair shook free, the silky veil sliding over her bared shoulders.

He gazed at her, swallowing hard. She was clad in shoes, stockings and drawers, and nothing else. Her breasts, pert with rose tinged nipples, peaked awaiting his touch. She reached for the string to loosen the drawers, and his heart leaped to his throat.

"Wait," he said. "Sit down first."

She frowned but did as he asked, sitting on the bed.

He kneeled before her and slipped off her shoes. "Lie down."

Doing as he asked, she stretched her arms over her head, her bosom swelling toward him. His fingers tingled as he loosened the ties of her drawers and slid them down her stocking clad legs. The dark curls at her core enticed him. He longed to dip his finger inside but didn't want to alarm her. He didn't know if she were a virgin.

She shifted her hips, writhing as he reached for her garters and peeled off her stockings, one by one. His hands glided over her silken legs.

"Oh, George," she breathed. Her eyes closed halfway. "Now, let me see you."

He rose to his feet and fingered the waist of his trousers. "Cassie, are you sure?" He bit his lip. "Have you ever done this before?"

"No." She shook her head against the pillow. "Never."

"Then maybe we shouldn't. Not yet, anyway."

She reached for him. "Let me undo them, if you won't." Grasping his hands, she helped him loosen the buttons, allowing his trousers to slide down around his ankles. "Now, the drawers," she breathed.

His pulse raced as he undid the drawers, allowing them to drop. Her eyes widened, but she didn't shy away or cower. She eyed him boldly and patted the bed. "Show me what it's like to be a woman, George."

He swallowed hard. "I reckon we'd better take it slow."

"I've got nowhere else to go." She smiled as he settled beside her on the mattress.

Knowing no other man had touched her in all these years, increased his yearning, but he'd have to be gentle. The last thing he wanted was to hurt her.

Chapter Seventeen

Cassidy arched her back as George settled on the bed. Although she practiced medicine, her father had always shielded her from viewing this part of a man's anatomy. She'd sneaked a peek now and again without her father's knowledge, and now examined males on a regular basis, but to see the broad plains of George's body for the first time, now he was healthy and whole, intrigued, and excited her. Even his scar didn't repulse her but only reminded her of the time she'd spent caring for him after their return. She couldn't tear her gaze away.

He leaned over and took her mouth, sending a thrill straight to her belly. Although she wasn't a stranger to a man's kisses, the feel of his hot skin so close to her own heated body sent delicious sensations racing through her. She wanted more. Much more.

His hand moved down her throat to her breast. He cupped one in his hand, sending her pulse spiraling. He took a hardened nipple between his teeth. Liquid heat rushed to her core. She thought she'd die of the sheer excitement the act brought.

Her breath came in gasps.

He fingered her nipple and slid his hands down to her waist. "I'll show you what it feels like to be a woman, but anytime you want to stop, you tell me."

She nodded, not trusting herself to speak.

His fingers slid up and down her inner thighs, slowly, bringing an unbearable ache. All her senses were heightened by his touch, his scent, and the knowledge of what they were about to share.

His hand moved over her nub, increasing the wave of pleasure. A soft moan escaped her lips.

Was it possible to die of wanting?

The lightness of his fingers moving over her caused her breath to hitch. A series of moans escalated as the wave grew, threatening to drown her in its murky depth.

"Do you want me to stop, Cassie?"

She heard the question as if from the end of a long tunnel as the wave enveloped her.

"No," she rasped.

"Don't be afraid," he whispered. "Just relax."

His finger pushed inside her, increasing her want. A hot shaft of desire pierced her as the intensity of the wave coiled inside her body. When she feared she could stand no more, an explosion of pure hot pleasure sent shudders racing through her. She'd never felt such an intense feeling before. Wetness seeped between her thighs as she collapsed on the mattress.

"Are you all right?"

George's concerned gaze brought her back from pure rapture. She whooshed out a breath. "It was wonderful." She frowned. "But that's not all that happens between a man and woman. I want to pleasure you, too."

"That doesn't matter right now."

"Yes, it does." She pushed him flat on his back and licked and kissed his chest, the way he'd done to her, losing herself in his scent, the texture of his skin, and the light hair peppering his chest. As she licked his flat male nipple, his breath hitched.

"I think we should take it slower," he rasped.

She shook her head. "I want to feel everything...with you." She kissed his lips. "I've waited much too long."

"Well, then...if you're sure."

"I'm very sure. Show me everything." Fingering

the tip of his shaft, she smiled as his eyes closed.

"If you keep that up, darlin', there won't be much left to show you. At least not right now."

"Oh." She released his shaft and slid her body against his, slipping her arms around the rock hard muscles of his broad back as they rolled to face each other. His desire danced against her belly. Her breath grew shallow as her longing increased.

Gently, he rolled her onto her back. Again, he fingered her, causing tingles to build to intense spirals. A hoarse scream ripped from her throat. He lifted her legs, positioning them, and braced himself on top of her, his shaft between her thighs.

"Last chance to back out," he whispered. His hot breath sent a thrill racing over her body.

"I don't want to stop," she breathed.

"This may hurt a bit. I'll take it real slow." He slid into her. Resistance built, but she tried to ignore the slight pain and breathed deeply, concentrating on him. Just him.

"The pain should just last for a moment," he rasped.

She opened her legs wider as he slid farther inside, pushing slowly. After a moment of pain, she relaxed, relishing the feel of his chest against her breasts. She reached up and cupped his nape, fingering his thick hair, inhaling his male scent.

When he glanced at her, she nodded. He pushed again, and she writhed beneath him, enhancing her pleasure. Her gasps and moans built, until the upward spiral burst into release. She lay gasping under his weight, certain she'd never feel this good ever again.

He brushed his thumb against her cheek and rolled beside her. "Cassie, are you all right?"

She smiled. "This is the best I've ever felt." She rolled over and cupped his face in her hands. "Don't ever leave me again, George. I couldn't bear it."

"I won't, darlin'. Never again."

****

George sneaked Cassidy out of his room and down the service stairs at the back of the hotel. Maybe they'd be lucky and no one would notice the couple as they made their escape out the kitchen entrance.

He noted the clang of pots and pans and voices conversing. Pulling Cassidy aside, he lifted a finger to her lips to indicate silence. She nodded, grinning. Apparently, she enjoyed the secrecy and intrigue. But how would she feel if they were caught and word got back to her family, as it surely would?

He scowled. She giggled but covered her mouth to hide the sound. He led her out the back door and glanced around. No servants were outside at the moment. He motioned for her to follow around the side of the hotel, down the alley.

At the front of the building, she sagged against him. He righted her, and she brushed the front of her skirt.

"George..." Her green eyes crinkled. "That was such fun."

He grinned, not sure if she meant their lovemaking or their escape. "I think we'd best get you home, Cassie."

She nodded but covered her mouth to suppress another giggle.

George turned and gulped. His contact, Mrs. Claymore, strode toward the hotel, likely on her way to deliver a note to him. If Cassidy saw her...

He grasped Cassidy's arm. "You'd best go on home alone. I have something I have to attend to immediately."

"George?" Her dark brows knitted. "What's wrong?"

"Nothing." He backed into the alley, but Mrs. Claymore had spotted him.

"Mr. Masters," she called. "I've something for you."

Cassidy stared at the woman, then turned and faced him, her face contorting. "I see what important business you have to attend to!" She crossed her arms over her chest. "And I thought you'd changed." She slapped his face and strode across the road. A carriage driver halted his horse to avoid hitting her.

"Cassie, wait!" he called. She never looked back.

Mrs. Claymore approached, her puzzled gaze following Cassidy's departure. "A problem, Mr. Masters?"

He sighed. "Nothing I can't handle. I hope."

She handed him a note. "Mr. Pinkerton wants you to leave as soon as possible for Philadelphia. There's been a new development in the case." She glanced at the paper he held. "Your instructions are in the note."

"Philadelphia," he repeated.

Mrs. Claymore nodded, then left. He cringed. *How the hell can I fix things with Cassie now?*
****

Monday morning, Cassidy set up the exam room, preparing for her first patient of the day. The warm memory of her morning in George's arms, followed by the encounter with the woman from the boardinghouse confirmed her worst fears. He'd used her like he used all women. To cover for the time spent with him, she'd told her mother she'd been detained in town by a patient who needed immediate care. She hoped her mother wouldn't ask any more questions, but she seemed too busy with her baking to inquire further.

Cassidy sent a note to Dr. Madison asking him to stop by today, too, since she wouldn't have time to call on him. In truth, she didn't want to show up at his house, in case the maid wasn't there. Her pulse raced as she wondered how she'd hide what she knew from the doctor.

An hour later, her mother led Dr. Madison into the room. A bandage covered his nose, black smudges lined his eyes, but he twisted his lips into a smile.

"Miss Stuart, I'd like to thank you again for coming to my rescue Saturday night."

"Not at all, Doctor." She gestured toward a chair. "Please, have a seat."

He settled his long frame in the chair, resting his hat on the table beside him. "I'm grateful I didn't run into Masters this morning. He might've given me a bloody lip to match the nose."

She chewed on her lower lip. Images of George's naked body and the sensations he'd aroused sent her stomach fluttering.

Madison's brow arched. "You seem more than a bit distracted, Miss Stuart."

"Do I?" She swirled around to locate a pair of shears. "I've had a rather busy morning."

He grasped her wrist.

Her breath caught. She turned back to face him.

"You have a certain glow about you today." His amber gaze roved over her.

"I...it's just such a glorious day. Why wouldn't I be glowing?"

Madison grinned. "Why indeed?"

Cassidy quirked a brow, lifting the shears. "Let me just take a peek at your nose, Doctor."

He stiffened but allowed her to proceed.

****

George tossed clothes in his suitcase. The note from William Pinkerton ordered him to leave for Philadelphia to interview a Miss Mildred Strunk. She'd worked as a nurse for the Madisons, both father and son, at the father's still thriving practice in Philadelphia, but she'd resigned her position. He'd checked at the station to find no train available until

Monday morning and he'd reckoned Cassidy was none to happy with him right now, so had stayed away yesterday, but how would he explain his sudden absence? Or should he? Maybe he should have left her out of this whole investigation.

The spot on the bed beside him held her scent, lilac and woman. He sighed. Maybe he shouldn't have taken advantage of her, but she'd seemed eager. He hoped she wouldn't regret what they'd done, after this apparent misunderstanding. They'd waited five long years, because of his stupidity. But because he couldn't trust her with his true identity, he may have ruined his chances with her again.

He lifted the feather pillow she'd lain on, inhaling her scent. His mind drifted back to the day he'd returned from prison camp. The day he'd asked her to be his wife.

After his release from the prison in Richmond, he'd hitched rides and trudged the rest of the way home. Although he had nothing to return to in Burkeville, he had nowhere else to go.

He'd plodded up the road with her house the first he passed. He slowed and saw an angel, his angel. She'd raced to the end of her garden to the gate. Tears glistened in her eyes.

"What's *this* all about?" he'd asked.

"I thought you were dead, and I wanted to die, too. I've been denying my feelings for a long time..." She took a deep breath. "I love you."

He blinked, taken aback for a moment. "You don't know how many times in prison I dreamed of this moment. I should have told you before I left how I felt, but I was afraid."

"Of me?" Cassidy opened the gate and stepped toward him.

He took her by the shoulders and grazed his lips over her forehead.

"Cassidy Stuart," he whispered, "I've loved you

for a long time. I'm not ever letting you go again. Marry me."

She pulled away.

He smiled, but his smile faded as she hesitated. His stomach tightened as he realized she was going to say no.

"Forgive me," he said. "I presumed too much."

She clasped her hands together. "Oh, no it's not that...I never expected this."

"I'm rushing you." He backed away a few paces.

She grasped his hand, her warmth and scent enveloping him. "Please, don't misunderstand. We've had too much of that already."

He gazed into her beautiful green eyes. "Thinking of you was the one thing that kept me alive."

She shook her head. "I should've done more. If only I could've written you..."

He shushed her with a finger on her lush lips.

"Yes," she said.

"Yes, what?"

"Yes, I'll marry you, but first—" She smiled and patted his ribs. "—I've got to fatten you up. You look like your pa's scarecrow."

George glanced across the hotel room and stared at the patterned wallpaper. That day had been the happiest of his life and, until now, he'd been living in hell without her.

He vowed he'd never leave her again, and he sure as hell swore to keep his promise. When he returned from Philadelphia, he'd make things right.

Chapter Eighteen

Before leaving his room, George penned a hasty letter to Cassidy explaining he must leave but would be back as soon as possible. He didn't want to divulge any more in case the letter landed in the wrong hands. He didn't have time to hand deliver it.

He sealed the post, then splashed water on his face and shrugged into his vest and coat.

He grabbed the packed bag and thudded down the stairs, stopping at the front desk. His jaw still ached from his encounter with Madison, and he'd spent a good portion of Sunday night pacing his hotel room worrying about Cassidy.

The clerk, Mr. Stanton, glanced up as George dropped his suitcase and handed him the sealed note. "You look like you got run over by a train, Mister."

George ran a hand over his stubble. "Reckon I feel like I have."

The clerk leaned on the counter and eyed him. "Are you checking out, sir?"

"No. I'll just be out of town for a few days. I hope you can hold my room until I return."

The man nodded. "Either that room or another. We don't see much business."

George grinned. "Thanks. I will be back."

"You the one had the run in with Doc Madison?" Stanton narrowed his gaze.

George scowled. "Word does get around."

"Over Miss Stuart, wasn't it?" The man's salt and pepper brow arched. "Fighting over the little lady, you were."

George detected admiration in the man's gaze. "Maybe I didn't like the way he touched her."

Stanton grinned. "Well, sir, I wish you luck." He squinted. "Folks here tell me you used to live in Burkeville."

"A long time ago, but I left just after the war." George handed Stanton the letter. "Could you please be sure Miss Stuart gets this?"

The man smiled. "I'll take it to her myself." He nodded. "Yes, sir, I'll get this right out for you today."

"Thank you." George reached into his pocket extracting a few coins, thankful the clerk didn't ask any questions.

As he turned to leave, Stanton warned, "You'd best get some rest, sir. Maybe you should get Miss Stuart to give you a look over before you leave." He winked.

"Don't have time. Have to catch the next train out." George turned away.

He strode to the train station, wishing he'd had more time to explain to Cassidy. As he neared the platform, he caught sight of a well-dressed woman with chestnut hair standing by the ticket office, suitcases beside her.

Mrs. Claymore.

He stepped to her side. "Don't tell me you're going to Philadelphia too?"

She smirked, then her face colored. "No, Mr. Masters, I'm headed for New York. But I will be joining you in Philadelphia in a few days so I can relay your findings back to the agency..." She sighed. "You know we can't risk—"

"I know," he said. "Can't risk telegraphs or the mail." He lifted his suitcase as well as one of hers. A porter grasped the other one.

"After you, ma'am," George said.

She nodded and preceded him into the train. He

hoped to hell this wouldn't get back to Cassidy, but knowing this town as well as he did, was sure as hell it would.

****

After treating Dr. Madison, Cassidy saw him to the door. "I'd like to apologize for what happened, Doctor."

He lifted her hand and grazed his lips over her knuckles. "No need, my dear. What that ruffian did wasn't your fault."

She shook her head. "But he had this misguided idea he was protecting me, so I feel like it *was* somehow my fault."

"Forget about him." He didn't release her hand. "Have dinner with me this evening."

"I don't know. Your nose...you're still not recovered."

"Nonsense. I feel fine, and my doctor's given me a clean bill of health."

"If you're sure." She licked her lips. "I *would* like to discuss a medical school my brother told me about...in Philadelphia." His smile faded, but he nodded. "Of course, if you'd like. Over dinner then?"

"All right."

He released her hand and placed his bowler on his head as he opened the door. "I'll be by at six to escort you."

She nodded and stood by the door until he'd descended the porch steps. George would have a conniption fit when he found out she was having dinner with Madison. But the image in her mind of him and Mrs. Claymore sent hot prickles of indignation up her spine. She'd help George discredit the doctor, but afterward, he could go back to New York or wherever he came from, and she'd be more than happy to never see him again.

****

Dr. Madison arrived to escort Cassidy to town in

his carriage. As he led her to the conveyance, she balked. "Whatever did you hire a carriage for? It's a short walk to town. I walk it all the time."

He smiled, extending a hand to help her up. "Ah, but I never said we were having dinner in Burkeville, did I?"

Her heart sped up at the implications. "Where are we going then?"

"It's a surprise, my dear. Trust me."

She smiled, but prickles of unease raced over her. Maybe she should turn and race back to the safety of her house.

At her hesitation to board, he quirked a brow. "I promise to behave as a proper gentleman. I fear I may have imbibed a bit too much the other night and let my animal instinct get the better of me."

Cassidy flinched as George's words of warning came back to her. Was she making a mistake?

After a quick glance back at her house, she made her decision, extending her arm so he could assist her.

After a pleasant ride through farmland extending beyond town, the carriage stopped at a stone, two story house with a long wraparound porch. Gigantic oak trees and colorful flower gardens graced the outside of the building.

"It's beautiful," Cassidy said.

Dr. Madison took her hand. "After our meal, I'll escort you through the gardens. They're breathtaking."

She alighted from the carriage and glanced around. "However did you find this place?"

"A patient of mine who lives at the boardinghouse dines here regularly."

He led her onto the wide porch. Rocking chairs invited patrons to lounge and enjoy the scenery. Flower pots perched alongside chairs and on the wide railing. Once inside, she delighted in the interior view, as inviting as the outside. The dining area was set with a number of tables. The ones in the middle of the room seated about ten, while the tables bordering the walls were of a size to seat four. Flowers and candles adorned each of the tables, with gas lamps on windowsills lining the perimeter, although the large windows allowed enough sunlight so they weren't yet lit.

Dr. Madison leaned toward her. "Do you like it, Miss Stuart?"

"Oh, yes. This is a beautiful inn."

"I've heard the food here is excellent as well."

And likely expensive.

A gray haired woman approached, a broad smile on her face. "What may I do for you, sir?"

Madison patted Cassidy's hand settled in the crook of his arm. "I'd like your finest table for my lady and myself."

"Of course, sir." The woman waved them into the dining room. A few patrons were already seated, with the majority of the tables still empty.

The woman led them to a table near the wall. Madison pulled out a chair for Cassidy. After she'd settled and brushed out her skirts, he took the seat across from her.

"Would you care for a menu, sir, or do you know what you and your lady would like?"

"This is my first time dining in your fine establishment, madam. So, yes, I would like to peruse a menu if it's all right."

She inclined her head. "I'll be right with you, sir."

Cassidy's mouth gaped as the woman retreated.

Madison smiled and reached for her hand. "I take it you don't get out of Burkeville much."

Startled by his remark, she straightened her shoulders. "Sir, I'll have you know I've traveled to Gettysburg and as far as Washington City."

His brows rose. "You've been to Washington?"

"Well..." She shrugged. "It *was* during the war. I worked in the hospitals alongside my father."

"Oh, yes, so your brother said." He shook out his linen napkin and spread it on his lap. "The capital wasn't a pretty sight during those years."

The woman returned with the menu. "Here you are, sir." He glanced over it, while she stood at his side.

"Well, now, this looks very tasty." He pointed to something on the menu and the woman nodded.

"Very well, sir." She glanced at Cassidy. "For you and the lady?"

"Yes, madam." He grinned.

As the woman strode off, Cassidy tilted her head and crossed her arms over her chest. "What did you order?"

"A surprise. I'm sure you'll love it."

She pursed her lips, annoyed he hadn't asked her what she wanted. "If you must know, sir, I have a mind of my own and am capable of deciding what I'd like to eat." She snapped her napkin across her lap.

He seemed oblivious to her agitation as he glanced around the room. *Is he that dense, or does he treat all women this way?*

A waiter carrying a decanter of wine approached. He set their glasses right side up and filled them.

After he retreated, she said, "You ordered wine?"

"Why, yes. Is there a problem? If you'd like something else..."

"It's fine," she ground out between clenched teeth. She lifted her glass and took a sip. The fruity warmth glided down her throat. But she'd be sure not to take too much. She wondered what mother would think of her getting into a carriage with the doctor sans chaperone. She'd left the house without telling anyone.

After another sip, she felt decadent. She'd often done outrageous things, but to go off with the dashing doctor alone in a carriage would earn her more than a share of gossip in town. Of course, they all thought the world of Dr. Madison. A man beyond reproach.

After wiping her lips with the napkin, she leaned forward. "Doctor, my brother thinks I should apply at the *Female Medical College* in Philadelphia. What do you think?"

His brows furrowed. "I'd hoped you planned to take me up on the offer of working with me. Why would you need to attend medical school?"

She sighed. "I need better credentials than I have now. I've assisted my father for years, but people don't take me seriously."

"If you think a degree would help, Miss Stuart, but I really don't think it necessary. Surely, you plan to marry someday."

"Well." She hesitated. "I suppose, if the opportunity arises."

He quirked his full lips. "You'd make a wonderful wife and mother, Miss Stuart."

Prickles shot up her spine. The conversation grew too personal. Next thing, he'd be proposing.

She breathed a sigh of relief when the waiter reappeared setting their meal before them.

Cassidy inhaled the spicy aroma of roasted beef, potatoes, and glazed carrots on her plate.

"You do eat beef, I assume." The doctor eyed her, the corner of his mouth tilted upward.

"Of course...it's just...this has to be expensive." She frowned.

"Nothing too expensive for my lady."

She bristled, not liking his possessive attitude. Sitting back, she lifted her fork, poking one of the red potatoes. She sampled a bite of potato, then sliced off a piece of the beef. Lifting her fork to her lips, she bit into the morsel allowing the succulent juices to melt in her mouth. When she glanced at the doctor she found, to her consternation, his gaze fixed on her.

"Do you like it?"

"It's excellent." She reached for her wine glass.

"Then you're pleased with my choice of meal. I didn't want to assume but felt certain you'd enjoy my selection."

She sipped her wine, then replaced the glass. "Yes, you chose well."

He leaned forward. "I can help you, Miss Stuart. I have connections in Philadelphia. If your dream is to be a practicing physician, stick by me, and I'll see you accomplish everything you dream." He raised his glass, nodding for her to do the same.

She lifted her glass, and he clinked his against it.

"To our union," he said.

Saying nothing, she took another sip and replaced her glass on the tabletop as unease crept over her again.

What union is he talking about?

Chapter Nineteen

Tuesday morning Cassidy stood at the stove, scrambling a batch of eggs. After Dr. Madison had brought her home last night, she'd lain awake for hours going over their conversation. He seemed to trust her, but how would she ever get him to reveal his indiscretions? Her one chance would be if they spent time alone. Her skin crawled at the thought.

She scooped the eggs onto a plate and set them on the table. Sarah slouched in her usual seat, but Ma and Matt hadn't yet arrived downstairs.

Sarah helped herself, then gazed at Cassidy as she took a seat across the table.

"Tell me, Cassie, what's it like?"

Cassidy squinted. "You mean, the inn?"

"Yes." Sarah sat up. "Mrs. Bigsley saw you ride through town in the doctor's carriage last night. And after you'd gone rumors were spreading all over town. Where did you go?"

Cassidy shrugged. "The Westside Inn."

Sarah sighed. "That's the fanciest eatery around." She served herself eggs, then glanced up. "He didn't propose, did he?"

Cassidy scowled. "No, he did not. It's way too soon anyway. I hardly know the man."

"It's because of George, isn't it? You're still not over him."

"I am so." She glared at Sarah, but heat crept up her face at the memory of their lovemaking.

Sarah lifted her fork, pointing the utensil straight out. "Well, reckon it's for the best, since he left town yesterday with that woman from the boardinghouse. Mrs. Clayton...Clanton?" she waved her fork around. "I'm not sure of the name."

Cassidy's face heated. "Mrs. Claymore?"

"That's the one." She lifted a forkful of eggs to her mouth. While chewing, she tilted her head, then swallowed. "He didn't tell you he was leaving?"

"It's his business, I reckon, and I couldn't care less." Cassidy shrugged and spooned eggs into her mouth. She'd not allow Sarah to see how his departure had rattled her, but a lump rose in Cassidy's throat. She chewed slowly, hoping she didn't choke.

Her sister frowned. "I think you're still in love with a man who can't give you anything. It would be for the best if George leaves and never comes back."

Cassidy managed to swallow her eggs, then sighed. "Can we talk about something else?"

Sarah shrugged but said nothing. She polished off her plate and rose from the table, angling her belly over the tabletop. "I guarantee now George is gone, you'll start to see things in a new light."

I very much doubt it. Why didn't he tell me he was leaving? Her face burned, and she hoped Sarah didn't notice. Cassidy didn't want to field more questions about George.

After her sister left the room, Cassidy shoved her plate aside. Ma and Matt strolled in chattering. They sat and filled their plates with eggs and biscuits.

"Cassie, are you all right?" her mother asked.

She glanced up to find her mother and brother staring at her. "Oh, yes, Ma. I ate with Sarah. I'll go out and tend to the garden, then come back in to clean up after you two are done."

"I'll take care of the kitchen," her mother said. "You go on ahead. I'm sure you have something to attend to in the office, anyway."

Cassidy frowned. "After I'm finished in the

garden, I suppose I could check my appointment book and get the examining room ready for the first patient...if I have one."

She left them to finish breakfast and retreated to the front garden, snatching the claw on the way. She planned to yank out any weeds invading the flowers. Although still early, bright sunlight promised a warm May day. As she surveyed the petunias and hyacinths, searching for weeds to pull, her mind drifted back five years to a month after the war ended.

George disappeared near the end of the war, and she'd received word he'd been taken prisoner. She'd spent countless hours worrying about him and wondering if she'd ever see him again. After the surrender had been signed, she waited every day for word of him. But nothing.

The day he returned had been a bright sunny day like this, and she'd been in this very spot, working in the garden. When she spotted a lone man walking up the road in a soldier's uniform, she gathered her skirts and raced to the gate.

Her heart rose to her throat at the sight of George. Although he'd lost weight and looked like a scarecrow in his oversize uniform, he never looked better. He asked her to marry him, and she said yes.

Not long after, everything had gone wrong. He seemed agitated and unsure of himself as she and her family discussed wedding plans. And two days before they were to be married, he told her he was leaving. He didn't feel worthy of marrying her.

She tried to convince him otherwise, but he left anyway. After a period of mourning for him, she decided to go on with her life. And she'd been doing just fine until he showed up again.

Now, knowing he wasn't a changed man, just a man who'd perfected his gambling skills and womanizing while away, her face burned in shame for allowing him to bed her. She hated him. He'd completely disrupted her ordered life, and she didn't know how she'd react if he returned. The memory of his dark eyes, tobacco, and leather scent and lean-muscled frame sent her traitorous pulse tingling. Why had she trusted him? Was he really investigating Dr. Madison? What if all he'd told her and Quinn had been a lie?

****

Cassidy sat in her office reading over patient files. What few she had anyway. She needed something to take her mind off George. How could she have been so stupid?

The raw hurt and anger set her teeth on edge. The words on the files swam before her eyes.

She folded her arms atop the desk and sank her head down. She'd allowed him back into her heart, but this was worse, far worse than when she'd accepted his proposal five years ago.

She bit her lip, willing herself not to give in to tears. Her mother and Sarah were right. He was no good. Not the marrying kind. If not for this investigation he'd involved Quinn and her in, she'd break all ties with him.

A light rap at the door caught her off guard. "Yes?" she called, patting her hair and wiping any tell-tale smudges from her eyes.

"Cassie," her mother said.

"Come in, Ma."

Her mother peered in, a frown crossing her face. "The hotel clerk has a letter for you. Says he was told to hand deliver it."

Cassidy sighed. "I'll be right there."

Once her mother left, she gathered herself, smoothing her skirt and checking her appearance in the mirror. Deciding she looked presentable, so no one would sense the turmoil of the past few hours, she descended the stairs and stepped to the door.

"Good afternoon, Miss Cassie." Mr. Stanton tipped his hat.

She smiled. "Hello, Mr. Stanton. My mother said you've a letter for me?"

"Yes, ma'am." He handed her the note. "I promised I'd deliver it."

She frowned. "Promised who?"

He waved his hand toward the letter. "I'm sure you'll know once you read it." He tipped his hat again. "Good day."

She watched as he strode down the porch steps and garden path whistling a tune.

She glanced at the letter, recognizing the handwriting. *George.*

She had a sudden urge to throw the paper in the fireplace, but her hand stilled when she realized the hearth wasn't lit.

What good would throwing the letter in there do? Her heart fluttered and she swallowed, clutching the paper to her chest.

A glimpse of skirts told her Ma stood nearby, likely curious about who sent the letter. She strode to her office and closed the door.

Settling into her desk chair, she lifted the letter and broke the seal. Unfolding the paper, she hesitated. She didn't care what George had to say.

But curiosity won out over anger.

Dearest Cassie,

I regret I have to leave for a bit. But I promise when I return I'll explain and set things right.

I love you,

George

She crumpled the paper into a tight ball and threw it across her desk.

The son-of-a-bitch!

Every time they got close, he ran.

And his assurance that he'd return meant nothing.

He'd taken everything she had to give, and now he'd left with no explanation.

If and when he did come back, she'd tell him to go to hell.

Chapter Twenty

Wednesday afternoon, Quinn pulled Cassidy aside and invited her to take a walk with him into town.

"Have you talked to George about Madison?" he asked as they strolled toward the center of town. "I've been too busy catching up on patients to pay attention to what he or Madison is doing. Has George found anything out?"

"Nothing, I'm afraid. At least, nothing incriminating. Now that I've volunteered to work with the doctor, maybe I can get him to admit to something that will aid the investigation, if George even comes back."

Quinn yanked her to a stop. "What do you mean, if he comes back?" He lifted his hat and raked a hand through his rusty-colored hair. "George would never allow you to be alone with that man and neither will I."

Cassidy shrugged. "George left two days ago on the train in the company of Mrs. Claymore." Her cheeks burned.

"Two days ago? I wondered why he wasn't coming around. Why didn't you tell me?"

"What difference would it have made?"

"I would have been more vigilant, instead of preoccupied with my workload." Quinn scowled. "Who's Mrs. Claymore, anyway? And stop squeezing my elbow so tight." He moved his arm to help release her grip.

"A mysterious and beautiful woman staying at the boardinghouse. I met her last week, and she's been seen in town talking to George. Now, she's left with him for God knows where." She propped her fists on her hips and faced her brother.

"He didn't tell you where he's going? Cassie, I'm sorry. I really thought he'd changed."

She sighed. "So did I, but he and I are through now."

"What about the investigation of Dr. Madison?"

She shrugged. "George's story may have been a ruse to get to me."

"I don't understand." Quinn raised his brows.

She shook her head. "Doesn't matter. I'm done with him."

"What about Madison? Are we finished with him, too?"

"Of course not. No matter what else, he's trying to take all our patients. We have to stop him before we don't have a practice left to call our own." She gazed at her brother. "If you still want to rebuild Pa's practice, that is?" The thought occurred to Cassidy that Quinn might have been offered a place on staff at the hospital, although he hadn't hinted at that since he'd returned, but he had so little to come back to town for.

Quinn gazed across town square toward the mercantile. "I want to see this thing with Madison through whether George is with us or not."

"I'm so glad, Quinn." She clasped his arm. "I think you and I can expose him."

He scowled. "But I don't like that you're getting so close to him. Ma told me he's been courting you. You shouldn't be alone with him."

"I'm afraid you don't have a choice in the matter. I started seeing him on a social basis to try to draw him out."

"If I hadn't been so busy, I would have talked you out of such a dangerous venture. I'm surprised George allowed you to do that."

Cassidy scowled. "He has no say in the matter."

"Well, I'm sure old George was none too happy." Quinn narrowed his gaze. "He didn't try anything, did he?"

Cassidy's face heated. "You mean Madison?"

"Of course, I mean Madison. Who else..." Quinn allowed the sentence to die. "Were you and George, ah, er...?"

"Not your business, Quinn." Cassidy swallowed the lump in her throat.

As they strolled to the center of town, her hand resting on her brother's arm, she noticed his attention drawn to a couple of young women with ribbon-laced straw hats and baskets hung on their arms.

Following his gaze, she smiled. Miss Elizabeth Baker, the schoolteacher, stood at the fruit stand, fingering a peach.

"Why don't you go and talk to her?" She poked her brother.

His throat worked as he gazed at the teacher with a lost puppy dog expression. "You sure she doesn't have a beau?"

"I'm certain." She gestured for him to approach the woman.

"Maybe she has one back where she came from."

"You'll never know if you don't ask." Grasping Quinn's arm, she steered him in the schoolteacher's path.

Colliding with Quinn, Miss Baker gasped and dropped her basket.

"Begging your pardon, Miss," Quinn said. "Allow me to get that." He retrieved the basket and glared in Cassidy's direction. "I'm afraid my sister is feeling pushy today."

Miss Baker straightened her hat and accepted the basket from Quinn's hands. Cassidy couldn't help but notice the shy, appraising glance the woman gave her brother.

"Oh, Miss Stuart," she said.

"I'm so sorry, Miss Baker," Cassidy apologized. "My brother's right. This is all my fault."

"So good to see you again, Dr. Stuart." Her hazel eyed gaze roved over Quinn again.

"Ma'am." Quinn tipped his hat.

"I haven't seen you around town lately."

"Oh, I've been here, but I've been immersed in catching up on Cassie's patient files, since I'll be working with her now. I'm eager to help Cassie rebuild our father's practice."

"That would be a fine tribute, sir."

Quinn grinned. "Thank you, ma'am. My sister and I think so too."

"Your sister has already treated me for a cut on my arm. I've told her I want to keep seeing her for other ailments." Her skin turned a bright pink, and she batted her pale lashes.

"Cassie's a fine physician, ma'am, despite what anyone around here says."

Cassidy caught her brother's gaze, giving him a thankful smile.

"I'm sure I'll be seeing both of you again, then." Miss Baker lowered her lashes as she stepped forward to ascend the steps to the mercantile.

As she disappeared into the store, Cassidy gripped Quinn's arm. "I'd definitely say she's intrigued by you, big brother."

He frowned. "You reckon so?"

Cassidy grinned. "You are so dense. Of course she likes you. Did you see the way she looked at you and batted her eyes?"

He lifted his hat and scratched his head. "Women. Guess I'll never understand them."

Cassidy sighed. "If you don't go after that woman, I'll..."

"You'll what?"

She threw up her hands. "Invite her to the new ice cream parlor at the edge of town."

"You sure? I don't want to seem too forward."

She patted his forearm, then threaded her hand through the crook of his arm. "Let's go home, and I'll tell you all you need to know about women."

****

Wednesday night, George felt almost presentable after a bath, a shave, and a clean set of clothes. He'd arrived in Philadelphia, early in the evening and obtained a room at a hotel off Chestnut Street. He felt horrible about not telling Cassidy the truth about his post as a Pinkerton agent, but if word got to Madison, the man would likely run or take even more devious measures to prevent his downfall.

Since nothing could be done about the doctor until George returned to Burkeville, he decided he needed a night on the town to clear his mind for the work ahead. He hated like hell to hurt Cassidy. He'd done far too much in that regard. He may have lost her forever, but he hoped, once he could explain, she'd understand and take him back.

One of the hotel clerks apprised him of a tavern down the street that held a nightly poker game. He excelled at poker. Had learned to play as a lad and the game whiled away the endless hours of waiting while in camp during the war. Soldiering was nothing but intense anxiety before and during a battle, followed by exhaustion and boredom. Poker eased the strain then and would so now. He'd even engaged in a few games in a back room of the local tavern in Burkeville. Gambling turned out to be a good cover for him, since as far as the townsfolk knew, he had no job. This way he could appear to be earning his keep at the hotel. Before joining the Pinkerton agency, his sole income had been winnings from card games. After a few games in the

159

Philadelphia tavern with two different locals, who he cleaned out, he sat back and surveyed the tiny, smoke-filled room.

He still worried about how he could draw Doc Madison out, since his only source of information was the school teacher. According to Cassidy, she didn't want to see Madison as her doctor anymore but wouldn't say why. He hoped this new lead would give him something to go on. A nurse, who once worked for both the Madisons, now taught a class at *Female Medical College.* His assignment was to interview her and find out anything she knew that might help the case.

His heart skipped a beat at the thought of Cassidy being anywhere near the man while he was away, but he couldn't do anything until he got back.

Idly, he shuffled the deck of cards, then sensed someone standing over him. He glanced up at a thin, full-bearded man. He looked vaguely familiar, but George couldn't place him.

"This is my brother, Nate," one of the other card players, who'd introduced himself as James Bartholomew said. "He sits in on our games when he comes out for a visit."

The man scowled.

"I seen you in town earlier. You're staying at the hotel, but I thought I recognized you from somewhere else." He nodded. "George Masters. I served with you in the 83rd. I done thought the Rebs killed you."

Oh, hell! Bartholomew had gotten into a fight with him and Josh over a poker game in camp. Although Josh was forever raring for a good fight, George had talked their way out of a brawl. Otherwise the three of them would have landed in the guardhouse. But he also swore he'd seen the man in Burkeville, just hadn't recalled their past association.

Nate leaned his hand on the table, a slight wobble to his gait. His breath reeked. George turned away to avoid the stench and resumed shuffling cards.

"Can I do something for you?" George asked.

"I see you're still cheating folks out of their hard earned cash," Nate slurred.

"You've no call to accuse me of that." George gestured to a chair. "Have a seat and we'll discuss this like gentlemen."

"You're no gentleman, Masters." Nate waved his hand in the air. "In fact, I think you're a damn thief!"

Before George could respond, a tavern worker approached and laid a beefy hand on Nate's shoulder. "Sir, if you could lower your voice."

Nate shoved the hand away. "I am just stating facts." He pointed at George. "This man is a thief. You shouldn't allow him in here."

George set the cards down and stood, glaring at James. "Reckon you should take your brother outside."

"C'mon Nate, why don't you go on home and sleep it off?" James grinned but made no motion to rise.

Nate shoved the table into George, propelling him backward against the wall. The table upended and cards and glasses spilled over the floor. "I want all my money back, Masters."

"What money?" George raised his hands.

"All the money you stole from me while we were in camp."

"I won the money fair and square."

The tavern worker grasped Nate's shoulder. "Sir, I have to ask you to leave."

"I will not!" Nate shouted. He pushed back his coat, revealing a revolver at his hip.

The man's face paled. "Please, sir. You know we

don't allow guns in here."

James groaned and swiped his hand in the air. "Nate, I told you to go on home."

Nate ignored his brother and grinned. "So, that means *he* don't have a gun?" He motioned to George.

George carried a firearm, because of his profession, but the last thing he wanted was to reveal he had one. "No, I don't." He gritted his teeth hoping Nate wasn't stupid or drunk enough to pull his.

The tavern worker glanced at George, then Nate. "Please, sir. If you have a problem with Mr. Masters you'll have to settle this elsewhere. Our patrons aren't allowed to bring weapons in here."

Nate closed his coat and nodded. "All right, Masters. I'll wait, but you'd best be on your guard." His brother rose and grasped Nate's arm. The pair wobbled out the back door.

"Are you all right, sir?" the tavern worker asked.

"Sure am. He doesn't bother me. Just drunk is all." He helped the man set the table back in place.

"I'd be careful when I leave here, sir," he said. "He may be outside lying in wait. You can go through the tavern and out the front door, if you'd like."

George nodded. "I've dealt with men like him before. His brother likely got him home, or he's passed out in the back alley."

"Best be on your guard anyway, sir."

****

"George, wake up." George opened his eyes and gasped. Cassidy lay in the bed beside him, her dark hair loose around her shoulders. Her filmy nightgown exposed the creamy swell of her lush breasts.

"What are you doing here?" He stared at her through the dim lantern light. Hadn't he extinguished it? And how the hell had she gotten in his room anyway?

She leaned down. Her hair tickled his face, smelling of lilac. "I'm getting married," she whispered.

A low laugh drew his gaze behind her. In the shadows, the form of a man edged forward. Scott Madison stretched out his hand to rest on Cassidy's shoulder. "She's mine, Masters. Reckon the best man won."

George jerked his head back, and they both disappeared. What a horrid dream. He grasped his pillow. He'd turned off the lantern, but pale moonlight revealed an empty room.

He rose and paced, shoving a hand through his hair. As a trained agent, he couldn't allow his frustration over having to play act in front of the doc and the whole town, get to him. As soon as he could get the proof he needed against Madison, this whole nightmare would be over. He and Cassidy could start over again.

Locating his basin in the pre-dawn light, he poured tepid water from the pitcher and splashed his face. After he'd toweled himself off, he paced until sunlight seeped into his window.

How am I going to catch the bastard without anyone getting hurt?

Chapter Twenty-One

Scott dined alone at the tavern Thursday evening. He'd asked Miss Stuart to join him, but she claimed to be otherwise engaged. And he knew why. Tillie told him Mrs. Bigsley had seen Miss Stuart and Mr. Masters by the pond having a picnic last Saturday. And Miss Stuart had never said a word. According to Tillie, Masters had the audacity to lean over and kiss her. Tillie knew Scott had been courting her and feared Miss Stuart was deceiving him.

He assured Tillie Miss Stuart was through with Masters but caught the knowing smirk on the housemaid's thin lips. The bitch! Perhaps he should think of dismissing her and hiring someone younger.

His thoughts strayed to the schoolteacher. An image of her ivory skin and golden hair caused an erotic throbbing in his groin. He grimaced. He'd deal with those urges later, in the privacy of his room.

Weeks had passed since his encounter with the lovely teacher, and Miss Stuart seemed to be stringing him along. And now she cavorted with Masters.

He sliced off a hunk of beef and raised the morsel to his mouth. He nibbled, musing how he'd love to have both women tied down, at his mercy. He'd have his fill again and again, then when done, he'd dispose of them both.

The waitress approached, distracting him. Her dark-eyed gaze settled on his plate. "Have you had enough, Doc? You hardly touched your beef?"

He glanced down at the juicy hunk before him,

then back up. The waitress had a beautiful smile and a plump, voluptuous shape.

But alas, she was married to the tavern owner. The beefy man would have Scott's hide if he so much as made an improper gesture to his wife.

"My dear, could I trouble you to bring me a bottle of bourbon?"

She smiled and nodded, ambling away. He studied her posterior. He'd have to console himself with liquor tonight.

****

Cassidy tossed and turned, her mind on George and his betrayal. She slid from her bed, lit the lantern, then descended the stairs. She crept to the kitchen and gasped. A shadowy figure sat at the table.

A lantern illuminated the table top, revealing Quinn. His face lay in the shadows.

"Quinn, what's wrong? Couldn't you sleep either?" She set down her lantern and joined him at the table.

He grinned. "Just not used to this house again, I reckon." His gaze held hers. "What about you?"

"Been thinking too much on my future." She leaned on her elbows. "Tell me, when were you planning to visit the hospital in Philadelphia?"

"Tomorrow." He frowned. "Why?"

"I think I'd like to go with you, if it's all right."

He shrugged. "Fine by me. You can put the few patients you have on hold. In case of an emergency, Madison could see them."

"If just for a few days, I reckon it would be all right." She bit her lip. "I don't like giving Madison any more business though."

She straightened her shoulders, feeling giddy. "We could tour the *Female Medical College*."

"Excellent idea, Sis." He beamed. "And while we're there, we'll spend a little time digging up

165

Madison's past."

She smiled. "We don't need George to find out what we need to know."

"Well..." Quinn sat back and lifted his hands behind his head, "if we can dig up anything on Madison while we're in the city, you'll be doing old George a favor."

She scowled. "If he comes back."

"Sorry, Sis. Didn't mean to bring up old wounds."

Cassidy sighed. "I'm beginning to hope he never returns."

****

Scott retreated to his room cradling the bottle of bourbon. All day he'd gone over in his mind ways to make things right with Miss Stuart, but the thought of her with Masters enraged him. The bitch had ruined his plans. If she and her brother reopened the Stuart practice, more than a few of his patients might move back. And where would that leave him?

So for tonight, he'd drink himself into a stupor. Maybe in the morning, he could come up with a plan. His one other option, move on to another small town and start over.

The bourbon warmed him but didn't ease his agitation. The image of Miss Stuart and how he'd love to make her pay ate at him. He'd start by ripping off every stitch of clothing and showing her what a man could give her. Then he'd beat her black and blue, so she'd never dare defy him again.

Oh, yes, he'd love to keep her locked up all to himself.

As the bourbon worked its way down his gullet, he warmed to the idea of taking Miss Stuart for his. Lying on his bed, he stroked his groin, imagining her sweet ivory skin pressed against him as she begged him to take her again and again.

In the vision, he gave her what she wanted, long

and hard, until she gasped for him to stop. Then he slapped her. Over and over, until she cowered, begging him to stop hurting her.

He took another swig from his bottle, spilling a good portion on the quilt covering his mattress. He ached to go to the Stuart home and take her now. But he had to bide his time. He'd come for her after he had time to conceive the perfect plan.

****

Cassidy finished cleaning the exam room after the last patient, Mrs. Ames, left. She had no one else scheduled today, so planned to wash and start packing for the trip to Philadelphia. She opened the door and stepped into the hall.

"Oh, Cassie, there you are." Her mother caught her gaze. "Would you have time to see one more patient before you close for today?"

"I suppose, who is it?"

"Miss Baker. She's not feeling very well."

Cassidy raised her brows. "Of course, Ma. Show her right in." She retreated back into the exam room and waited.

"She's right in there," her mother said from the hall.

Miss Baker poked her head inside, a shy smile flitting across her face.

"Come in, Miss Baker." Cassidy motioned to the exam table. "What seems to be the problem?"

The teacher settled herself on the table and coughed into her gloved hand. "I've been feeling a bit poorly, Doctor Cassie. Might be something I caught from a student."

Cassidy frowned. "It's quite possible. Let me take a look." She lifted the jar of tongue depressors and fished one out.

"I'm so sorry I came unexpected. Your mother said you were closing for the day."

Cassidy grimaced. "Seems I've been closing early

167

a lot. Dr. Madison now has a monopoly on most of the patients."

She noted Miss Baker's indrawn breath at the mention of Madison.

"Open wide," she said.

The teacher complied. Afterward, she felt her glands.

Miss Baker's gaze followed her every move. "What's wrong with me? Is it serious?"

"No, of course not." Cassidy smiled. "You have some minor redness on your throat, nothing more. I'll give you some cough elixir, and I want you to get extra rest."

"Yes, Doctor."

Cassidy cleared her throat. "Dr. Madison has asked permission to court me, but I'm not quite sure about him. Tell me, what did you think of him when he treated your arm?"

Miss Baker stiffened. "You shouldn't allow him to court you."

Cassidy frowned. "Why not?"

"There are things about him no one in town knows."

"What kind of things?" Cassidy held her gaze.

She shook her head. "I can't..."

Cassidy grasped the teacher's slim shoulders. "Did he hurt you?"

"No, I can't..."

"Cassie?" A male voice called from the hall. The door opened a crack. "Oh, I'm so sorry."

"It's safe to come in, Quinn." Cassidy sighed and motioned to her brother. With the sudden interruption, she hardly expected Miss Baker to reveal anything. "We're about finished up in here."

Quinn opened the door wide. "Miss Baker, what a pleasure to see you again."

The teacher nodded and ducked her head. "Good to see you as well, Doctor."

He stepped into the room. "I didn't know Cassie had any patients scheduled this afternoon."

"I didn't." She glanced at the teacher. "Miss Baker's feeling poorly."

"I'm sorry to hear that, ma'am," Quinn said.

"Just a little sore throat," Cassidy explained. "Nothing some cough elixir and a little rest won't cure."

Quinn smiled. Miss Baker beamed in return. At this point Cassidy felt a little extraneous.

"I suppose I should be on my way." The teacher slid from the table and accepted the bottle of cough elixir Cassidy held out. "I don't want to hold you two up. You must have tons of work to do if you're going to reestablish your father's practice."

Though she'd spoken to them both, Cassidy couldn't help but catch the batting of eyelashes in her brother's direction.

"Not at all, Miss Baker," Cassidy said. "You're welcome here any time. And if I'm not here, I'm sure my brother can see you."

The teacher's cheeks colored.

"Thank you both."

After she left the room, Cassidy caught her brother's gaze.

"I'm trying to get her to admit to what Madison did to her. I'm afraid George's suspicions are right. The weasel hurt her, and now she's either too embarrassed or too scared to talk about what happened."

"Then what'll we do?" Quinn quirked a brow.

She bit her lip. "Maybe..." She paced the small room. "Maybe..."

"Maybe what?" Quinn spread his hands.

"Well..." She glanced at her brother, then to the open door leading to the hall. "She seems to like you. Maybe you should court her, and she'll open up."

He shook his head. "I'm not sure..."

"You like her, don't you?" She tilted her head. "What could a little flirtation hurt? After we get back from Philadelphia, why don't you take her to the ice cream parlor?"

He grinned. "You sure?"

"As I said, what could it hurt?" She turned to the wash pan and scrubbed her hands. "I've got to get to my room and pack."

****

Cassidy shifted in her seat as the train chugged across the countryside. Beside her, Quinn sat reading the newspaper oblivious of the changing landscape, but she couldn't take her gaze from the scenery passing by. She hadn't traveled beyond town since the war. After she'd come down with quinsy throat, Pa had sent her home to recover. Since then, she hadn't been outside of Burkeville.

When they arrived at the station, Quinn collected their bags and led her through city streets. Six years ago, in Washington, many of the streets had been unfinished, and the city resembled a vast military camp. She marveled at the tall buildings in the central part of Philadelphia, packed so close together.

Quinn dropped their baggage to the ground and hailed a coach. After hoisting Cassidy to her seat, he settled beside her. "Not like our little town."

"No. It's rather exciting being in a big city. I envy you attending medical school here."

"We'll get a hotel room near the *Female Medical College*. It's on Arch Street." He leaned over to ask the driver where he could find a room.

"I know just the place, sir," the man assured him.

Leaning back, Quinn squeezed Cassidy's hand. "If you'd like, we'll arrange for a tour of the college after we settle in."

She nodded. Glancing out the window, she

focused on the trolleys, carriages, and pedestrians. The narrow streets and attached rows of brick and stone houses seemed to caress her. She wouldn't mind living in a big city like this. And if she liked the college, perhaps she could apply.

Friday afternoon, Cassidy stood beside Quinn in the hall of the *Female Medical College*. A dark-haired woman escort, who introduced herself as Mrs. Simmons, motioned them to follow.

"Well, Sis, what do you think so far?"

"This is marvelous! I'd love to be a student here."

She grasped her brother's arm as the escort led them through classrooms and patient rooms where students learned to care for the sick and injured.

She swiveled her head left and right, trying to take in all the activity. Female physicians directed female students. No condescending male doctors in sight. The few men, who taught here, treated the women as equals.

The tour complete, Mrs. Simmons turned to them and smiled. "If you're interested, Miss Stuart, I'll take you to the dean's office where you can fill out your application."

"Oh, yes." Cassidy's breath caught. She'd not leave without turning in her application.

Chapter Twenty-Two

George stepped from the hotel lobby, clutching the post from Pinkerton with the name of the nurse who worked at the *Female Medical College.*

Mrs. Georgiana Hirsh. His thoughts strayed to Cassidy. She'd surely learned of his departure by now. He could only wonder how she'd taken the news. He sighed. More than likely, she now hated his guts.

He'd make everything up to her when he got back, but how to explain without spilling the truth? He had to wait until the investigation was over in order to keep her safe.

He entered the hospital lobby and introduced himself to the woman at the desk. A short, round woman led him to the second floor and down the polished wood hall to a classroom. She opened the door, allowing him to peer inside. A young woman, with sable hair piled atop her head, sat at a desk at the front of the room. The student desks were vacant.

"Mrs. Hirsh?" He stepped into the room.

"Yes?" She glanced up at him.

"I'm George Masters. Mr. Pinkerton is investigating your former employer, Dr. Scott Madison."

The woman scowled. "I haven't set eyes on either of the Madisons for three years."

"Would you mind telling me why you left their employ?"

"Both of them were too demanding. And I didn't trust the son one bit. When the senior Madison was away, the son would call me into his office when no one else was about, touch my hand, make unseemly suggestions..." Her voice trailed off.

George's pulse quickened. "What type of suggestions, if I may ask?"

The woman blushed. "Nothing I would want to say in the company of a lady or gentleman, if you take my meaning."

"Did he do anything to hurt you, ma'am?"

She frowned, rising from the desk. "I made sure I was never alone in that house with him..." She waved a finger. "Oh, he tried to get me there saying he needed me to stay late. The servants, you see, didn't live in the house. Only came in during the day. But I refused to work nights, even when his father was home."

"What about patients?" George asked.

"What about them?" She frowned.

"Did he have a lot of female patients? Young ones?"

She took in a breath. "He did. I was supposed to be in the room when he examined them, you see, but he always would send me out to fetch something in another room."

"Do you, by any chance, remember Miss Audrey Wellingham?"

"Wellingham?" She frowned. "I'm afraid I don't remember her, sir. I resigned over a year ago."

George sighed. "Sorry to have bothered you, ma'am." He stepped toward the door. "But you have been a great help in the investigation."

She brightened. "You work for the Pinkertons, you say?"

"Yes, ma'am."

****

After filling out her application, Cassidy stepped down the hall on Quinn's arm as Mrs. Simmons pointed to the classrooms along the second floor corridor. "Most of them are empty right now, but I'll see if any classes are in session."

Voices sounded from an opened door at the end of the hall. A man and a woman conversing. Before they reached the room, a man stepped out. Cassidy halted in her tracks.

George! A woman stepped out to take his hand. A young, lovely woman. Cassidy clutched Quinn's arm and turned on her heel, not wanting to see any more.

****

Saturday afternoon, Scott arrived at the Stuart home with a fresh bouquet of blossoms for Miss Stuart. She was an enigma, not easy for him to read. She grew hot and cold from one instant to the next. But now, he felt it necessary to swoop in for the kill. If she agreed to marry him now, in time, he'd push her brother out of the practice. Convince him he'd do better working at a city hospital. Scott wouldn't take no for an answer.

He paused at the door and adjusted his coat. Pasting on his most sincere expression, he rapped on the door. After a few moments, the door opened and a young man peered out. Miss Stuart's younger brother. Scott racked his brain for his name.

"Dr. Madison, I'd invite you in, but it looks like you came to see my sister." He gestured to the flowers. "She's not home."

"Did she go into town?" Maybe if he hurried he could catch up with her at the mercantile or wherever else she'd gone.

"No, sir. She's gone to Philadelphia."

"Philadelphia?" Scott's blood ran cold. Why on earth would she go there?

"Who's there, Matt?" a woman's voice called. The door opened wider to reveal Mrs. Stuart.

"Oh, Dr. Madison." She glanced at the bouquet. "I'm afraid Cassidy's not here."

"So your son's told me." He gestured toward Matt.

"You can go on now, Matt," his mother said. "I'll take care of the doctor."

Matt nodded to Scott and retreated down the hall.

"May I come in anyway?" Scott asked. "I'd like to hear where's she gone off to and why."

Mrs. Stuart hesitated. Just as he wondered if she'd turn him away, she opened the door wider and lifted her arm. "Come into the parlor."

Scott preceded her into the room and set the flowers on the table. Mrs. Stuart reached for them. "I'll put them in water and be right back."

Sighing, Scott sank onto an upholstered chair and set his hat on the table where he'd placed the flowers. If Miss Stuart had gone to Philadelphia, she might overhear gossip about him. Or worse yet, maybe she'd already heard rumors about his indiscretion and had gone to investigate. But she surely wouldn't have gone alone.

Mrs. Stuart returned with two glasses of lemonade on a tray. "It's hot today. Thought you might be thirsty."

Scott leaned over to retrieve one of the drinks. "Thank you, ma'am."

After settling herself, she looked him in the eye. "Cassidy obviously didn't tell you she was going."

"No, ma'am. Was it something sudden?"

"Well..." She folded her hands in her lap. "Her brother was going to Philadelphia to study some new surgical techniques at the hospitals. And she wanted to see the medical school for women."

Scott nodded. *"Female Medical."*

"Yes. She thought she could tour the facility while there and maybe put in an application." Her gaze caught his. "I hope this doesn't go against your own plans."

"Well..." He chuckled. "Your daughter is a head strong woman. Far be it from me to tell her what she can and cannot do." He took another sip of his drink. "But I had hoped she'd accept my proposal and settle with me."

Mrs. Stuart's hand rose to her throat. "You've already proposed?"

He shook his head. "Not straight out, ma'am, but I did imply that I was interested in her hand. She couldn't mistake my intentions. But every time I think I'll ask her proper, she pulls away."

"Well, you must understand, Doctor, she's had a rough time of it with the Tasker incident. She was very upset."

"Of course, ma'am. Entirely understandable, but it surely wasn't her fault."

"As her brother also told her."

"Well..." Scott glanced at the clock on the mantel. "I'd best be going." He stood. "When do you expect your daughter to return?"

Mrs. Stuart rose. "They should be back Monday. I'll keep the flowers in water until she returns."

"Thank you, ma'am."

She showed him to the door. Only after settling into his carriage for the ride back home, did he allow his temper to rise.

Blast it! He could only hope she'd be so focused on her own goals, she wouldn't hear any gossip about him. But he wondered about her brother, Quinn. He seemed like a sharp man. What if he found out about Scott's past?

****

Monday afternoon, George lurched forward as the train stopped at the tiny Burkeville station, his first thought for Cassidy. He'd hated leaving her, even though Quinn was home. Disappointed he hadn't gathered anything damning enough to stop Madison grated on him. He hefted his bag and descended to the platform.

Fatigue slowed his steps as he plodded toward the hotel. As he scanned the street, he caught sight of Cassidy stepping from the mercantile, a basket slung over her arm. Her gaze caught his, and a scowl formed on her face.

He stepped toward her, but stopped dead. "Cassie, I need to explain what happened. Why I left."

She fisted her hands, propping the one not holding the basket on her hip. "I know why you left."

He grasped her arm. "How do you know? Who told you?" He racked his brain, but outside of Mrs. Claymore, now in New York, no one knew.

"I saw you in Philadelphia talking to that woman at the hospital and also know you left town with Mrs. Claymore." She glanced around. "Where is she? Did you leave her for that woman at the hospital?"

"Cassie, you don't understand."

"Like hell I don't." She wrenched her arm from his grasp and turned on her heel. "Goodbye, George. And don't come calling again. You're no longer welcome in my home."

She strode down the road not looking back.

George scratched his head. When had she gone to Philadelphia? And why? She wouldn't have followed him just to see where he'd gone. But she knew about Mrs. Claymore. He'd have to come up with a plausible story. He hoped, once her anger cooled, she'd allow him to speak to her. For now, relief flowed over him knowing she was safe.

His gazed followed until she disappeared behind the courthouse, then he turned toward the hotel. He'd drop his bag there and deal with Cassie later. But the mercantile door opened, grabbing his attention. Miss Baker emerged and peered around, seeming pensive. She dropped one of her parcels and bent over to retrieve it.

He strode across the street, dropping his suitcase at his side. "Allow me, ma'am." He lifted the packet. "I could walk you home, if you'd like."

She blushed. "No, sir, that won't be necessary."

"No, it won't, Mr. Masters. I'll be happy to see the young lady home."

George turned. Madison stood behind him, scowling.

The teacher's face turned scarlet. "I...I'm fine. I can handle it myself."

"But I insist, Miss Baker." Madison reached for the parcel in George's hands. He jerked back, gathering the package against his chest, not willing to release the bundle. "I don't believe the lady wants to take you up on your offer, Doc."

Madison frowned. "She needs help. I'm going in the direction of the boardinghouse anyway."

Miss Baker glanced down. "Please, I don't need any help, from either of you."

George handed her the package. She balanced it on top of the other one she held. "Yes, ma'am. If that's what you want." He glared at Madison, daring him to touch her or try to wrench the parcels away.

"If it's what the lady wants, who am I to argue?" Madison smirked.

Miss Baker looked away. "If you gentlemen will excuse me?"

George backed away and allowed her to pass. Madison stood his ground but followed the teacher with his gaze.

She scurried away, struggling to balance the parcels, not looking back.

The doctor smirked. "She's a real beauty, but a bit skittish, wouldn't you say?"

George scowled. "I wouldn't know, sir." He held his breath, wondering if Madison had somehow found out about his visit with Miss Baker. Did he have some hold on the woman?

Madison shrugged. "Perhaps she's just bashful around men."

George didn't answer.

"Now, Miss Stuart is a woman who knows what she wants. She just needs a man to tame her wild urges." The doctor leered.

George stepped close, keeping his voice low. "If you know what's good for you, I'd advise you to stay away from the lady."

"You, sir, gave up your right to her." He wagged a finger. "And don't threaten me, if you know what's good for *you*. She has a mind of her own."

George leaned away, crossing his arms over his chest. "Are you saying she's chosen you over me?"

Madison smirked. "I'm saying whoever she wants to be with is entirely up to her. Fighting over her won't do you a bit of good."

George rubbed his jaw. "You may be right, Doc. I've known Cassie a long time, and she's always done what she wanted. You'd best remember that."

Madison gaped.

George turned away. His hand clenched around the handle of his bag, the urge to throttle the doctor close to the surface. He kept walking and didn't look back.

Chapter Twenty-Three

Late Monday afternoon, after Cassidy and Quinn had settled in, her mother told them about Dr. Madison's visit.

"He seemed upset you hadn't told him you were going to Philadelphia," she said.

Cassidy glanced at Quinn. "As well he should be." On hearing the news, he likely worried they'd find out about his past, but in truth, she still didn't have any solid proof. She suspected, as George told them, his family had hushed up the matter.

And she still wasn't over the sight of George conversing with the woman at the hospital, as well as his departure with Mrs. Claymore. Quinn tried to convince her to talk to George. His visit may have been part of the investigation. But why had he gone without explaining? And what about the mysterious note he'd left?

"What did he want, Ma?" Cassidy brushed off her gown. She needed to wash before eating the light meal her mother had prepared for her and Quinn. Her stomach growled in anticipation.

"He brought you flowers. I have them in a vase in the parlor." She glanced at her two children. "Go wash and we'll discuss this over lunch."

Cassidy fumed as she approached the kitchen sink to wash the grime from traveling off her hands and face. She hated the idea he'd come here with only Matt in the house. What if he'd harmed her mother or Sarah?

She dried her hands and turned from the sink. Her mother had already laid out the lunch. Her stomach grumbled again as she caught the delicious scent of fresh bread, cold chicken, and potato salad.

"Ma," she said, "you've outdone yourself."

Her mother glanced up from laying out plates on the table and smiled. "Nothing's too good when my children return to me. I miss all of you so when you're gone."

Cassidy slid out a chair and smoothed her skirts. Her mother poured three glasses of lemonade. "Where has that brother of yours gone?"

"He likely got caught up talking to one of the neighbors," Cassidy said. "You know how Quinn likes to talk."

Her mother smirked. "Well, let's just start without him. I know you're hungry."

Cassidy nodded.

Her mother pushed the plate of chicken in front of her. "While you were away, the schoolteacher, Miss Baker, came by. She seemed upset when I told her both you and Quinn were gone."

Almost choking on the piece of chicken she'd put in her mouth, Cassidy swallowed hard and took a gulp of her drink. "Miss Baker? Is she all right?"

Her mother raised her brows. "I don't believe she was physically ill, but she did want to see you about something."

"How do you know?"

"Well, I told her she could see Dr. Madison if she had an emergency. That seemed to upset her more, and she told me she'd wait until you came back."

Cassidy stared at her mother as she spooned potato salad onto her own plate. "Ma, how upset was she? Did she seem to be hurt?"

"I don't think so. Why do you ask?"

Quinn entered the room and sat next to Cassidy. "What's wrong?" He picked up a chicken leg and bit into it.

"Ma told me Miss Baker came by," Cassidy said,

"and she seemed upset."

Quinn raised his brows. "Oh." He glanced at his mother. "Reckon I should pay her a call?"

Her mother frowned. "What's this all about? What's wrong with Miss Baker?"

A knock at the front door startled all of them. Her mother rose. "I'll see who it is. You two sit and eat."

After she departed, Cassidy shook her head. "Do you think Madison got to her while we were away?"

Quinn shrugged. "With George gone too, it's quite possible."

Cassidy propped her elbow on the table and cupped her chin. "This whole situation is worrying, Quinn. I'm at a loss what to do."

"Why don't I pay a call on Miss Baker, and you see if George is back? Find out if he's uncovered anything new."

She groaned. "Yes, he's back and the last person I want to speak to right now."

****

Scott bathed, shaved, and dressed in his most expensive suit. Earlier, he'd asked his landlady to arrange a bouquet of assorted flowers from her garden.

He'd made a horrible mistake with Miss Stuart but wasn't ready to give up on her or the chance of inheriting all the patients from her father's practice. The thought of moving on and starting over grated on his nerves. He'd not allow her and her brother to rebuild and ruin his well laid plans.

The news George Masters left town with another woman had temporarily lifted his spirits, but now the scoundrel had returned. Scott had to convince Miss Stuart that Masters was no good. Once Scott had her in his grasp, he'd propose. As his wife, he'd force her to cease practicing medicine. But first he needed to be sure she hadn't learned anything damning about him while in Philadelphia. If not, the one obstacle left would be her brother.

He halted in front of the house and alighted from the carriage, adjusting his coat and hat. He rapped on the front door, but no one answered. Silence surrounded him. *Someone* had to be home. Edging along the porch, he glanced to the space at the rear of the house. He spotted Mrs. Stuart hanging laundry on a line.

Stepping down from the porch, he rounded the side of the house. "Ma'am," he called. He didn't want to startle the woman.

She poked her head around a bed sheet, her eyes widening. "Dr. Madison."

"I'm sorry, ma'am. I knocked at the front door, but no one answered. I saw you back here and thought I'd let you know I was here."

Her gaze drifted to the bouquet. "Was Cassie expecting you?"

"No, ma'am." He held up the flowers. "I wanted to surprise her."

"Well..." She eyed him, frowning. "I expect she's tired from traveling and don't know if she wants to see anyone right now. Perhaps you could stop by tomorrow."

Scott sighed. "I was rather upset that your daughter neglected to inform me about her trip to the city. I'd like to talk to her, if I may, to see if I've done something to offend her."

Mrs. Stuart's hand rose to her throat. She swallowed, obviously at a loss what to do. Scott gave her his most charming smile. "Please, ma'am, if she's home, I need to see her."

The creaking of the back door drew both their gazes.

Miss Stuart stood in the open door, a scowl marring her lovely features.

"Miss Stuart." Scott strode toward her.

She held up her hand. "What are you doing here?"

Scott hesitated but held up the flowers. "I'd hoped you'd agree to have dinner with me tomorrow night."

"I'm afraid I won't have time." She planted her clenched fists on her hips.

"Cassie..." her mother warned.

"Miss Stuart..." He edged closer, hoping to lure her sentiments with the fragrant bouquet. "I was a bit perturbed to learn you'd departed for Philadelphia without telling me. I wasn't aware I'd done anything to upset you."

Mrs. Stuart nodded. "Why don't the two of you sit in the garden? It's a lovely day. I have to go inside and start dinner." She glanced at Scott. "You're welcome to stay, if you'd like."

Miss Stuart glared at her mother.

Scott bit his lip. "I think we'll leave the decision up to your daughter."

"Of course." Mrs. Stuart brushed a hand along her daughter's sleeve. "When you come inside, you can let me know."

After she'd retreated into the house, Miss Stuart turned to him and waved her arm. "Well, let's sit, and you can tell me what you came to say before you leave."

Scott grinned. He'd known this wouldn't be easy, but he felt certain any slight she'd imagined he'd committed, he could smooth over and charm his way back into her life, and in time, her bed.

She settled on one of the iron chairs, glaring up at him. He noted she'd neglected to offer him a seat. He handed her the flowers. She lifted them to her nose, but eyed him warily.

He sank onto the seat beside her and studied the flower garden. "I see you've been tending your plants well."

She shrugged. "It's one of my chores."

"But you seem to have a knack." He waved his hand over a bed of impatiens and daffodils. "To have a wife who could tend my garden would be an absolute blessing."

She huffed. "Please don't tell me you're proposing marriage?" She tilted her head, her gaze boring into his.

He sighed. "I know you spent time with George Masters before he left. Why didn't you tell me?"

She lifted a hand to her throat. "It's not what you think. George and I have a past, but I no longer trust him."

Scott grinned. "I'm very glad to hear that. I recognized the man as a scoundrel the moment I first met him. I hope we can resume courting."

She glanced away.

"I'm sorry my animal instincts got the better of me the night in the alley, and my coming here harmed you professionally. I know the difficulties of women trying to break into medicine are having. Male doctors don't respect their talents and try to push them out of the profession." He reached for her hand. She flinched but didn't pull away. "I don't wish to see you hurt."

Now he'd swoop in for the kill. He brushed a thumb over her delicate cheek. "If you wish to practice medicine, I'll be with you every step of the way."

"I, ah..."

"Please, Miss Stuart, I couldn't stand it if you sent me away now." He gazed at her with what he hoped was an earnest expression. She had to believe him.

Lifting the flowers to her nose again, she took a delicate sniff. He reached up around her nape and pulled her to him for a kiss. Unlike the first time he'd kissed her, she didn't resist.

He kept the kiss gentle and brief. When he pulled away, her eyes were closed. Her tongue darted out to lick her lush lips.

"Ah...I'll go tell Ma we're having a guest for dinner." She rose and smoothed her skirts.

"Why thank you very much, Miss Stuart." He stood, then followed her into the house.

****

After dinner, Dr. Madison took his leave. Cassidy paced the kitchen. Her stomach clenched at the memory of his touch, but she had to gain his confidence. The kiss they'd shared repulsed her. She'd curbed her urge to recoil and slap his smug face. She had to see this through.

And after George had left town without notice or any explanation, she could no longer trust him. Quinn was all she had left. Her brother would help her see this through. They had to prove Madison was a monster if they were to go on with their lives.

Although she'd agreed to see him tomorrow night, the thought of sharing dinner with him again sent her stomach roiling. Her mother seemed quite taken with him, as well as Sarah, and Cassidy regretted she couldn't warn them off the man without absolute proof.

After she helped her mother clean up the meal leavings, Cassidy decided to take a break before going to her office. Quinn was out on a call, and her mother had saved some ham and potatoes for when he returned.

She found Sarah fanning herself on the porch seated in a rocking chair. "Reckon it's gonna be hot today?" she asked.

Cassidy placed her hands on her hips and surveyed the clear, blue sky. "Feels like it, but it's not summer yet."

Sarah scowled. "Don't know how much heat I can abide right now. How much longer until this

186

baby comes?"

"Just a few more weeks, by my reckoning." Cassidy sat across from her sister. "Won't be long at all."

"I hope you're right, Cassie." She grimaced.

"You all right?"

"Just a little kick, is all, but I'm scared, Cassie."

"Scared of what?"

"You know...of childbirth. How hard will it be? Will the baby survive? Will I?"

Despite the warmth of the afternoon, a shiver raced down Cassidy's spine.

"Cassie..." Sarah held out her hand. "I need you to be here for me when the baby comes."

"Of course, I will, but Quinn will too."

Sarah gripped Cassidy's hand. "But I want you to deliver the baby."

"Why me?"

"I trust you. Quinn can assist, but I don't want any other doctor. Just family."

"Sarah...I don't know if you'll want me there at all."

Sarah squeezed her hand. "You're a good doctor, Cassie. One of the best around. I trust you."

"Maybe you shouldn't." She eyed her sister. "Maybe I can't do this."

"You can." Sarah patted her stomach. "You're in charge of this baby. No one else."

Cassidy bit her lip. Although she wanted to be around to witness the birth, the thought of delivering the child scared the hell out of her.

Chapter Twenty-Four

Tuesday evening, George decided to give himself a little leisure time before trying to explain the situation to Cassidy. The only way he could convince her he hadn't betrayed her would be to tell the truth. Did he have a choice now? He had to tell all or risk losing her.

He paid a visit to the small gambling den in the back room of the tavern. After all, as far as the town knew he earned his living gambling. And so did Cassie and her family. He didn't have much hope of winning big with nothing but locals for players, but maybe a few hands would relax him. If he could get Madison in here, how he'd love to clean the smug doctor out.

He spent the evening playing three rounds of cards with five different patrons, but he didn't win enough to pay for a meal at the tavern. George excused himself. He needed to stretch his legs.

A carriage drove up as he stepped to the side of the building. A man emerged and held his hand out to the passenger.

Madison!

George held back waiting to see who the doctor had stashed in his carriage. Cassidy descended on Madison's outstretched arm.

Damn her!

He waited, out of sight, until they'd entered the tavern. Footfalls behind him, spun him around. He reached inside his coat for his revolver, but halted as he caught sight of the bartender.

Jake strode up, wiping his beefy hands on his

apron.

"A bit jumpy tonight, aren't you Masters?"

George sighed. "I just got an eyeful of something ugly." He poked his thumb toward the front tavern entrance. "Doc Madison's courting the woman I almost married five years ago. I'm still not sure I did right by her the way I left, and I don't trust Madison one bit."

Jake shook his head. "The Doc's all right. I don't think you have to worry..." He stood back and folded his arms across his barrel chest. "Or is it jealousy rearing its head?"

George grinned. "I've loved that girl since I was a lad. Reckon it's hard to let go."

****

George crept into his hotel room toward one o'clock in the morning. He'd stuck around to be sure Madison didn't do anything to hurt Cassidy. Of course, once they'd left in his carriage, he couldn't follow or check on her to be sure she'd arrived home safe. A feeling of utter helplessness gutted his stomach. How could he protect her if she insisted on seeing the doctor?

He spent the remainder of the night pacing, trying to decide if he should go to the Stuart home and see if she were all right. But he'd have to wait until morning. He mustn't appear a jealous fool or an over controlling ass. Cassidy was already angry over his unexplained departure and thoughts of him philandering with other women, even if he hadn't. Maybe she delighted in allowing Madison to court her to pay George back for his imagined indiscretions.

He had to decide what to tell her. He might have to fess up to keep her safe.

As he drifted off to sleep, he conjured up an image of Cassidy. Her midnight dark hair loose around her shoulders, her green eyes bright and animated as she laughed at something he said, then half closed in passion as he kissed her ripe lips.

He loved her with all his heart and would be damned if he'd chance losing her again.

****

Wednesday morning, George left the hotel, catching sight of Cassidy entering the mercantile. Seems he didn't have to go to her home, after all. He strode over, trying to maintain the appearance of just chancing on her. She stood in the aisle inspecting and sniffing lavender and rose soaps.

The memory of her on the arm of Madison vexed him. Although he knew she had no love for the doctor, the thought of the bastard touching her in any way, caused a physical ache. He had to bring the man down.

The swish of a woman's skirts drew George's attention to the door. Cassidy slipped out. Hadn't she seen him?

George raced to the door and caught the flurry of black skirts as she raced down the street.

Oh no, you don't. He raced after her, catching her arm.

She turned toward him, eyes wide.

"Are you running from me, darlin'?"

She gaped. "Of course not. I didn't see you."

"I saw you at the tavern last night. With him."

She frowned.

He released his grip on her arm.

Taking a step away from him, she adjusted her felt hat. "Well, yes. I'm still trying to gather information, if you even care about the investigation anymore."

He caught the ire in her tone. "Did you?"

She shook her head. "Not anything that will help."

"I don't want you involved in the investigation any longer. It's too dangerous."

"But we can't just allow him to go free." Her fists clenched.

"I didn't say I'm abandoning the investigation, but there's more to it than you know."

Cassidy frowned. "What do you mean?"

He shook his head. "I can't tell you right now...but I don't want to see you anywhere near the man." He raised a finger. "I mean it, Cassie."

Her gaze darkened. He almost swore her eyes would spit fire. "I can't promise anything, George. You aren't being honest with me. How can I trust you? I'll do what it takes until he's brought down."

He grasped her arm. "You are being reckless. If your mother knew the risk you take by allowing Madison to court you, she wouldn't permit you to leave the house."

She yanked her arm from his grasp. He lifted his hat and raked a hand through his hair. "I can't take the risk that he'll harm you when I'm not there to protect you."

"George, please, people are staring."

Cassidy's face flamed as she scanned the street. "I don't want to see you anymore."

"How can I protect you then?"

"You have to understand. He heard we spent time together by the pond. He suspects you and I were on the verge of getting back together."

"All for the good. He'll stay away from you."

She shook her head. "It won't help our cause."

"You said yourself Quinn may be able to pry damning evidence against Madison from the school teacher. Then you won't have to use yourself as bait."

"George, please I don't want to talk about this. Or talk to you ever again." She wheeled around and strode down the street.

"Cassie, please..." he called out behind her.

She refused to turn in his direction and hoped

he wouldn't follow her and create another spectacle like he had outside the mercantile. He'd hurt her for the last time, and if word got back to Madison, he'd know she was through with George. She'd have a better chance of luring him into making a mistake that would condemn him and ruin his practice.

Footsteps behind her sent heat to her face. Unable to run from him in her long skirts, she clenched her fists and turned to face him. "Leave me be, George."

"I can't." His dark eyed gaze sought hers. "Just how involved with him are you?"

"I know how to take care of myself." She scowled.

"Cassie, I..." He reached up as if to touch her but dropped his hand to his side.

"I'll deal with this in my own way." She noted passersby gawking as they strode past on their way to or from the store. "I have to go."

The look in his eyes burned her soul. He had to know how deep he'd hurt her, or was he that dense?

"Before you go, just oblige me in this..." He glanced around, then held her gaze. "Don't allow him to take you anywhere alone."

"Do you think I'm a complete fool?" She lowered her gaze. "Goodbye, George."

She spun on her heel and kept walking, afraid to look back. When she finally did, he strode in the other direction.

****

When Quinn arrived early in the afternoon, Cassidy took him aside. "Swear to me you'll be here when Sarah's time comes."

"Of course I will, Sis." He glanced down the hall. "Where is everyone?"

"Ma's gone to the grocer's to buy some fresh vegetables for dinner tonight, Matt's not back from the bank, and Sarah's likely napping."

"When will Wes be back from the west coast?"

"Should be any day now. I know he doesn't want to miss the birth of his first child."

"Course not." Quinn studied her. "And what about you? You don't seem yourself."

"It's George. We had an argument outside the mercantile." She gestured toward the kitchen. "But forget about him. Come on out and wash. I made lemonade."

Quinn grinned. "Sounds good. Lead the way."

While her brother washed at the sink, Cassidy poured two glasses of lemonade and settled at the table.

Quinn joined her and took a long draught. "Ah, I sure missed your fine lemonade, Cassie."

She laughed. "It's just lemonade. How could I make it any different from anyone else?"

He grinned. "Don't know. You just do."

Cassidy sighed. "Maybe you should've taken a position at the hospital in Harrisburg. As you can see, we don't have much in the way of patients here."

He shrugged. "Nothing we can't fix. If George can drive Madison out, all the better. We'll be the only physicians left in town."

Cassidy frowned. "I'm not sure what George is doing. He's being so damned secretive."

Quinn bit his lip and searched her gaze. "I know George hurt you deeply, but you can't allow Madison to win."

"I don't know." She shook her head. "I didn't expect George to show his face in town again. I don't trust him." She caught Quinn's puzzled gaze.

She pushed back her chair and paced the room. "I don't know about anything anymore." She turned and eyed her brother.

Quinn gazed toward the window. "I don't know what's going on with George either. Maybe I should talk to him."

She pursed her lips and leaned her back against the counter. "Thank you, Quinn, but I have to do it."

Quinn rose and grasped her shoulder.

"Everyone's told me from the start he's no good for me, a born drifter who can't stay in one place too long, but despite all these years of trying to forget him..." She shrugged. "I can't. When I thought he'd left me again, I wanted the earth to swallow me up whole. Am I being foolish?"

Quinn settled his lanky frame against the counter at Cassidy's side and took a long swallow of his drink.

"I don't know what to tell you, Cassie. I'm not experienced in love and marriage."

Cassidy swallowed. "I don't understand George. I still can't believe he actually got into a fist fight with Madison."

"After knowing George as long as I have, I must admit, I wasn't surprised." Quinn's eyebrow arched. "What's hard to imagine, is that he lost control when he's been investigating the man. Don't tell me they were fighting over you?"

Her face heated, but she laughed to cover her embarrassment. "I'm not sure what they were fighting about. Seems they had words, and I just assumed George was jealous of the attention the doctor paid me."

Quinn grinned. "I believe ol' George has never quite gotten over you after all these years."

Cassidy flushed recalling the morning she'd spent in George's room. If Quinn knew, he'd likely be on his way to sock George in the jaw.

"I was all set to marry him right after the war." Cassidy spread her arms and stepped back to the table. "*He's* the one who left me at the altar. Not the other way around." She slid out a chair and sat. "And now I fear he's cavorting with other women behind my back."

Quinn shook his head, pulling out the chair he'd vacated and sat across from her. "Not sure what to tell you, Cassie, but I feel sure he's regretted his decision to leave every day of his life since."

She bit her lip. "I just don't understand the man. He acts like he loves me but can't stick around long enough for anything to develop."

"And what about you and Madison?"

She shrugged. "He thinks he's courting me, but I'm only after information. Maybe he'll slip up."

"I don't like it much." Quinn shook his head. "He could hurt you."

She sighed. "As I told George, I'm being careful. I won't allow him to get me alone anywhere. If we're courting, as he thinks, it wouldn't be proper anyway."

"Good." Quinn leaned back, lifting his hands behind his head.

She cradled her chin in her hands. "George is a complicated man. I thought I'd come to finally know him before he left. But now..." She straightened her spine and spread her hands. "The picnic took me completely by surprise."

Quinn quirked a brow. "Seems to me the man is smitten."

She huffed out a breath.

"So, what's the plan of attack against Madison?"

"I'll continue to allow him to court me, and you have to get busier with Miss Baker. She should be over her throat ailment by now. Maybe you could catch her in town and inquire as to how she's feeling."

Quinn grinned. "Better if *you* did that."

Cassidy tapped his forearm. "Go on. I suspect she'll be thrilled to see you again and welcome your attention."

Quinn sat back. "I'll tell her you sent me by with your blessings."

"There you go." She sipped her drink. "We have to flush Madison out. Between the three of us..."

Quinn set his glass down and cupped his chin in his hand. "You're including George, I reckon."

She nodded. "I know he's still with us. At least, I hope he is."

"Despite everything going on, you're still in love with him." He pointed a finger. "That's why you've never married."

"And who are you to talk?" She glared.

"I've been too busy studying medicine to look for a woman I could settle down with."

She smiled. "I'll bet once you call on Miss Baker she'll have you eating out of her hand. I've seen the way you look at her."

"You're absolutely sure she doesn't have a beau hidden away somewhere she's been writing passionate letters to?" He grinned.

"Not that I've heard." She tapped his arm again. "After you examine her throat, invite her to the ice cream parlor."

He laughed. "I thought Sarah was the matchmaker in this family."

"Seriously, Quinn. We have to draw her out before Madison drives our practice into the ground." She bit her lip.

"In the meantime, I want you to try to stay out of the good doctor's clutches."

"I will." She stood and hugged her brother around the neck. "We work well as a team, don't we?"

Chapter Twenty-Five

Cassidy kept company with Sarah in the parlor through the evening. Her sister muttered and sighed, attempting to knit a cap for her coming baby. Cassidy tried to help, but the end result had to be pulled out and redone.

"Oh, I'm just no good at this!" Sarah complained. "Wes assures me I'll be a good mother, but I just don't know." She stood and stretched her back. "I can't abide this much longer." She rubbed her hand over her stomach. "He kicks all the time, and I can't ever get enough sleep."

Cassidy laughed. "Means you're going to have a healthy, active child. You should be glad."

"But babies are such hard work. Poor Wes can't afford help right now, and he has to travel so much." She turned her mournful gaze on Cassidy. "He used to take me with him, but now I'll have to stay home with the baby."

Cassidy reached for her sister's hand. "It's called responsibility, Sis. You should have known once you'd married Wes, this would be the end result."

Sarah frowned. "I guess. But I'd always thought of children coming way ahead in the future. This happened much too soon for me."

"Well...Wes is just getting his business dealings started. In time, I'm sure he'll earn enough for you to get some help. Then you can leave your children behind and go on trips again."

Her sister heaved a harsh breath as she settled on the chair. "Children? I'm having a hard enough time dealing with *this* little one."

Cassidy sighed. "That's what marriage is. You make a home with your husband and have little ones." She yawned and stretched. "I think I'll just go on up to bed."

Sarah glanced at the clock. "It's too early, Cassie. I'm the one who should be tired."

"Well, I do need to catch up on my reading."

"You're not reading those medical journals Quinn gave you again?"

"No...as a matter of fact, I'm reading a novel by Elizabeth Wetherell called *The Wide, Wide World*."

"Is it good?" Sarah's brow quirked.

Cassidy rose and smoothed out her skirts. "I don't know. I've just started reading."

"When you're done with the book, pass it on to me." Sarah rose too, arching her back. "I could use a good novel to read."

Cassidy nodded and bade her sister goodnight.

In her room, she tried to read, but the words swam before her eyes, her thoughts a jumble. George was the love of her life, but she feared to trust him again. Would he stay in town once this business with Madison finished? George *had* said he planned to ask her to marry him again, but he may have used the ploy to charm her into his bed. She'd made a big mistake by succumbing to his charms. He said he loved her, but she'd always have doubts about him straying. What if he left again? After all the heartache he'd dealt her, he shouldn't be the only man who made her heart leap and pulse race with anticipation of just catching a glimpse of him.

****

Monday while Cassidy, Quinn, and her mother were having lunch, a knock sounded at the front door. Quinn excused himself and reappeared to announce. "We have a guest." He turned, his scowl focused on Dr. Madison standing behind him.

The doctor smiled at her mother, but when his

dark gaze settled on Cassidy, his lips curved downward. Her mother ushered him to a seat. As he sat, she set up a plate for him and poured a glass of lemonade.

Cassidy tried to keep her expression neutral, but his gaze seemed to bore into her. His brow knitted, and his lips thinned to form a rigid line.

Her mother resumed her seat and glanced at Madison. "A pleasure to see you again, Doctor."

"Thank you, ma'am, I mainly dropped by to see if your daughter was all right."

"As you can see, she's fine." Her mother frowned. "Why are you so concerned?"

"I discovered Mr. Masters had returned to town. I'm not sure what he's up to, but I'd hate to see Miss Stuart taken in by such an unsavory man."

"Tell me, Doctor, why are you so concerned for my welfare?" Cassidy asked candidly.

Her mother's brows rose. Cassidy glanced at Quinn. His gaze fixed on Madison.

"I'd hoped we had something special between us," the doctor said. "I was puzzled when you neglected to tell me you were going on a trip." He held Cassidy with his gaze. "And at dinner Saturday night, you changed the subject every time I inquired about your jaunt to Philadelphia. I've spent the last few nights tossing, wondering what I'd done wrong. I stayed away yesterday but made the decision that I must speak to you today. I'd like to know where I stand with you, Miss Stuart."

She shrugged. "I haven't decided yet."

"Perhaps it would be best if we discussed this at another time." Dr. Madison's face turned pink.

She glanced sidelong at her brother. Quinn set down his fork.

"Well," her mother said. "I think we should talk about what you two did when you were in the city."

"Yes." Madison leaned back in his chair. "I'd like

to know what you two did there also."

Quinn saved Cassidy from having to answer. "I learned a few of the new antiseptic surgical techniques at Pennsylvania Hospital not yet available at Harrisburg, and Cassie applied as a student at *Female Medical College.*"

"Interesting." Madison poked his fork into his potato salad. "I do recall you saying you wanted to apply to that school, Miss Stuart."

"And you implied you'd help me get in." She scowled.

"Ah, so I did. You must forgive me. Apparently you were unhappy with me at dinner over this misunderstanding. I promise to make it up to you." He sipped his drink. "I'd have been more than happy to take you to Philadelphia."

"Is that so?" Cassidy folded her arms across her chest.

"Cassie!" her mother scolded. "Mind your manners at the table."

"Sorry, Ma." But she stared Madison down, daring him to answer her question.

Quinn cleared his throat. "If you'll all excuse me, I have things to look after." Her brother rose from the table and gave her a pointed look before leaving.

Her mother started talking about her vegetable crop in the garden. Dr. Madison politely engaged her but kept stealing glances across the table at Cassidy.

She decided the best course would be to wait until after lunch and have a private talk with the doctor.

****

After lunch, her mother invited Dr. Madison to dinner, but he begged off, explaining he had work to attend to. Before he left, he asked Cassidy if she would go for a walk with him in the early evening. She agreed, because she wanted to set things straight between them.

He arrived bearing another bouquet of flowers. Her mother scooped them up to place in a vase, while Cassidy pinned her new straw hat on her head.

"I missed you when you were away. You grow more beautiful every day, Miss Stuart." He lifted his elbow for her to take.

For mid-May, the evening was breezy and cool with a clear blue sky. The sun wouldn't be setting for a few more hours.

They strolled down the path and turned toward the center of town. Dr. Madison tipped his hat to all the ladies passing by, and Cassidy caught more than a few knowing smiles. Did everyone expect her to marry this man?

Her thoughts were in such a whirl she didn't notice they neared his home. Instead of escorting her up onto the wraparound porch, he edged her around the side of the house. A colorful garden of roses, petunias, and marigolds left the small area awash in color.

"I hadn't realized you had such a grand garden," Cassidy said.

He led her to a bench set up amidst the blooms. "The perfect place for the two of us to have a private talk." He inclined his head. "Unless you'd like to go inside?"

She licked her lips. "Is the maid still working?"

He chuckled. "I'm afraid she's gone home for the day. You'd likely think it improper to go inside with her away. Or would you?"

She bristled. "I most certainly would."

Did he want to talk about the real reason she'd gone to Philadelphia or something else?

He settled on the bench beside her and draped his arm across the back above her shoulder. She stiffened. Several yards away stood his nearest neighbor's house, but no one seemed out at this hour. Surely someone would hear her if she screamed.

"Miss Stuart..." He leaned in close. The strong scent of tobacco threatened to choke her. "Over the past few weeks I've come to care a great deal for you."

"Oh." She sat up straighter to discourage him from brushing against her.

"I hoped you'd come to feel the same for me." He frowned.

"I-I'm not sure about anything right now."

"But you're of an age where you need the comfort of a husband, a home of your own, and children."

Her face heated and she stood, dislodging his arm. It plopped onto the seat.

He jumped up beside her and grasped both her hands. "Miss Stuart...or may I call you Cassie?"

"I-I don't think it would be proper."

"It will be soon, my dear." He smiled and she shivered, fearing his next move.

He lifted her arm and led her down the garden path, toward the back of the house. He plucked a red rose and presented the fragrant bloom to her.

She took the offering, but the sharp prick of a thorn bit into her thumb wrenching a gasp from her.

"I'm so sorry," Madison said. "I should have removed the thorns before handing it to you."

He took the rose from her and lifted her injured hand. He pressed his lips against the spot. A warm tingle accompanied his touch, but she had the urge to recoil.

"Dr. Madison, please..."

"Call me Scott."

"I don't think..."

He leaned in and planted his heated mouth on hers. She tried to pull away, but he held tight, trying to force his tongue between her lips.

Twisting away from him, she broke free and sprinted toward the front of the house, hoping to catch *anyone's* attention.

He grasped her hand and yanked her back. "Cassie, don't leave. I have something very important to ask you."

She swallowed hard but didn't dare allow him to lead her back into the garden. She glanced toward the front of the house. She wouldn't allow him to force her inside.

His gaze sought hers. "I care for you very deeply, Cassie. I want us to combine our medical practices. You'd be an excellent assistant."

"But what about Quinn?" She racked her brain for a way to extract herself from this whole situation.

He frowned. "Surely, your brother could do better by finding a position at a city hospital. I'd like you to marry me."

She bit her lip, glancing to and fro. "I can't."

"You can't?" He frowned. "You can't or you won't?"

"Dr. Madison... Scott...now isn't the time to discuss this." She pulled her hand away from his and turned to the front of the house.

Rough hands spun her around. She glanced up into his reddened face.

"You *will* marry me. I've planned the whole thing out. You'll move into my home, and we'll work together. Your brother can go off and find a position wherever he likes."

She shook her head. "Quinn already turned down a position in Harrisburg. He wants to revive our father's practice." The doctor's hand on her upper arm tightened. "You're hurting me. Let go!"

He gripped her, pinching into her flesh.

"Ow!" She kicked him in the shin, then yanked her arm away.

"We have nothing more to discuss." She spun on her heel and raced up the path.

"Come back here, you bitch!" he ordered.

She gathered her skirts and raced down the cobbled path. As she rounded the front of the house, a man and woman strolling by stopped to gape.

Her face hot, she hurried past them toward the center of town. A shout caused her to turn her head. She caught sight of Dr. Madison kicking the fence post at the front of the house.

She turned and strode ahead, not daring to look back again.

Chapter Twenty-Six

George left his hotel room and strolled to the tavern for a bite to eat. He'd agonized most of the night before over what to do about Cassidy. He didn't want her socializing or being anywhere near Madison. If he told her he worked as a Pinkerton agent, would the revelation redeem his actions in her eyes, or would the fact he'd lied to her, hurt his chances of ever getting her back? Although he wanted her in his life, his main purpose right now was to see her safe.

As he exited the building, he spotted a dark-haired woman in black racing up the street.

"Cassie!" he called.

She didn't answer. He sprinted after her, caught her arm, and spun her around. Puffiness around her face and stained cheeks told him she'd been crying.

"Cassie, what's wrong?"

She pulled on the brim of the hat, half concealing her face. "Nothing, George. Go back to whatever you were doing."

"I am not leaving you like this." He glanced down the street. "Did Madison hurt you?"

She shook her head. "All he did was propose marriage."

George's blood heated. "And what did you tell him?"

"I told him, no, of course." She scowled.

Relief surged through his body. He pulled a handkerchief from his vest pocket and offered it to her. "Good for you. Now dry your eyes."

She dabbed her face with his hanky, then her

205

face puckered. "George, I don't know what to do. I want this to be over."

He wrapped an arm around her shoulders. Being close to her and inhaling her sweet scent brought back all the passion of the morning in his hotel room.

"Come with me," he said. "I need to talk to you." He glanced up and down the street, searching for a place they could converse in private and not be gawked at. He spotted the alley beside the hotel, hoping no workers were out there now.

He steered her into the narrow space, expecting her to protest, but she allowed him to guide her.

After propping her against the brick wall, he searched her face. Her lower lip trembled, and the urge to kiss her overwhelmed him. He leaned in close and, pushing the brim of her hat back, touched his mouth to hers. She tensed for a moment, then softened, leaning into him.

Encouraged, he deepened the kiss, tracing his tongue along her lush lips. She opened to him, and he reveled in her sweet taste.

She stiffened, breaking the spell. He came up for air and followed her gaze. A man walked by the alley, but continued on.

"It's all right," George whispered. "He's gone."

She lifted her gloved hand to stroke his face. Her light touch sent waves of fire through his body. His shaft throbbed with want. If they didn't get out of this alley, he'd be tempted to take her right here. But it wouldn't be right. Not for a lady like her.

"Cassie, I need to get you home."

"No, George. You're not being honest with me. I have to know you won't leave me or take up with someone else."

He sighed. "You're still worried about my trip to Philadelphia...the nurse at the hospital."

She lifted her chin. "I won't be strung along

again. Not by you or anyone." Her lower lip trembled.

He leaned forward to kiss her again, but her downcast expression halted him. He had to tell her the truth, whether it redeemed or damned him in her eyes.

"Cassie..." He placed a finger under her chin, forcing her to meet his gaze. "Since I returned to town, I haven't been entirely honest with you."

She lurched away from him, but he held her fast.

"You're still the same man you were before the war. My mother and sister warned me, and now you've proven them right."

He shook his head. "No. You don't understand at all. No one in this town does." He took a deep breath. "The reason I'm investigating Dr. Madison is not because the colonel hired me, although it's true the doctor did assault the colonel's daughter..." He hesitated, knowing he had to tell her, but afraid of the results.

"So why are you investigating him?" Cassidy's glare pinned him.

"I...I'm working for the Pinkerton Agency. William Pinkerton sent me to investigate at the colonel's request."

Cassidy sank against the wall. "You're a Pinkerton agent?"

"Shh." He pressed a finger against her lips. "I don't want this getting around town, at least until my investigation is finished. That's why I couldn't tell you."

She lifted a hand to cover her mouth. "I can't believe this. How long have you been an agent?"

"Not long. About six months. Before that I earned my living as a professional gambler."

"George, this is just too much for me to take in." She frowned. "The reason you went to

Philadelphia..."

"Was because Mr. Pinkerton sent me an urgent message. He wanted me to interview a nurse who once worked for the Madisons."

She scowled. "And Mrs. Claymore?"

"She works for the Pinkertons as a messenger. She stayed in town to relay messages back and forth for me."

Cassidy swallowed. "You couldn't telegraph...?"

"Too risky."

She wrapped her arms around his shoulders enclosing him in her scent. "I'm so sorry I doubted you. Please, stay with me. I need to learn more."

"All right." He pushed her away with a gentle grasp of her shoulders, then glanced down the alley. "But I think we need to talk about this somewhere else."

"We could go to your room." She caught his gaze, her intent clear.

"No, Cassie, I don't want to ruin your reputation."

"Blast my reputation! All it's gotten me is a proposal from a man who attacks women under his care." She grasped his shoulders. "Please, take me to your room."

"All right. But just to talk."

As he led her from the alley, he wasn't sure if he could keep his promise. With the woman of his dreams in the privacy of his hotel room again, there was no telling what might happen.

****

After Cassidy ran off, Scott lost the little composure he had left and kicked three pickets from his fence. He would have knocked down the entire blasted thing if passersby hadn't stopped to gawk.

His only choices were to go inside and stew or go after the woman who ruined all his plans. Glancing down the road, he caught sight of her skirts as she raced away. He'd go after the little bitch and force her to listen to reason.

He strode down the road, ignoring the stares of townspeople, but before he could reach her, another man raced forward, stopping her flight.

Scott halted, trying to get a closer look at the man. He might be one of the local shopkeepers, in which case Scott would stroll up and take over. But as the man turned his way, Scott's face heated.

George Masters! Damn it! I was right about the two of them.

Scott flattened himself against the nearest building and watched. He hoped she'd send Masters away, and he could catch her before anyone else did.

Miss Stuart leaned into him. He put his arm around her and led her back this way. Scott glanced from side to side. He couldn't allow either of them to see him, but he had to know where they were going.

He crouched to stay out of their sight, relieved when they entered an alley next to the hotel. He moved to a better vantage position to wait them out.

A few minutes later, they left the alley and stepped around the other side of the hotel. Racing across the street, he watched as they walked around to the back.

Blast it all! He's sneaking her into his room!

His jaw clenched as he realized he could do nothing to stop them, but, by God, they would both pay for this.

****

Cassidy woke to a shaft of sunlight in her face. She frowned as she realized this wasn't her room. Moving her hand to her side, she found a hard, warm body beside her.

George!

Her heart lurched. She hadn't meant to fall asleep. Grasping the sheet against her bared bosom, she scanned the room for the clock.

"Oh, no!" *Seven in the morning.* Her mother and Quinn would be frantic.

George stirred beside her. He opened an eye as she surged out of bed searching for her clothes.

"Cassie?" he croaked.

"I've got to get home." She settled her chemise over her head and tied on her drawers. "We fell asleep. My family..."

He lurched from the bed. "I'm sorry, Cassie. I should've taken you home last night before it got too late."

She hesitated, eyeing his naked body. Heat crept up her face. He grasped his drawers and yanked them on.

Finding her stockings, she rolled them up, then fastened her petticoats, all the time fearing the reception she'd have once she arrived home.

"What will I tell my family?" She searched George's face. His frown told her he didn't have an answer.

"We'll think of something." He pulled on his trousers. His gaze swept the floor, and his hand wrapped around his wrinkled shirt.

By the time she'd settled her gown over her head, he shrugged into his coat. He reached for her and kissed her, his scent and taste causing Cassidy's breath to catch.

He stroked her cheek and searched her gaze. "I'm so sorry, Cassie. I've likely ruined your reputation beyond repair."

She smiled. "I don't care anymore. I love you, George. I reckon I've always loved you, even when we were children and you teased me without mercy."

He smirked. "I was in love with you then, but you wouldn't give me the time of day. I was afraid if I went too far, you'd bust me in the nose."

She laughed at the memory. "I think all the boys were afraid of me."

He brushed a hand over his jaw. "If they didn't want you to sock them. We were all afraid of Josh, too."

"I know." Her eyes misted as memories surfaced of her oldest brother. "I miss him, George."

"So do I." He glanced at her hat on the ottoman. "You'd best get yourself presentable, so I can walk you home."

"Reckon we can get out of here without the whole town knowing?"

"I'll see if I can sneak you out the back."

She pinned on her hat and reached for his hand. "No matter what happens, George, I'll never be sorry for this."

He nodded and lifted her hand, allowing his lips to brush her knuckles. Delicious anticipation sent her stomach fluttering, but she couldn't stay.

He opened the door, glanced outside, then reached for her hand. "Let's get you home."

****

By afternoon, Cassidy could stand no more questions from her mother and retreated to her room. She and George concocted a story of his being ill and her staying to be sure he was all right, but her mother and brother didn't seem convinced. Quinn's stern gaze swept over them, while her mother sniffed into her hanky, eyes red rimmed from crying the night before.

Cassidy apologized for making them worry, but caught Ma's scowl at George. She had to suspect what had happened last night. Cassidy believed her brother knew, though he wouldn't betray his suspicions to Ma. Should she just admit they'd found solace in each other after so long and had given in to lust?

But their tryst hadn't been pure lust. She loved George. And he'd promised not to leave her again. Now she knew he was working as a Pinkerton agent, the pride she felt for him added to her trust. She felt sure he wouldn't leave her now. But she had to take care she didn't reveal his identity to anyone else in town, including Quinn.

A knock at her door roused her from her thoughts. "Who's there?" she called.

"Cassie," her mother called through the door. "Someone's come to pay you a call."

"George." She slid from the bed and patted her hair into place before the mirror, then opened the door.

Ma eyed her and shook her head. "It's not George."

"Then who? I don't want to see anyone else right now."

Her mother sighed. "Dr. Madison. He insists he must see you."

Cassidy's heart lurched. "He wants me to accept his marriage proposal and I can't."

"I can see that." Ma searched her gaze. "But you must see him and tell him outright. You're obviously in love with George. Just tell Dr. Madison, so he'll leave you be."

Cassidy reached for her mother's hand. "Are you very disappointed in me?"

Ma's gaze dropped, but a soft smile played about her lips. "What I want is for all my children to be happy. If George makes you happy, who am I to argue?"

Leaning forward, she kissed her mother's cheek. "Thank you, Ma. It means a great deal to me that you have faith in my choices."

"Of course, dear. Now, go see Dr. Madison and let him down easy."

"I'll try."

She found him in the parlor, gazing at the family daguerreotypes. When she entered, he turned her way and lifted one of the photos. "Your oldest brother, I surmise."

She gazed at the photo of Josh, standing tall and proud in his uniform. "Yes, he was killed at Gettysburg." She stepped toward him and waved an arm for him to take a seat.

After setting the photo back, he sat and waited for her to do the same. She perched across from him, smoothing her skirts. She didn't want him near enough to touch her. Just the thought repulsed her.

His gaze darkened as he held hers. "I've been patient with you, Miss Stuart, and bowed to your wishes of taking our courtship slow, but now..." He waved his hand. "I see why you won't accept my proposal of marriage."

"I—I don't know what you mean?" Her heart leapt into her throat as he glowered.

His voice lowered, taking on a dangerous edge. "I saw you and Masters last night after you ran from me. Sneaking into his hotel. You were with him last night, weren't you?"

She swallowed, but she should have known someone would see them. By now, no doubt, gossip engulfed the town. Smoothing her skirts, she tried to think of what to say.

"I was with him, yes." Her gazed locked with Madison's. "I love him, and that's why I can't marry you."

His face colored and he rose to his feet, grasping his hat. "I thought you were a moral, respectable woman I would be proud to have as my wife, but now I see you're nothing but a strumpet."

She rose to face him, her face heating. How dare he after what he'd done to other women? "I'd like you to leave *now*, Doctor."

"Oh, I will." He waved his hat. "But you'll be sorry you humiliated me like this. Both you and Masters. You'll pay for this."

She scowled. "How dare you insult me in my

own home? You can spread whatever gossip you like, but I'll not have you threaten me or Mr. Masters." She waved her arm in invitation for him to exit the room. "Now, please leave!"

"With pleasure." He strode to the door, set his hat on his head, and stormed out.

Once he'd gone, she glanced down the road, but she didn't see him or his carriage, if he'd brought one. She let out the breath she'd held, closed the door, and leaned against it.

Just what did Madison's threats mean? Would he dare to harm her...or George? She had to warn him.

Chapter Twenty-Seven

After the incident with Madison the day before, Cassidy paced the floor, unable to relax. She sent a note with Matt to deliver to George at his hotel warning him about the doctor.

Her mother, although she could tell she didn't quite believe her story concerning the night she'd spent with George, kept her peace, but she did tell Cassidy Dr. Madison was angry that she'd turned down his proposal, and her mother feared he'd react badly.

Quinn told her he'd seen Miss Baker, given her a clean bill of health, and talked her into an outing at the ice cream parlor. The teacher admitted to Quinn she feared Dr. Madison but wouldn't tell him why. He planned to gently pry it from her.

Late Wednesday afternoon, Cassidy walked into town to pick up the mail but glanced over her shoulder at every sound. She didn't think the doctor would try to accost her in public but also didn't relish the idea of the whole town talking about her and George.

She sighed. Seems she had no choice but to show her face in town and get it over with.

On her stroll through the streets, she noted a few women with their heads together whispering behind their hands. She ignored them and called out a greeting to everyone she passed.

She stepped onto the walk of the post office, looking over her shoulder for any sign of Dr. Madison. Once inside, she stayed on guard, her gaze sweeping from the counter to the door, while the clerk, Clyde Johnson, checked for her mail.

"Here you are, Miss Cassie." Mr. Johnson handed her three posts, two addressed to Quinn and one for her. She gasped as she read the return address, *Female Medical College of Pennsylvania.*

Her hands trembled as she held the post.

The clerk eyed her. "Aren't you gonna open it?"

She pursed her lips. "Yes, I guess I should." Her hands shook so bad, she had trouble breaking the seal.

"Hope it's not bad news, Miss," Mr. Johnson said.

"I surely hope not." She turned her back to him and straightened out the fold of paper. Her eyes misted, and she had trouble making out the type.

"Focus," she whispered. Blinking her eyes, she scanned down to the body of the letter.

Dear Miss Stuart, we are pleased to accept you as a student at the Female Medical College of Pennsylvania for the class starting September 1870.

Cassidy whooped and spun toward the startled clerk.

"Good news, Miss?" he guessed.

"The absolute best! I've been accepted to medical school."

"Glad to hear it, Miss Cassie! I know you'll make a great doc."

"Thank you, Mr. Johnson." She had the urge to throw her arms around the man but held back, instead clutching the post against her chest. She gathered her brother's letters and turned toward the door.

A gasp escaped her when she caught sight of Dr. Madison outside. She should have known she wouldn't get home without bumping into him. Thoughts of retreating back into the post office were thwarted when he caught her gaze.

"Miss Stuart." He tipped his hat. "I'm glad I've

run into you. I wanted to see you today...to apologize for my behavior yesterday."

She frowned. "Why bother?"

"Cassie..." He shook his head. "I was hurt, and understandably so. I felt betrayed. But last night I realized Masters isn't the type to stick around, even to make a woman respectable."

She swallowed. The last thing she wanted to do right now was to stand here conversing with Madison in front of the post office. "Doctor, if we could discuss this later?" She glanced up and down the street, noting people eyed them.

He sighed. "Please, I've asked you to call me Scott."

She bit her lip.

"But there's still time to quell all the gossip." He reached for her hand. She pulled away.

"Cassie, I can make you respectable if you'll only accept my proposal. You know from past experience, Masters won't stay in town long. He'll leave and you'll be disgraced." He glanced at her stomach. "Or worse if he's left you with child."

Her body heated with fury at his implications. She slapped his face. Her hand stung, but it felt good.

He gaped at her. She spun on her heel and strode away.

****

Early evening, Cassidy stepped into the lobby of the hotel. She no longer cared what anyone in town thought. She had to see George tonight.

Earlier, when she'd first returned home, she showed the post from the college to her mother and Quinn. Her brother was ecstatic, assuring her he knew she'd be accepted. They both congratulated her, but her mother didn't seem thrilled with the idea of Cassidy going off to study in Philadelphia.

"Cassie," Ma had said, "you'll be so far away for

217

so long."

"Only one semester at a time, Ma. And Quinn will be here to keep up the practice."

Her mother glanced up at Quinn. "Tell her it's not the same."

Quinn rose and placed his hand on their mother's shoulder. "I think this will be a good thing for Cassie. She'll be studying with other women, after all. I happen to think, with formal training, she'll make an excellent physician. I'll have a well-trained partner when she comes back."

Cassidy smiled at her brother, silently thanking him for always standing up for her.

"You don't know how much this means to me, both of you."

"I do." Quinn nodded toward her mother, who bit her lip. Now, she wanted to share her good news with George and also be sure Madison hadn't threatened him. No telling what would happen if those two ended up in a showdown, especially if the doctor learned George was a Pinkerton agent.

She approached the desk and asked the clerk if he could have Mr. Masters come downstairs. She didn't want to stir up any more gossip by going straight to his room.

Moments later, she turned at the sound of footsteps on the stairs. She caught George's gaze, warmth spreading from the crown of her head to her toes at the look of desire in his dark eyes.

He strode toward her and took her hand. "Cassie, what is it? I got the note from your brother."

She shook her head and smiled. "This isn't about that. I wanted to share my good news."

He frowned.

She extracted the post from her reticule and handed it to him. He scanned it, then caught her gaze, his eyes wide. His lips curved into a smile.

"You did it! I'm so proud of you."

Cassidy glanced around the room, catching the curious glances of the clerk and hotel patrons.

"Can we go for a walk? It's lovely outside."

George nodded. "Of course." He crooked his arm and escorted her outside. The heat of the day had dissipated with the sun now low in the sky.

A gentle breeze caressed Cassidy's cheek. She longed to have George wrap her in his arms, but not here. They had to find someplace private.

He seemed to read her thoughts. "Let's go around to the back. There's a grove of trees where we might find some privacy to talk."

She nodded and allowed him to lead her to the grove, the air in the shelter cool against her face. She propped her back against a sturdy oak and raised her arms. "I'd like a congratulatory kiss, sir."

He stepped into her embrace and took her mouth, his hunger obvious. His scent and taste sent heat swirling through her. She longed to lie down right here and allow him to take her, but they had to be careful.

After he released her mouth, she held his gaze. "Are you really happy I'll be going off to Philadelphia to study?"

"As long as I can continue to see you." He squeezed her hand and helped her arrange her skirts so she could sit on the cool grass. He settled beside her. "And one day soon, you're going to be my wife."

Her heart lurched. "You're serious?"

"Of course." He frowned. "Otherwise, I'd have never let it go as far as it did in my room. I don't want to take advantage of you. I love you and want you by my side always."

"Even when you go back to New York?"

He chuckled. "Guess I'll have to find a new occupation. My experience as a Pinkerton agent will surely land me a job in local law enforcement."

"You'd quit being an agent for me?" Her breath caught.

"I don't want to have to leave you to go off on long term assignments in other locations. Once we're married, I'll resign." He held her gaze.

Her eyes stung as she realized the implications of his words. "We're really going to get married?"

He shrugged. "Have to now. I wouldn't have it any other way."

"But medical school—"

He took her hand. "You go off to that school and do me proud. Once you've finished, we'll make our marriage plans. By then I hope to have a job lined up right here in town. The sheriff's deputy is getting on in years." He lifted her hand to brush his lips over it, sending tingles down her spine. "And once you've completed your doctor training, we'll settle down, and you can start a practice in town if that's what you want."

"Oh, George." She leaned over and kissed his cheek, then slid her lips over his. Half-reclining, she allowed him to ravage her mouth. Delicious sensations shot straight to her core. Afterward, they lay side by side on the grass.

"Well," George said, "I think we should put a hold on this right now. We don't want to fuel any more gossip in this town."

She laughed. "Tell me, George. Won't you miss being a detective?"

He lifted his arms, hands cupping his head. "I don't rightly know, and I haven't done it all that long, anyway. I think I'd enjoy working as a deputy here." He scowled. "Would sure hush up all those older folks who said I'd never amount to anything."

She smiled, lifting on an elbow to lean over him. "Anything you want to do is fine with me, as long as you marry me, Mister."

He reached up and pulled her down to lie on his

chest, then kissed her again.

****

George held Cassidy against him and took her soft, sweet mouth yet again. He grew hard. He had to stop before things went too far. This wasn't the place, and now wasn't the time. He lifted her off of him and set her on his side.

Her dark brows lifted as she gazed down at him, lips swollen from his kisses.

Sitting up, he brushed dried grass from his coat and trousers, then stood and reached a hand toward her. She placed hers in his and he pulled her to her feet.

"It's time for you to get on home, Cassie."

She nodded. "I know."

Before they left the grove, he brushed his thumb along her mouth and planted a soft kiss there. She licked her lips and smiled. "I want to go back to your room, George."

"I know, darlin', but you have to go home now." He swallowed hard but took her hand and led her from the cool shelter of trees, glancing about to make sure no one saw them emerge from their hiding spot.

By the time they'd reached her house, the sky darkened to twilight. George had a hard time seeing but held Cassidy's hand like a life line. He didn't want to allow her to go but knew she'd be safe at home with her family.

After ascending the porch steps, he turned to her, squinting to make out her face in the muted glow from the gaslights in the windows. "I love you, Cassie." He brushed his finger along her rose petal cheek.

She reached to caress his nape, her sweet breath within an inch of his mouth. "I love you, George. I always have."

His lips itched to smother hers in a passionate kiss. Voices drifted from inside the house and he pulled away. "I'd best get out of here, before your family finds more disfavor with me."

"I wish I could tell them who you really are."

"I know, darlin', but it'll all come out after Madison is disgraced for good."

She blew him a kiss goodbye and turned to the door. George hurried down the steps and out the gate convinced Quinn would throttle him if he caught him alone with her.

Chapter Twenty-Eight

Scott shifted behind the wide oak where he hid out of sight of Miss Stuart and Masters. He'd spotted them in town earlier and followed them. He picked up gossip about the two of them, convinced she'd shared Master's bed.

His blood heated as he watched them caress, then Masters hightailed it away, brushing Scott's hiding spot. He held his breath and waited until the man disappeared down the street before emerging. Miss Stuart hesitated on the porch.

He bounded up the steps, drawing a startled gasp from her. She peered at him. "George?"

Using darkness to his advantage, he didn't speak but strode up the steps and grasped her hand.

"Dr. Madison." She yanked against his grip. Before she could make a sound, he clamped a hand over her mouth.

****

Madison's iron grip held Cassidy fast. She had to get to the door, alert her family.

But he grasped her around the waist and forced her back down the steps and out the gate. She struggled but couldn't free herself. He propelled her toward the wooded area beyond the house.

Pulling to a stop, he released her mouth and spun her around. "You whore!" He hauled back and slapped her so hard, tears stung her eyes.

"Must you continue to humiliate me before the entire town? I saw you together. You Jezebel!" He pulled back his arm again, but this time she was prepared and ducked the blow.

"Come here!" He grasped her wrist before she could run and yanked her against him, squeezing her chin.

"I've already told you I love George, and there's nothing you can do about it. So, let me go."

He shoved her, then struck her again. Losing her balance, she tilted backward and crashed to the ground.

"What's going on?" A man carrying a lantern appeared.

Relief coursed through her when she realized he was her brother. "Quinn, help!" she called.

As Quinn raced toward them, Madison backed away, then broke, disappearing into the night.

"Cassie, are you all right?" Her brother set the lantern down and gathered her into his arms. "Who *was* that?"

"Dr. Madison." She reached around Quinn's neck, pulling him close as relief coursed through her.

"Did he hurt you?" Quinn raised his head as if trying to see where the doctor had gone. "If he did, Cassie, I'll kill him. I swear I will."

"It's all right. He's gone now." She grimaced as her brother helped her to her feet. "Please, take me home."

As he escorted her back to the house, a new fear gripped her. Would Dr. Madison go after George?

****

After seeing Cassidy home, George stopped at the tavern for a lager. After their encounter, he doubted he'd get a wink of sleep without something to numb his ardor. He'd wanted to take her back to his room and make love to her all night but didn't dare. She belonged with her family, at least until he proposed properly and married her.

The thought of having her as his wife after so long brought a smile to his face. He sipped his beer, savoring the taste, then set the mug on the counter.

The bartender sauntered over, eyeing the glass. "Ready for a refill?"

George shook his head. "No, thanks. After this one, I'm heading back to the hotel."

"I reckon, by that big grin on your face, you'll likely be dreaming of Miss Stuart."

George frowned. "What are you implying, sir?" He placed both hands on the counter.

The bartender raised his hands. "Didn't mean nothing insulting. Any man would consider himself lucky to have a feisty lady like Miss Cassie. And she's right pretty, too."

"Don't I know it?" George sighed into his glass.

"I hear tell you were once supposed to marry the lady. Just after the war."

"You heard right." George nodded. "But I made a big mistake and left her. I'm still kicking myself but am sure glad she's forgiven me."

"She gonna take you back?" The bartender's bushy brows rose.

"Reckon so. All I've got to do is propose to her proper."

"Well, congratulations in advance. I'd say it deserves a drink on the house."

"Ummm... I should be heading back."

The bartender poured more lager into his glass. "I won't take no for an answer. Special occasion like this deserves a celebration."

George watched the man pour his drink. Wouldn't be right to spurn his hospitality.

"Thank you, sir. Reckon one more will help me sleep better."

"That's the spirit." The bartender rose with a flourish. "Enjoy." He stepped aside to attend another customer.

George half turned at a rush of air behind him. He twisted around to find Quinn standing behind him, breathing hard, his rusty colored hair mussed.

"George, Cassie wanted me to find you right away...to warn you..."

George rose and planted his hand on Quinn's shoulder. "What is it, man? What's wrong?"

"It's Doc Madison. He's gone berserk. Came after Cassie and..."

George's pulse raced. "Did he hurt her? Where is she?"

Quinn gulped. "He knocked her around, but she's not hurt. She's safe at home...but she's afraid he'll come after you."

George frowned. Had Madison gone off after seeing George and Cassidy together? He grasped Quinn's arm and guided him into an alcove, so they could have at least a bit of privacy.

Quinn's gaze narrowed. "He knows about you and Cassie. It's what got him so riled. He wanted to marry her."

"I know." George sighed. "This is my fault. I should have been more careful with her. I fear I've already ruined your sister's reputation." He glanced at Quinn. "Your mother must hate me."

Quinn grinned. "Well, she did have a few choice words for you, but I think she knows you and Cassie love each other."

"What about Madison?"

"I don't think he's caught on that you're investigating him, but he did set his sights on Cassie, and now he must feel thwarted. There's no telling what he'll do." He glanced toward the door as a customer exited. "I wish I could have found out more about him in Philadelphia, but no one seemed to know or was willing to reveal anything. I reckon you didn't have much luck either."

George scowled. "No. The nurse I interviewed worked for them before the incident with Miss Wellingham, but she *did* resign because of amorous treatment by Scott Madison. She feared to be alone in the house with him. If his father is as influential as Colonel Wellingham led me to believe, I'm sure he's instigated a cover up to hide his son's indiscretions so as not to tarnish his own reputation in the city."

Quinn nodded. "So, what are we going to do?"

George patted his shoulder. "We're going to keep your sister safe and away from the man."

"What about you? Do you think he'll come after you?"

George clenched his teeth. "If the bastard comes after me, I'll be more than ready for him." He stared off into the outer room. "And if he comes after your sister again, I swear to God, I'll kill him."

****

Cassidy paced the length of the kitchen awaiting Quinn's return. After tending to her scratches and scrapes, her mother wanted her to go to her room where she'd be safe. Cassidy insisted she was all right and had to be sure Madison hadn't gone after George.

Matt vowed to stand guard so the deranged doctor couldn't get to her again.

When the entry door opened, she raced from the room, her mother on her heels. Quinn entered, glanced behind him, and shut and locked the door.

"Did you find him?" she burst out. "Is he all right?"

"He's fine, Cassie." Quinn's gaze swept from her to their mother. "He's more worried about you and assured me he can take care of himself."

She wrung her hands. "But he was so violent. He knows I was with George." Her face flushed. "I have to see him, be sure he's all right."

Her mother grasped her arm. "Young lady, you are going nowhere but to your bed. George can take care of himself, but you're no match for Madison. It's up to your brothers to be sure he doesn't get to you again."

Her heart hammered. "But I can't sleep until I see George."

A knock at the door drew a gasp from her. Quinn cracked open the door, then swung it wide. "It's George," he announced.

Cassidy raced into his arms. "I'm so glad you're all right. I was so afraid for you." She buried her face in the comforting scent of his coat.

"Shh." His hand brushed over her hair, sending shivers down her spine. "We'll all take care of you." He lifted her chin, studying her face. "He hurt you."

She gazed into his eyes and read the raw anger there. "He saw us together. Followed us to the house. As soon as you left, he came after me."

He raised his brows. "I'm sorry." He gathered her into his embrace. "I should have made sure you were inside before I left. This is my fault."

"No. It's not your fault."

"It is." He eased her back. "Are you sure you're all right?"

She rubbed her arms. "A few scratches and bruises. But Quinn came to my rescue. He heard us."

George glanced at her brother. "Thank God for that."

Quinn cleared his throat. "Matt and I will be here to see the women are safe." He clapped a hand on George's shoulder. "You'd best get back to your hotel room and be cautious."

Cassidy glanced up at George then at her brother. "Maybe he should stay the night. Just to be sure he's safe?"

Her mother shook her head. "I don't think it would be wise, dear." She frowned in George's direction.

He patted Cassidy's back. "Your mother's right. I'll be heading back." He looked from her mother to Quinn. "Just keep her safe."

"We will," Quinn said.

Once George left the house, the trembling started. She'd held herself together since the assault and now knew he was a trained agent, but with Dr. Madison so out of control, her heart refused to slow. What could a man so deranged do to George?

Chapter Twenty-Nine

Late Monday morning Scott stepped from the train at the Burkeville station. He'd spent the last few days at a medical conference in New York City and was anxious to get home and find out if anything had changed since he'd left town. His plans to wed Miss Stuart and combine their practices had been thwarted by Masters. The man not only meddled in his plans but also seemed to be hounding him, ever since he'd first set foot in his office to talk about Miss Stuart. He'd obviously been baiting Scott, but why? And now the sight of Miss Stuart and Masters together proved too much for him to bear.

He accepted his bag from the porter and strolled down the short platform. After spending time in New York, he realized just how small this town was. Did he want this for his future? Maybe he should cut his losses and move on.

Arriving home, he found Tillie, who he'd left to care for the house while away, in an uproar. She rushed up to take his bag from his hand.

"Sir, you have to know what they're saying about you."

He scowled. "What the devil is wrong?"

The woman's thin lips quivered. "There's rumors you mistreated a patient under your care. A young woman."

"That's absurd!" Scott's blood ran cold. "Who's spreading these ridiculous rumors?"

"It's the Stuarts. Miss Stuart said you laid hands on her and her brother backs her up. They've been saying horrible things about you."

"Well, I'll just have to put a stop to this." He stomped down the hall. Heated, he stripped off his coat, dropped the garment, then unbuttoned his vest.

Tillie raced after him, scooping his coat from the floor. "Sir, what if the town believes them?"

Scott twirled around. "They're obviously after the patients who flocked to me after Miss Stuart showed the town what a bungler she is, and now her brother wants to get them back."

"They're lying?" Tillie raised her brows.

"How can they prove what they say? It's their word against mine." Scott racked his brain, trying to recall who'd seen him that night.

"What about the patient you mistreated?" Tillie lifted her gnarled hands to her mouth.

Could they have found out about Miss Wellingham or had that bitch, Miss Baker, talked? He'd thought he had her cowed, but she may have spoken up when he'd left for New York.

"They can't have proof for any of these wild accusations." He stepped on the bottom stair. "Have a glass of bourbon ready for me when I come back down."

"Sir?" Tillie frowned. "It's ten o'clock in the morning."

"I didn't *ask* you, Tillie. On second thought, bring it to my room." He turned and ascended the stairs, not looking back.

After quenching his thirst, he decided a trip to the tavern would be in order, while Tillie prepared his dinner. If gossip about him had spread through town, he'd find out and see if he could nip the whole thing in the bud.

As he sat at the bar sipping bourbon, a man slid into the seat beside him. Scott glanced over at a thin, blond haired, clean-shaven, man eyeing him with interest. He took a sip of the drink the bartender laid before him and swallowed.

"You're Doc Madison ain't ya?" the man murmured. "I've seen you in here before but haven't had the pleasure..."

"I believe I'm at a disadvantage, sir." Scott extended his hand.

The man smiled. "Nate Bartholomew." He reached out and shook Scott's hand. "Heard you'd gone out of town for a spell."

Scott glanced around the tavern. This early in the day, only the bartender and a serving woman dealt with a handful of patrons. "I was in New York City...for a medical conference."

Bartholomew leaned toward him. "The Stuarts have been spreading gossip about you since you've been gone."

"So, I've heard. False gossip, I might add."

"Seems likely they want to drive you out of town, so they can get all their patients back." Bartholomew frowned. "But I've seen you courting Miss Stuart. What'd she do, go sour on you, Doc?"

Scott scowled. "Seems her old beau, George Masters, showed up in town and stole her away from me."

"Masters? He's a liar and a cheat. She'd be better off with you."

"So I'd thought." He lifted his glass, allowing the warmth of his drink to stir up his embers. "Seems she's chosen him."

Bartholomew shook his head. "If I see him, I'll sock him in the jaw. He cleaned me out about a week ago when I stayed at my brother's in Philadelphia. We have a running poker game here in the back room, too. He's there whenever he's hurting for cash. A real pro at raking it in too." He inclined his head, and Scott followed his gaze to a door on the left side of the kitchen.

Scott turned back. "So, you know him." He leaned toward the man, keeping his voice low. "Sounds like you have a serious grudge against the man."

Bartholomew turned and spat in the spittoon on the floor beside his stool. "Sure enough do, Doc. In fact, if I get my hands on the scum, I wouldn't want to say in polite company just what I'd like to do to him."

"I wouldn't mind sharing in a bit of retribution on the man myself." Scott relaxed, knowing he'd found a kindred spirit.

"He's a cheating bastard. Learned all those fancy card tricks in New York City. Served in the war with him, too. Still the same son-of-a-bitch back then. Took all my money, then told me I just had back luck." He leaned toward Scott and lowered his voice. "If I had my druthers, Doc, I'd be happy to take care of him for you, so you can get the little lady back."

Turning to his drink, Bartholomew lifted his glass and swallowed the last drop, then slammed the empty container on the bar. "The one room I can afford in town is a small room behind the kitchen. I would've left this hell hole by now, but he took all my money, and the only job I could find is cheap labor that doesn't pay enough for train fare out of here."

"What if I told you I could help you out?" Scott smiled, pulling out a wad of money.

The man's brows lifted. "I'm listenen'. What I have to do?"

"I'd like to discredit the Stuarts so they're the ones forced to leave town, but for George Masters, I need someone skilled in the art of revenge."

Bartholomew leaned in close. Scott caught the scent of whiskey and tobacco on his breath.

"Tell me, do you own a firearm, Mr.

Bartholomew?"

****

With his plan for revenge in motion, Scott decided it was time to pay Miss Baker a call. Find out if she'd told the Stuarts what he'd done to her. If she hadn't, maybe he'd just spend a little more time with the schoolteacher. Then he'd deal with Miss Stuart and her brother.

He waited, like he had the last time, for the school day to be done. He hoped to find her in the school house alone. Anticipation of seeing her again and touching her petal soft, ivory skin, threading his hands through her silky hair, sent his pulse racing.

He stopped a few yards from the school house. The door stood open, but he didn't see any children. He hoped she was inside getting ready to depart for the day.

Stepping around the side of the one room structure, he peered into a window. She stood at a desk setting slates in a pile. He opened the door and walked in.

Her eyes widened and she backed away. "Miss Baker, I thought it time to see you again and be sure our agreement is in order."

Her gaze shifted to her left. Movement in the corner of the room caught Scott's attention. A man strode toward him. Quinn Stuart.

"What the hell are you doing here, Madison?"

Scott swallowed. "I could ask you the same thing, sir."

Miss Baker's face paled. "He's helping me clean up and seeing me home."

Scott licked his lips. "I wish to speak to you, Miss Baker. Nothing more."

"About what?" Stuart's scowl deepened, and he stepped menacingly close. "What business do you have with her anyway?"

"I...I saw Miss Baker a few months ago as a

patient. She'd cut her arm."

"I know all about that. My sister treated her. She's Cassie's patient now. You have no business coming here, and I suggest you leave." He raised a fist.

Scott backed away. "Are you planning to cuff me like that brute Masters? I heard your sister's his whore now."

Stuart stepped to within an inch of Scott and grasped his shirt collar, twisting the fabric. "Get out of here, now, or I swear to God, I'll..."

Scott raised his hands in surrender. When Stuart released him, he backed out the door. "I'll leave, but you'd better get a handle on your sister."

As Scott strode back to town, rage burned within him. Apparently, Miss Baker hadn't told the Stuarts what he'd done, but would she now? And how could he get to her to be sure she didn't?

****

George stopped by Cassidy's home to be sure she was all right. He'd learned Madison had returned from a trip to New York City. He had to be sure the bastard wouldn't come after her again.

He found her in her office, cleaning up after a patient visit. Her mother let him in, and he noted acceptance and relief in the woman's gaze when she greeted him.

Cassidy glanced up when he entered the room. She dropped the rag in her hand and ran into his arms. Her hair smelled of fresh rainwater and herbs.

"He's back," George said.

"Who?" She searched his eyes. "Dr. Madison?"

He nodded, setting her away from him.

"Seems he's been at a medical conference in New York. I'd kind of hoped he'd left town for good."

"Quinn talked about going to the sheriff, but it would be Madison's word against ours. I'm not sure what we can do."

"Likely, he'll try to discredit you and Quinn. Make it look like the two of you are in cahoots to get your practice back."

She frowned. "Do you really think so?"

"I truly believe the man's capable of anything, Cassie, after what Colonel Wellingham told me he did to his daughter."

"How will we ever get any proof against him?" She chewed her lower lip.

"Can't say I know, but we have to stay vigilant. I won't allow him to harm anyone else, especially you." He stepped close and spread his arms.

Cassidy smiled, melting into his embrace. Soft and pliant. He'd keep her safe, no matter what.

"George..." She pressed her face into his coat, so he had trouble hearing her muffled words. "...you promised never to leave me again."

"I won't, darlin'." He kissed her hair. "I won't."

****

Tuesday evening, Scott invited Nate Bartholomew to his home so they could talk without being overheard. He'd told him to come late, after the housekeeper left for the day.

Bartholomew strode in the door and followed Scott to the parlor where he slid into an upholstered chair. As Scott perched on the settee, he noted the man's scowl. He certainly looked capable of killing a man.

"Now, Doc..." Bartholomew rubbed his calloused hands together. "...just how much would you pay me to take care of Masters for you?"

Scott frowned. "Well, if truth be told, I'd say you wanted him gone just as much as I. Makes us partners of a sort."

Nate frowned. "If I'm the one pulling the trigger, I'm taking all the risks. Reckon I should be compensated, is all."

Scott smiled. "My good man, you will be. First

off, I'll be paying your train fare out of Burkeville. Until then, you can stay here, and I'll provide all your meals."

The man rubbed his chin. "What about your housekeeper?"

"Simple. I'll tell her I'm renting you a room until you can get back on your feet."

"She won't be suspicious?"

"Tillie knows to keep out of my business. Otherwise, I'd be forced to dismiss her."

Bartholomew scrubbed his face. "And after I've done the deed?"

"You'll be paid handsomely for your part." Scott waved his hand. "I'll make sure you get out of town, and then you'll be free to go anywhere you wish."

Nate squinted. "I've always wanted to go out west. Reckon that's where I'll head."

Scott nodded. "A good choice. A man can lose himself on the west coast." He scowled. "I don't know who'd care about Masters' death, anyway."

"What about that gal he's taken up with?"

"Don't worry about her." Scott rubbed his palms together in anticipation. "I have my own plans for Miss Stuart."

Chapter Thirty

Late Wednesday morning, George trudged in the direction of the Stuart home. Madison back in town put his nerves on edge. He couldn't get past the thought the bastard plotted and planned something malicious. He didn't worry so much for himself, but if Madison harmed Cassidy, he'd never forgive himself.

He found her in the garden at the back of the house, pulling weeds. When she caught sight of him, she smiled.

"I worried so about you, George."

"And I worried even more about you." He reached for her hand and set down the basket. "Has Madison contacted you?"

She frowned. "No, but...I've spoken to Quinn. He stayed with Miss Baker at the school house after her class left and Madison showed up wanting to see her."

He gulped. "What happened?" He searched her eyes.

"Quinn threatened him and chased him off. Afterward Miss Baker seemed scared. He tried to comfort her. That's when she told him..." She swallowed.

"Told him what?"

"Madison forced himself on her."

George's pulse thundered. "In his office?"

"No." Cassidy shook her head. "He touched and kissed her in the office, but later, he came to the school house when she was there alone..." Her gaze glazed over. "I can't believe anyone could be so horrible! Miss Baker is the sweetest woman."

George gathered her in his arms. "It's all right, Cassie. We have him now. We'll take Miss Baker to the sheriff."

"No." She mumbled into his chest. "Quinn wanted to take her, but she refuses to go." She gazed up at him. "She fears revealing what he did will damage her reputation beyond repair."

"Blast it all!" George backed away, ruffling his hand through his hair. "We have to tell the sheriff..."

"But it will be her word against a respected doctor," Cassidy protested.

"What about the attack on you?" George paced the room. "You and Quinn can see the sheriff..."

She spread her hands. "Without absolute proof, the sheriff would have to take our word against his. And rumors are already spreading through town that we're trying to discredit him and drive him out."

"There has to be something we can do. I couldn't live with myself if he got to you before I could stop him."

She turned away and planted her fists on her hips. "What about you? He's no more happy with you than me. Miss Baker, Quinn, you and I...we're all in danger."

George sighed and grasped her shoulders, turning her to face him. "We all have to be on guard. But I don't know how to keep watch on you when I can't be with you all the time."

She smiled and stroked his cheek. "The hours I spent in your room were the most wonderful hours of my life." Her face lifted, so he could feel her sweet breath on his face. His own breathing quickened. "I want you to make love to me again."

"Cassie...no..." He swallowed hard. "This isn't the time. Your mother and Quinn already suspect..."

"I don't care, George. I don't know if it's the excitement of all this going on with Madison or just being here so close to you. My senses are tingling." She stood on her toes, her tongue flicking out to lick his lips. He opened his mouth and she kissed him, probing with her tongue.

His arms tightened around her. An image of the two of them naked, alone for the night, sent his shaft hardening. How could he deny her?

She pulled away and smirked. "Will you, then?"

He shook his head, but grinned. "You drive a hard bargain, Cassidy Stuart."

She glanced around, then lifted her lips to his ear. "I'm supposed to tend to one of my patients in town after dinner. I'll look in on her, then sneak to the back of your hotel. Meet me there at eight o'clock."

Before he could answer, she snatched the basket and dashed into the house. George sighed and licked his lips. He wasn't sure this was a good idea, but for right now, having her in his bed the entire night caused his body to hum with anticipation. And he wouldn't have to worry about Madison getting to her while he wasn't around to protect her.

****

By late Wednesday afternoon, Scott and Nate had their revenge all planned out. By allowing Nate to do all the dirty work, Scott would be left free to keep his practice. And with Masters gone and the Stuarts discredited, he'd have complete control. Since Miss Stuart had spurned him, he'd take up with that little schoolteacher. He'd keep her as a mistress until he found a suitable woman to pursue for a wife.

Once Nate settled in, Scott stepped into his room to go over the plan.

Nate glanced around, smiling. "Nice place you have here, Doc. My room at the tavern's a dump!" He flopped on the bed and lifted both legs onto the quilt.

Scott scowled, noting he still wore his boots.

"You must focus on your task, and as soon as the deed's done, I'll have your money waiting, and you can board a train out of town."

"Long as you're paying." Nate propped his upper body against the headboard.

Scott stiffened, not liking the man dirtying the quilt his late mother had sewn, but let it go, not wanting to aggravate him.

"Once you've taken care of Masters, you'll be free to leave."

Nate grinned.

"I do hope you've got your weapon ready and loaded."

"Sure do." Nate patted his vest pocket. "Got me a derringer all ready for the bastard."

Scott scowled. "A derringer? You'll have to stand at close range to shoot him."

A slow grin spread over Nate's face. "Oh, I surely intend to. I want him to look me right in the eye, so he knows who killed him."

"So long as he doesn't get you first." Scott waved his hand. "But I do want to be apprised when he's been taken care of. Once he's out of the way..." He trailed off, a thrill racing through him at the thought of what he'd do to Miss Stuart.

Nate grinned. "You're gonna go after that gal, ain't ya?"

Scott scowled. "She's no concern of yours."

"I see." Nate rose and circled Scott's chair. "If what you're planning is what I think, I'd like to have a go at her too."

"Absolutely not!" Scott glanced up at the man. "Once Masters is taken care of, I'll pay you, and you'll be on your way."

Nate grasped the back of the chair, jostling Scott. "Fine by me, Doc." He leaned in close, the sour stench of his breath assaulting Scott's nostrils. "But you'd best not cross me, you hear?"

Scott clenched his teeth but nodded. "You'll get your money, Bartholomew, just do what I'm paying you to do."

Nate grinned.

****

Right after dinner, Cassidy excused herself, claiming she had to look in on a patient she'd treated the day before.

Quinn's brows rose. "Mrs. Welkie? Would you like me to accompany you?"

"No, it's nothing serious." She met his gaze as her mother cleared the table. "She just asked me to stop by, and I thought I'd go now. If there's any problem, I'll come back and get you."

Her brother nodded, but frowned, not looking convinced.

She ran up to her room, patted her hair in place, and changed into her best dress, wishing she could abandon the dreary mourning clothes. She hoped her mother and Quinn wouldn't notice she'd changed, but she had to look her best for George. Tonight must be special.

As she neared the hotel, townsfolk greeted her and wished her a good evening. She nodded and greeted them in return, but eyed them covertly to be sure no one saw her go around the side of the hotel to the back door. She hoped an employee wouldn't come out this way and think her a scarlet woman.

She waited a few moments, watching the door, ready to scurry if someone other than George emerged. Her hands trembled at the enticing thought of being alone with him...his naked skin against hers. Anticipation threatened to send her swooning.

A sound at the back door sent her head swiveling. Her breath caught. A sigh of relief escaped her when George stepped out, devastatingly handsome in his frock coat. His eyes widened at the sight of her. Had he thought she wouldn't come?

"Cassie," he breathed. "You look beautiful." He reached for her hand and led her inside.

As they crept up the back stairs, she remained silent. She waited until he'd closed the door to speak.

"I couldn't wait to see you, George." She grasped his hand and raised his callused palm to her lips. The scent of wool, leather, and man thrilled her.

"I wasn't sure you'd come...or would be able to get out of the house."

She smiled. "I told them I was going to look in on a patient I'd treated yesterday."

"Then, you can't stay too long..." He trailed off.

"Let's worry on it later." She led him to the bed and sat, pulling him down beside her. "I'm here now and I'm not leaving. I never want to leave you again."

He smiled, then leaned into her, taking her mouth. Delicious sensations shot to her core. She relaxed, allowing him to lower her until she lay flat on her back, cushioned by the feather mattress.

"You are so beautiful, Cassie." He pulled the pins from her bun. She stilled as he loosened her hair and arranged the strands over her shoulders. "I've dreamed of seeing you this way for so long." He fingered a length of her hair, then raised the strand to his nose.

A thrill sent gooseflesh racing over her. She wanted his hands all over her body, touching her bared skin. She wanted his clothes off, too, so she could run her hands over his chest, his arms, his lower region. She wanted this man so bad, her gut clenched.

He rose and peeled off his coat and loosened his braces. She didn't move, just watched, moistening her lips.

He leaned down and fingered the clasps at her bodice. Her breath caught when he popped the top one, then another and another. A breeze from the open window caressed her exposed skin, adding to her arousal.

The bodice out of the way, his lips brushed against the edge of her chemise just above the corset. Her breathing grew shallow, and she reached for the buttons of his shirt. She ached to see his naked chest, run her fingers over his skin.

Once they'd divested themselves of their clothing, she lay atop him on the bed, her lips pressed against his. He brushed his hands along her spine, and tingles raced down to the part of her where she wanted him most. Her breasts swelled against his chest.

He lifted her, kissing one breast, then taking the hardened nipple into his mouth. The act sent liquid heat shooting between her thighs.

"George!" she gasped.

Releasing her breast, he nudged her onto her back and settled between her legs. "Are you sure you want this, darlin'?"

She gasped for air. "Of course I do, you dolt."

He chuckled, then stroked her, almost causing her to erupt. When he, at last, thrust into her, she raised her legs, wrapping them around his waist. She wanted him closer. Closer.

His hot breath brushed her ear as they rocked together. At the height of rapture, when she thought she could bear no more, she completely shattered.

Later, she woke beside him. A rosy glow lit the room, the air humid and still. He lay on his side, his arm thrown over her waist. She relaxed in his warmth and strength. If she lost him now, she didn't know if she'd survive.

He stirred and opened his eyes. Glancing at the window, he started. He pulled his arm from around her taking his warmth.

"George? What's wrong?" She propped herself on

her elbows.

He reached for his pocket watch, opened it, and grimaced. "As much as I'd like you to stay the night, I think it best if you went home." He sighed. "This way your mother and Quinn won't be suspicious."

She bit her lip. "I guess." Not wanting to move from the warmth of his bed, of him, she stretched and sat up, clutching the sheet to her chest.

He slipped off the bed and climbed into his clothes. He threw her underclothes across the bed. She dressed, knowing she didn't dare alarm her mother again.

As she shrugged into her bodice, she glanced at him. He adjusted his braces.

"That was so much better than the last time, George." Her face flamed. "Will it be even better the next time we're together?"

He grinned as he reached for his vest. "I surely hope so."

She smiled and fastened the hooks and eyes of her bodice. "Then I can hardly wait for the next time."

"The next time..." He buttoned his vest, then reached for his coat. "...I plan for us to be legally wed."

A thrill raced through her at his words. "I'd like that." She flushed again and glanced around the room to be sure she didn't leave anything.

"I want to marry you as soon as possible, Cassie." His gaze sought hers. "How does next week sound?"

She nodded. "I'll tell my family as soon as I get home."

"Good." He reached for her hand and kissed her wrist at the pulse point, his lips starting another round of tingles racing through her. "You've just made me happier than I've been in my whole miserable life."

****

After the meeting with Bartholomew, Scott left the house to see a patient in town. Afterward he decided to take a walk. He needed to calm himself. The anticipation of taking revenge on Masters and having Miss Stuart at his complete disposal, without the protection of Masters or her family, sent his pulse racing.

As he passed the hotel, the thought of Miss Stuart and Masters, alone in his room, infuriated him. What if he went up there and confronted the man? She could be with him now.

He strolled through the lobby. The clerk glanced up and nodded, likely thinking Scott there to see a patient. After ascending the stairs, he realized he didn't know which floor Masters stayed on. Perhaps he should go back and inquire at the desk, but he might raise suspicions. He continued to the third floor, hoping he'd guessed right.

He stepped down the hall, unsure of what to do next. He couldn't just start knocking on doors. As he neared the end of the hall, footsteps sounded on the back utility stairs the service people used. He caught voices...a man and woman. They sounded familiar. He crept to the back stairwell and caught a glimpse of a woman's dark skirts sliding down the stairs. Ducking back, he flattened himself against the wall and listened as they continued to the first floor.

He peered over the railing and sneered. Masters and Miss Stuart. She must have been in his room again. He clenched his fists.

Where the devil is Bartholomew when I need him? He rifled through his medical bag but had no time to look for his knife. He cradled the bag against his body.

Slipping down the front stairs, he hoped no one else would appear and get in the way. He wanted to catch them before they left. Since they'd descended the back stairs, he should be able to catch them at the back entrance. He hoped no one was out this time of evening.

As he rounded the back of the hotel, he caught a glimpse of them entering the alley beside the mercantile. He reckoned they expected to get out of the hotel unnoticed.

He raced toward the alley, the bag still in his hand. He needed to get to the knife. He kneeled and opened the bag, glancing up.

Two figures embraced. Miss Stuart clung to Masters as they kissed. Jaw clenched, Scott located the knife. Fingering the sharp blade, he rose and raced toward them.

Miss Stuart turned her head, her eyes wide, lush mouth agape. He grasped her arm and flung her aside. Raising his knife, he lunged at Masters.

He grasped Scott's wrist, twisting his arm to wrestle the knife from his hand. Scott fought, faintly registering pain as he threw all his strength into plunging the knife in his victim's chest. Masters' weight against him threw him off balance and he fell. Masters landed on Scott's chest, knocking the breath from him.

Scott glanced to his side.

Where's the knife? He shoved against Masters, in an effort to throw him off.

Masters socked him in the face, the blow sending white sparks through battered senses.

"I will kill you," Scott hissed.

"Not from where I'm sitting," Masters said.

Scott looked again for the knife. The handle lay beyond his reach. He hoped Masters didn't catch sight of the blade and try to use Scott's own weapon against him.

He needed a distraction. A startled gasp from Miss Stuart did the trick.

"George!" she called.

Chapter Thirty-One

George glanced in Cassidy's direction. She stood against the brick wall of the hotel. He followed her wide eyed glance. Nate Bartholomew emerged from behind her holding out a derringer.

"What the hell are you doing here?" George asked.

Nate edged closer. "I've come to take out my revenge." He smirked, his yellowed teeth and thin face looking like a death's head.

"Revenge for what?" From the corner of his eye, he caught Madison's arm snake out. The knife he'd threatened George with lay on the ground just out of his grasp. "Oh, no you don't." He reached for the knife before Madison could.

"Batholomew," Scott hissed. "What are you waiting for? Shoot him!"

Cassidy gasped.

Nate smiled, waving the derringer. "If you have any brains, Masters, I'd advise you to get off my friend and give him back his knife."

George glanced from one to the other. "You're working with him?"

"The doc made me a proposition I just couldn't refuse." Nate chuckled, then frowned. "Now, get up."

George grunted as he rose and dropped the knife, trying to catch Cassidy's gaze. He wanted her to run, while he had Nate's attention, and get help.

But she stood frozen to the spot.

Nate raised his gun, aiming the barrel at George's chest. "I know you got a gun on you. Pull it out real easy and drop it here in front of me."

George eased the Colt from his pocket and laid it on the ground, then raised his hands. "Before you shoot me, Nate, I have one request."

"What is it?"

"Allow the lady to go. She has nothing to do with whatever quarrel you have with me."

Nate glanced at Madison. The doctor rose and brushed off his coat, his face flushed. "*I'll* deal with Miss Stuart."

"Cassie, run!" George's heart lurched. He didn't care what happened to *him*. Only her safety mattered.

She held his gaze, swallowed, and stepped toward them.

His heart sank.

"Please, sir," she asked Nate, "what quarrel do you have with George that you'd want to kill him?"

"He cheated me one too many times at cards." The man waved the derringer at George.

George weighed the possibility of wrestling the gun from him, but the sour scent of sweat tinged with tobacco and an audible exhale told him Madison stood inches behind him. George didn't need to see the knife to know the blade pointed at his back. If he could get Cassidy out of the way...

"Nate," he appealed, "she's got nothing to do with this. Let her go." He caught her wide-eyed gaze. Would she run this time?

Nate scowled and turned toward Madison. The doctor shook his head. "She's coming with me." He sneered at George. "I'll take her to my home. You just deal with *him*, then meet me there."

Nate grinned. "All right then." He pulled the trigger.

The blast hit George in the side, sending him to his knees. Numbness settled in as he fell forward, his last thought—regret for not saving Cassidy.

****

Cassidy's breath caught as the blast knocked George to his knees. As if in a nightmare, she watched him fall flat on his face. Her throat closed up, cutting off her scream. Madison grabbed her arm. "Let's go, Miss Stuart."

"No!" She wrenched away, but his grip tightened. "You can't just leave him here."

"Mr. Bartholomew will take care of him, won't you?" He smiled at his accomplice.

The doctor yanked her arm. She stomped on his foot. He swore and raised his hand as if to strike her.

Voices from outside the alley sent hope surging through Cassidy.

Nate turned to Madison. "I'm gettin' out of here."

As the voices drew closer, the doctor swore. He released Cassidy and raced down the back of the alley, followed by Nate. Cassidy watched them go, then slid to the ground by George's side. Turning him over, she gasped at the blood freely flowing from his chest.

Two men raced toward her. "What happened here, ma'am? We heard a gunshot." She pointed to George. "He needs help, but I'm a doctor. I need someone to get me a medical kit..." Glancing around, she spotted Madison's bag. In his haste to get away, he'd left it.

"Never mind," she told the men. She scurried over to grasp the bag, then pointed down the alley. "The men who shot him went that way. I'll take care of him until someone else shows up to help."

"Yes, ma'am," one of them said. Both men raced down the alley in the direction Madison and Nate had gone.

Cassidy parted George's coat and pushed back his shredded vest. She had to stop the bleeding. Lifting her skirt, she ripped off a section of her petticoat and pressed the cloth against the wound.

George moaned. "It's all right," she said. "I'm staying to take care of you."

Sorting through the medical bag, she looked for a probe. She didn't know if the bullet lodged in his body, but if so, she needed to extract it. Grasping the instrument, she prayed. "Don't die on me now, George." Wouldn't be fair if she lost him after all the years they'd spent apart. She couldn't bear the thought.

****

George cracked an eye. A throbbing pain in his right side grabbed his attention. He lifted his hand and probed. A thick layer of gauze covered his ribs.

Gasping, he raised his head and caught a glimpse of a woman's skirt. "Cassie?"

She stepped to his side. "I'm right here."

"This is my room." He glanced around the familiar setting. "How did I get here?"

Cassidy smiled. "I had a little help. Two men heard the shot and went after Dr. Madison and his friend. Then more men arrived and carried you up here."

"What about the bullet?" White-hot pain shot through his body. He gasped. "Is it still inside?"

She nodded. "I tried to probe it in the alley, but I couldn't see in the dark. I wish Quinn were here. He has more experience than I."

George reached for her hand. "If I had to choose my doctor, you'd be the one I'd ask for."

"But, George, I-I don't want to make things worse."

"Sweetheart, you could never make things worse. If not for you, I'd likely have died years ago in the Confederate prison."

She shook her head. "That's not true. I had nothing to do with it."

"Yes, you did, darlin'. The vision of coming home to you kept me sane. Otherwise, I'd as soon just lay down and died right there."

"But when you came home, why didn't you stay?"

He shook his head. "I was a fool. Thought myself no good and you deserved much better." He reached up and stroked her cheek.

Another shaft of pain shot down his side, causing him to grimace.

"Now, lie still," Cassidy said. "Besides likely having a bullet in you, one of your ribs is cracked."

"I'm a mess." George sought her gaze. "How can I protect you now?"

She shook her head. "I don't think you have to. Likely, Dr. Madison and his friend are on their way out of town, if they haven't already been caught."

George struggled to control his breathing. Every indrawn breath burned like the fires of Hell. But the thought of losing her burned worse. If Madison did come back, what would he do?

Chapter Thirty-Two

Scott and Nate separated outside of town. He paid Nate the rest of the agreed money. Thanks to forethought, he'd had the bills in his pocket to avoid returning home to retrieve them. Nate decided to hike to the next town to escape detection, to continue with his plans to catch a train and head west.

But Scott's dilemma was where to go. He couldn't chance going home, but all he had were the clothes on his back and the cash he still carried. He had to find a town where no one knew him and start over. He had skills as a physician. He felt sure he could find a town in need of a doctor.

An image rose in his mind, causing him to wince. His medical bag! He'd left it in the alley when he'd fled. Should he chance going back for the bag? The cost of having to replace his instruments made the decision for him.

He hoped the satchel still remained in the same spot. He'd snatch it back and catch the next train out of town.

****

Cassidy washed the blood from her hands. George's blood. After the men had carried him up here, she'd used the probe from Madison's bag to extract the bullet. Afterward she washed out the wound, pushing lint in and wrapped it securely. She'd have to watch over him for several days to be sure he didn't develop an infection.

Once her hands were clean, she stood over George, watching him sleep. His features relaxed, but every now and then he grimaced. She'd prepare

253

a pain tonic for when he woke. Stroking his hair from his forehead, she noted his skin cool to the touch. At least he'd awakened for a short period. A good sign. She'd leave him sleep for now.

Sighing, she adjusted her skirts and settled in the upholstered chair. She chewed her lip as her thoughts slipped to Madison. With George out of immediate danger, she allowed herself to wonder where the doctor had gone. Likely he and his accomplice had run right out of town, and they'd never see either of them again. Or perhaps the sheriff had caught them. She'd find out later. Right now, she just wanted to rest her eyes and maybe doze for a bit.

As she started to drift, her thoughts focused on the last time she and George spent here together. Her lips curved in pleasure at the remembrance of the sensations accompanying their lovemaking. She'd never imagined the act would be so wonderful.

She sank down into the chair, a comfortable buzzing sending her into a semi-conscious state, but a knock at the door brought her back. Opening her eyes, she stared at the closed door, not sure if she'd dreamt the sound.

The knock sounded louder. She roused herself, straightening her skirt. "Who's there?"

"Sis, you in there?"

"Quinn?" She rose and opened the door.

Her brother glanced from her to the bed. "I heard what happened...is he..." He motioned to George.

"I dug out the bullet, and he's resting now. I need to watch him for infection, though."

He reached out and grasped her by the shoulders. "Are you all right?"

"I'm shaken up, but not hurt. I'm concerned about George. He's lost a lot of blood."

Quinn swallowed. "I know you want to stay with

him, but Sarah needs you."

"Why?" Cassidy glanced from George to her brother. "Is it the baby?"

Quinn nodded. "The baby is coming and Sarah wants you."

"Surely you can—"

"I can, but she wants you, not me. You know how demanding our sister can be."

Cassidy bit her lip. "I can't leave him now. You'll have to explain to her."

"Look..." Quinn glanced at George. "You said you dug the bullet out. There's nothing more you can do for him right now. I'll stay with him until you come back."

A surge of panic set Cassidy's pulse racing. "Quinn, I don't think I can...not without you there."

"Cassie, you have to. Besides, it's the best way to get over what happened. And Sarah trusts you."

"But what if something goes wrong?" Her throat closed up at the thought of doing harm to her sister or her baby.

"You'll do fine, Cassie." Quinn settled in the chair she'd vacated. "I'll stay with George and if you need me, send Matt over."

"But what if—?"

"Go home, Sis." He glanced at George. "He won't even know you're gone."

Cassidy swallowed the hard lump in her throat. Circumstances were forcing her into a nightmare situation. She just hoped she wouldn't end up doing more harm than good.

Cassidy arrived home to find the household in turmoil. Matt attempted to calm Wesley, while Sarah's screams echoed from the spare bedroom on the first floor.

Wesley turned to Cassidy. "I'm so glad you're here..." Her brother-in-law's gaze slid to the blood staining her gown. "Oh, my. I heard about George, is he..."

"He's all right, for now. Quinn is staying with him. He insisted Sarah wanted me, not him."

Matt nodded. "She won't allow Quinn to touch her. She wants you."

Cassidy grimaced. "I promised her I'd deliver the baby when the time came." The fear surfaced again, causing her skin to chill. "I'm not sure I'm the right person for the job, though."

Wesley braced her shoulders from behind. "You'll do just fine, Cassie. Go in and see her. I'm sure your presence will calm her."

"All right."

Wesley guided her to the door. The screams had been replaced by the sound of moans and her mother's voice, low, trying to soothe.

Wesley opened the door, then retreated a step. "I'll be right outside if you need me."

Cassidy stepped into the room, and Wesley shut the door behind her.

Her mother glanced back, her frown melting to an expression of relief. "Cassie, I'm so glad you're here and all right. We heard what happened."

"I'm fine, Ma." She stepped close to the bed. Her mother mopped her sister's brow.

A grimace crossed Sarah's face. "I'm glad you're here, too. The baby is coming, and I hurt real bad."

She reached for her sister's hand. "We'll get you through this, won't we, Ma?"

Her mother smiled and nodded.

Cassidy kneeled beside the bed and placed her hands on Sarah's stomach. She felt the baby's head and heaved a relieved sigh. With the head in the down position, the birth should be free of complications. As least she hoped so.

Sarah's muscles tightened and she arched, a loud moan tearing from her throat. Cassidy reached for her hand, allowing her to squeeze. The pressure on her hand mounted, but she held firm until the contraction eased.

"Now, breathe deeply," Cassidy soothed. "I need to take a look under the sheet to see if you're ready to push this baby out."

Her sister frowned, but nodded. Her mother took her hand.

After a look, Cassidy decided it was time. She bit her lip, wishing for Quinn's appearance, but she couldn't wait. She had to do this alone.

"It's time to push. When the next contraction hits, take a deep breath and bear down as hard as you can."

Sarah's face paled. "I'll try."

Cassidy settled between her sister's legs as her mother stayed by Sarah's head, holding her hand, mopping her brow.

When the tightening in her sister's abdomen started, Cassidy said, "Now, Sarah. Push as hard as you can."

Her face contorted as she writhed and moaned.

"Again," Cassidy instructed.

After another push, she frowned, slight prickles sending icy cold fingers down her body. A fist clutched her heart. The baby's head wasn't coming out.

"Are you pushing hard?" she asked.

"I'm pushing as hard as I can," Sarah gasped.

Her mother glanced at Cassidy, a worried frown lining her face.

Another wave drew a scream from Sarah. Her mother jumped up to move to the end of the bed. "Cassie, what's wrong?"

She glanced at Sarah, then at her mother, warning her with her gaze not to say anything more. Fear chilled Cassidy to the bone.

A scream tore from her sister. Her body went rigid. Blood gushed from her womb and the baby, stained crimson, slipped out. Cassidy caught the small body in a towel.

Sarah's skin paled.

Her mother moved to help Cassidy with the baby but glanced back at her other daughter. "So much blood," she whispered.

Her breathing shallow, Cassidy willed herself to regain control. The nightmare she'd had for months seemed to be playing out in real life.

What do I do now? Panic threatened to overtake her. "I have to cut the cord," she told her mother.

She cut the cord then handed the child to her mother. "Clean him up."

Her mother glanced at the bundle she held. "Cassie, he's not breathing," she whispered.

Cassidy jumped up and took the baby, placing him on the table. She had to save the baby...and Sarah.

The world crashed down atop her shoulders. She wanted to scream and sob at the same time.

What am I going to do?

Chapter Thirty-Three

George woke from a fragmented dream about Cassidy. Her face so close to his, her sweet breath fanned his cheek. But before he could kiss her, Madison yanked her away. He stood over him laughing.

Jostling himself from the dream, George groaned. His side hurt. He lay in bed in his hotel room. Someone moved on the far side of the room by the curtained window.

"Cassie?"

A male voice answered. "It's Quinn." He stepped close to the bed, so George could make out his face. "She had to attend Sarah. The baby's coming sooner than we thought, and Sarah wanted Cassie at the birth."

"So, you're my doc now?"

Quinn grinned. "She did most of the work. Dug out the bullet and bandaged you up, so the bleeding would slow. I'm just here to make sure you don't try to get up too soon and don't develop an infection."

George grimaced. "I see." He wriggled on the bed, sending pain up his side. "It hurts when I move."

"So, don't move." Quinn pulled the chair closer to the bed. "I checked the wound. Doesn't look too bad. A few days of bed rest, keep the bandages clean, and you just might make it."

"That so." George studied Quinn's face. "Kind of reminds me of the war. At Gettysburg."

Quinn nodded. "When we lost Josh."

George sighed. "I'll never forget that day. You're

the one pulled me off him and got me off the battlefield. Reckon I should thank you."

"No need." Quinn grinned.

"Did Cassie go home by herself?"

"She wasn't about to leave you alone. And Sarah couldn't wait."

"I'm afraid Madison might still be around. What if he gets to her...?"

Quinn shook his head. "I'm sure she's all right. Madison likely skedaddled out of town. Everyone already knows what happened. He won't show his face here again."

George frowned, trying to ignore the nagging ache in his rib. If Quinn was right, he'd failed in his assignment. How could he gather evidence on a man who'd run? But his main worry was Cassidy. "I'd just like to see Cassie. To know she's safe."

"She is. I'm sure of it." Quinn patted George's shoulder.

"Do you have any idea how much I love and care for your sister? If I could've killed Madison today, I wouldn't have hesitated."

"I'm sure my whole family knows."

George shook his head. "Did you ever love a woman so much, the thought of losing her forever tore you up inside?"

"I haven't had much experience, but I have been spending a lot of time with Miss Baker..." His face flushed.

"You're sweet on her? Does she know?"

"She does by now. Especially after what Madison did. She thinks she's spoiled goods now. Told me I should find someone respectable."

"But?" George tried to hold back his grin.

"I told her there's no woman in town more respectable than her."

"Good for you, Quinn." George shifted in the bed, trying to get to a comfortable position. Pain shot up his side, forcing a grunt. "You're a good man."

Quinn shrugged. "I hope it's my charm that's convinced her and not just the fear she's spoiled for other men. Maybe you could school me with your expertise regarding women, George."

"After the way I failed miserably with your sister?"

Quinn shook his head. "You haven't failed as far as I can tell. She loves you and always has. I see a real future for the two of you."

"I surely hope you're right." George settled back against his pillow, hoping to God things would at last turn out in their favor.

****

Scott pulled his hat brim down, trying to escape notice as he scurried to the alley to retrieve his bag. He supposed his actions foolhardy, but if he had to start over, even if he had to leave his house and other possessions, he couldn't go without the bag. While on the run, he couldn't afford to replace the tools necessary to reestablish himself as a physician.

He'd hid out until dark, not daring to show his face in town in daylight. Once he got the bag, he'd have to hide in the woods until morning, then catch the first train out of town. His stomach tightened. Look what Miss Cassidy Stuart and that gambler, Masters, had reduced him to.

Was the man a gambler? Scott grimaced. His actions seemed more like those of a lawman, working covertly. If he were a detective, it would explain his sudden appearance and stay in town. He'd paid his respects to his father weeks ago, but Scott had supposed he'd stayed on to woo Miss Stuart. The possibility Masters stayed to investigate Scott hadn't occurred to him until now.

He sighed. He should have left when his relationship with Miss Stuart soured. He could have already been set up in a new town, pursuing another established physician's practice. Why had he stayed?

As he drew closer to the hotel, he averted his gaze each time he saw a townsperson. He couldn't afford to be recognized. His blood heated at the thought of Miss Stuart. If he got his hands on her now, he'd wrap them around her slender throat and choke the life out of her. He hoped Masters had passed on but didn't dare stay around long enough to find out.

****

Cassidy laid the child on a table top and massaged the tiny chest. "Breathe...breathe," she whispered.

Her mother looked on, her face lined, hands fisted against her mouth. "Oh, Cassie! Will he be all right?"

Cassidy's pulse thundered. "He'll make it." She glanced at her sister, lying too still in the bed. "See to Sarah."

She turned the baby over and allowed the fluids to drain from his lungs. Then she pressed her lips against his, forcing air into his lifeless body. "You can't die on me. You can't!"

She massaged his chest again, then lay her ear against it. A small movement up and down encouraged her. She blew into him again, her reward a gasp, followed by a small, whimpering cry.

Lifting the baby, she patted his rump. He drew in a breath and let out a lusty wail.

Her mother turned at the sound.

"I think he'll be all right." Cassidy handed the whimpering baby to her mother and moved to attend her sister.

The paleness of her face alarmed Cassidy. With the baby all right, she had to make sure Sarah pulled through.

Her mother strode forward, cradling the child.

"Sarah's lost a lot of blood." Cassidy stepped to

the foot of the bed and examined her sister. "Her bleeding seems to be slowing now, though. I think she'll be all right."

Her mother looked about ready to burst into tears, but nodded. "You've done a wonderful job, Cassie."

"We just have to keep her from moving and get fluids and food into her to replace the blood she lost. With round the clock care, she should be just fine."

"Can I tell Wes?" her mother asked. "I'm sure he's frantic with worry."

"Go ahead."

After her mother left, Cassidy sighed in relief. Fear drained off her like water. Her sister and baby would both be all right because of her. But there wasn't time to bask. She had to go to George.

When her mother returned, she instructed her how to care for Sarah and told her she'd send Quinn right over. "I'll be at the hotel."

Her mother frowned. "But it's late. You shouldn't be going out alone. Take Matt or Wes."

"Wes should be here with his wife and child. I'll ask Matt." Cassidy kissed her mother's cheek. "Everything will be fine now."

She raced out of the room. Wes stood in the hall, cradling and cooing at the baby.

"Cassie..." He swallowed. "Will Sarah be all right?"

She nodded. "Ma's in with her now, but you can go ahead and see her." She glanced around. "Where's Matt?"

"He ran out on a quick errand. Should be right back."

Cassidy sighed. She didn't want to wait. "I'm going to see George."

Before her brother-in-law could protest, she'd pinned on her hat and raced out the door. Raw fear for George's welfare erased any feeling of accomplishment at the delivery.

Please, let him be all right.

****

Scott sidled down the alley. Darkness blanketed the narrow space, broken up by dim gaslight seeping from the buildings. Struggling to see, he swore when his foot hit against a barrel.

Why can't these small towns have gas lit streets like they do in Philadelphia? Maybe he should go to Chicago or one of the other big cities and lose himself. Coming here had been nothing but a waste of time. He felt along the wall at the spot where he thought he'd left the bag but found nothing.

Did someone take it?

If so, he'd come back for nothing. By now, everyone knew he was involved with Masters' shooting. He'd taken a big risk.

The sounds of heels clicking on the planks in front of the hotel drew his attention. He ducked deeper into the alley, so the passerby wouldn't spot him.

At the swish of skirts, he adjusted his gaze, straining to see in the dim light. A woman rushed past the alley.

On a hunch, he emerged, strode up behind the lone female and grasped her wrist.

She gasped and turned. Even in this dim light, he recognized Miss Stuart. Her hat a bit eschew, she wore no wrap on this humid summer night.

Yanking her against his chest, he growled into her ear. "Where the devil is my bag?"

She sputtered. "Your bag?"

"My medical bag's not where I left it. Where is it?"

"I don't know anything about your bag." She struggled, but he held fast, his face heating.

"Then what are you doing here this time of night? Most men would take you to be a street walker."

"How dare you!" She yanked against his grip, glancing up and down the street.

"You're going to see Masters," he growled. "I'd hoped he was finished."

"If he dies, you'll be a murderer. And he's a Pinkerton agent. You'll have the entire force out looking for you now. Even if you didn't pull the trigger, you'll be responsible for his death."

"A Pinkerton agent?" Scott sputtered. "It's your fault all of this happened. I'll take care of you just like I did your father." He grasped her slender throat and squeezed.

Chapter Thirty-Four

George startled awake. He'd thought the voices below his window part of a dream. A male and female argued. He glanced across the room to the chair, making out the outline of Cassie's brother.

"Quinn," George rasped.

Quinn's shadowed form sat straight up. "George, what's wrong?"

"I hear voices outside. In the alley."

Quinn crept around the room. The gas lamp flickered to life.

George struggled to breathe as a sharp pain knifed into his rib.

"Don't move," Quinn ordered. "I'll see to it." He stepped away from the light toward the window and peered out. "Hard to see, but I think two people are struggling in the alley."

George's pulse raced. "Do you think Cassie would've come back?"

Quinn stepped back to the bed, so George could make out his expression in the dim light. His rusty brows rose. "I wouldn't think she'd come alone, but then again..." He bit his lip. "It *is* quite possible. I'd best take a look."

"Be careful," George warned.

After Quinn closed the door, George grasped his revolver from the bedside table and tucked the gun beneath him.

Heart thundering, his impulse was to leap from the bed and confront whatever awaited outside.

Damn it all! If anything happened to Cassidy, he'd never forgive himself.

****

Cassidy gagged as Dr. Madison's hands tightened around her throat. She fought to breathe. He'd said he'd taken care of her father. Had he killed him? Raising her foot, she kicked him as hard as she could in the shin.

"You bitch!" He released his grip, and she twisted free.

She turned, prepared to race from the alley, but another man appeared in the dim light.

Not knowing what to do, she stopped.

"Cassie?"

Recognizing her brother's voice, she raced into his arms.

"What happened, Sis? Who..."

Movement behind them caused Cassidy to turn her head. A blow sent her brother's body slumping against her. Dr. Madison stood in the shadows grasping a large wooden beam.

Cassidy gasped, teetering off balance as Quinn fell to the ground.

"You've got no one to save you now," Madison growled. Dropping the beam, he grasped her arm, twisting it behind her back as he smothered her screams with his hand.

****

Scott forced Miss Stuart down the alley toward the back entrance of the hotel. He'd make her take him right to Masters. Now he knew the man to be a Pinkerton agent, he'd have to make sure he didn't live to report Scott's involvement with the shooting. Otherwise, he'd end up on the run with nothing left to live for unless he took care of both of them. *Now.* Miss Stuart twisted, kicking at him, but he swiveled her body to and fro to keep her off balance. She opened her mouth and bit his hand.

"Damn it! I've got a derringer in my vest pocket. If you don't stay still, I'll be forced to use it on you."

She stilled and allowed him to lead her to the back door. "If you see anyone," he whispered in her ear, "you're to nod politely and not say a word." He twisted her arm for emphasis.

She nodded and he propelled her forward. As luck had it, no servants appeared at the back entrance. He forced Miss Stuart up the stairwell.

"Step lightly," he warned. "I don't want to alert anyone we're on these stairs." She trembled, her slight nod the only answer. He exulted in his feeling of power. Maybe once he finished off Masters, he'd spend a little time alone with Miss Stuart so she could atone for all her rebuffs.

She stopped in front of a door on the third floor.

"That it?" He nodded toward the door.

"Yes," she whispered.

"Open it," he ordered.

As she opened the door, he glanced up and down the corridor to be sure no one saw them enter.

He shoved her inside, then eased the door closed behind him, adjusting his gaze to the dim lantern lit beside the bed. A full-size body lay shrouded in a quilt.

"Go over there and lift the cover." He pointed to the bed. "No tricks, though." He waved his gun.

Miss Stuart eased toward the bed, glancing back once. She lifted the quilt, revealing Masters. His eyes were closed, his face relaxed.

"Please, Dr. Madison..." Miss Stuart turned toward him, her eyes wide. "You don't have to do this. Just leave town now. I won't tell anyone I saw you. You can get away before it's too late."

"Oh, my dear," Scott said. "It's already too late for me." He raised the derringer, pointing the barrel at Masters' face.

Chapter Thirty-Five

George kept his breathing even, peering beneath closed lids at Madison.

He'd heard them in the hall and covered himself, so the doctor would believe he slept. With his revolver still tucked beneath his body, he'd fire if he had to. But he didn't like Cassidy being too close. If only he could warn her to move away, but he didn't dare reveal he was awake.

The sky outside his window brightened. Morning had to be swiftly approaching. Folks would be up and about. He hoped that would work in their favor.

Madison raised his gun. George slid his revolver out. At the same moment, Cassidy stepped in front of him.

Damn, woman! He bit his tongue to stop himself from shouting at her to get out of the way.

"Don't do this," she pleaded.

Her skirts obscured George's view between his shuttered eyelids. A scuffling sound, followed by a grunt, and she'd fallen from his field of vision, revealing Madison. George aimed at the doctor's midsection and fired. The loud blast echoed in the small room.

Madison's gun slipped from his hand. His eyes grew wide. "You son-of-a-bitch!" he breathed, as he caught George's gaze. The doctor grasped his stomach and slid to the floor.

"George!" Cassidy struggled to rise. Her gaze shifted from George to the felled doctor.

"Get his gun," George said. "Bring it here."

269

She scrambled to her feet and lifted the gun, handing the weapon to George.

"Is he dead?" he asked.

She kneeled by the doctor's side and performed a cursory examination. "No, but he's not moving."

"Good. Get the sheriff."

She shook her head. "I won't leave you alone with him."

He caught her gaze. "I've got his gun. What's he gonna do to me?"

Leaning toward him, her soft lips found his mouth. After a brief kiss, he leaned back. "Now go!"

She nodded.

"And what the hell happened to that brother of yours anyway?"

"Oh...Quinn." She indicated the prone doctor. "Quinn tried to help me, and he hit him with a beam. He may have killed him." Her eyes widened as she met his gaze.

"Get the sheriff up here, then see to your brother."

She kissed him again, then left, shutting the door behind her.

George hoped she'd be able to get help in time, but if Madison revived and tried anything, he wouldn't be long for this world.

****

Cassidy raced through the hotel lobby, not caring what the patrons or workers thought. "A man upstairs needs help," she cried. "And another one in the alley. I'm going for the sheriff." She rushed out the door, not heeding the buzz of apprehension behind her. One of them would investigate and if not, she'd have the sheriff in tow when she returned.

Racing outside, she jerked to a stop to avoid running into a young woman carrying a parcel. "I'm so sorry." Glancing at the woman, she gasped.

"Miss Baker!"

270

"Doctor Stuart, whatever's wrong? You look as if the devil's on your tail."

Cassidy grasped the teacher's shoulders. "You've got to help me. My brother is in the alley beside the hotel. He's been beaten, and I'm afraid he may be seriously injured. I'm going for the sheriff right now. Can you see to Quinn until I get back?"

Miss Baker gasped, but nodded. "Of course."

Cassidy pointed toward the alley. "He's there. Should be just inside the alley. I'll be right back with help."

The teacher gathered her skirts and scurried toward the alley. Cassidy took a deep breath and raced to Sheriff Carson's office.

"Sheriff," she gasped as she burst inside.

A deputy strode forward to take her arm. "What's the problem, young lady?"

"A man tried to murder George Masters. He's a Pinkerton agent and staying at the hotel. He shot the man in self-defense and is now holding a gun on him in his room. Mr. Masters is recovering from a gunshot wound already and can't leave his bed. You've got to help him."

"Now, calm down a minute, Miss. The sheriff's in back." He steered her to a chair, then stuck his head in the back room. "Dan, we got a problem over at the hotel."

Sheriff Carson stepped into the room, his brow quirking when he noticed Cassidy.

She just then realized how disheveled she appeared. Her hat gone, hair falling from her bun, lying in a tangle on her shoulder and her skirt smeared with mud.

"What happened?" the sheriff asked.

Cassidy sighed in relief when the deputy explained for her. She didn't want to have to go into the long account again.

"The man who tried to kill Mr. Masters," she

added, "is Dr. Madison. Mr. Masters had been sent to town to investigate him. He also attacked me and my brother. Quinn's lying in the alley alongside the hotel. I don't even know if he survived the blow." She caught her breath and twisted her hands in her lap as the shock of what had occurred sank in.

"I'll check the hotel," the sheriff told his deputy. "You see to the man in the alley."

"I'm going with you." Cassidy jumped up.

Sheriff Carson shook his head. "You'll stay right here where you'll be safe."

"No, I will not." She stared the man down. "I'll take you to the room." She glanced at the startled deputy. "Please, see to my brother, sir. The schoolteacher, Miss Baker, should be with him."

Carson nodded and the three left the office.

****

George kept his gun trained on Madison, but the man hadn't moved since Cassidy left. Maybe he'd died after all. He sighed. He didn't wish to be associated with this mess. He'd have to answer a slew of questions when he returned to Pinkerton, but he'd fulfilled his main purpose to protect Cassidy. Knowing the bastard had put his hands on her enraged him. If Madison showed any indication he still lived, he might just be tempted to finish the job.

The door creaked inward, startling him. He took a breath and raised his gun, then lowered the barrel toward the floor when the schoolteacher entered, supporting Cassie's brother.

"He told me to bring him here," she explained. Her eyes widened when she spotted the body on the floor and the revolver in George's hand.

"Don't worry." He pointed to Madison. "I'm a Pinkerton agent. He's the one who hurt Quinn and tried to kill me. Cassidy's gone for the sheriff."

Quinn groaned.

272

"Put him in the chair," George told her.

After settling Quinn's lanky frame in the chair, she edged away, her back to the door.

"Close the door," George ordered. "I don't want anyone taking us unawares. I hope to hell the next one coming through will be Cassie and the sheriff, but we have to be prepared for the worst."

She nodded, eased the door closed, then leaned against it. After studying the prone doctor, she inclined her head. "He shot you, Mr. Masters...?"

"Feel free to call me George." He glanced at Cassidy's brother. "Is he all right?"

"He was hit pretty hard. I found him lying in the alley where Miss Stuart told me to look. I had a hard time getting him revived and up here. He has a fair sized gash on the back of his head."

Quinn groaned again and slumped forward, cupping his face in both hands. The teacher moved to his side, then eyeing a towel on the nightstand, dipped an edge of the cloth in the wash basin filled with water, and pressed the rag to the back of Quinn's head.

"Quinn?" George winced as he rolled to his side, trying to get a better look at him. "You still with us?"

"I've felt better." He peered at Madison. "The son-of-a-bitch popped me with something big. Knocked me flat out."

"As you can see, I've dealt with him. Cassie and the sheriff should be here any minute and hopefully, all this will be taken out of our hands."

"Is Cassie all right?

"Your sister is the bravest woman I've ever met." George grinned. "She actually tried to shield me from his gun, but when he yanked her out of the way, I got a clear shot before he got me. Then I sent her for the sheriff."

Quinn sighed. "I'm glad he didn't do her any serious harm." He caught George's gaze. "And did I hear you say you're a Pinkerton agent?"

George grinned. "I had to keep my identity hushed up. Didn't want to alert Madison. I did tell Cassie, but only after she suspected I'd been unfaithful to her."

"I'd say it's a very good thing you came back to town when you did."

The door flew open, causing his pulse to race, but the sight of the sheriff followed by Cassidy brought a sigh of relief.

Sheriff Carson kneeled by Madison's body. "He's still breathing, I see." He glanced up. "I sent my deputy to look on Miss Stuart's brother, but I see he's already here."

"Thanks to Miss Baker." Quinn grinned. "She helped revive me and get me up here."

Carson pointed to Madison. "I'll need a doc to examine him so I know how bad off he is."

Cassidy gathered her skirts and strode forward. "I'll take a look at him."

George settled back on the bed, relieved the ordeal was over. After Cassidy declared Madison not mortally injured, although he'd require care in a hospital, the sheriff sent Miss Baker to find the deputy and ask him to bring a stretcher.

"Sheriff..." Cassidy pointed to the prone body. "He told me he'd take care of me like he took care of my father." Her hand rose to her throat. "Could he have killed him?"

The sheriff frowned. "Your pa died in a carriage accident?"

She nodded.

"I'll question the doc here when he revives. Maybe your pa's death wasn't an accident after all." The sheriff's gaze shifted to George. "And once you're feeling up to it, Mr. Masters, could you and Miss Stuart stop by my office?"

Once Madison was removed and the sheriff left,

Cassidy embraced George gently. "I was so scared he'd kill you." She buried her face in his shirt.

Quinn's brows raised at learning Madison had somehow been responsible for their father's death. "I hope the bastard spends the rest of his life in jail." He glanced at Cassidy. "What about Sarah?"

"Oh...right! None of you know."

George and the others gazed at her.

"Sarah had a boy. Both mother and baby are in Ma's care right now. And I told her I'd send Quinn right over."

"What wonderful news!" Miss Baker hovered by Quinn's side.

"Reckon I'd best get over there, then," Quinn said.

"Get on home, Quinn," Cassidy said, "I'll come back later and take a look at your head."

"I may need a bit of help," her brother said.

"I'll be more than happy to see him home," Miss Baker said. "If it's all right?"

"I think that would be just fine." George caught Cassidy's gaze. "I need a few minutes to settle some things with Cassie before she goes."

Quinn studied both of them, but nodded. "We'll get out of here. I'd like to take a look at the new member of the family anyway."

Miss Baker helped him out of the chair and supported him until they reached the door. Once they'd gone, George turned to Cassidy. "'Bout time I finally had a few minutes alone with my future wife."

Chapter Thirty-Six

On the second of June, a week after Madison was shot, George shrugged into his best coat and hat and descended the stairs of the hotel on his way to the Stuart home. Under Cassidy and Quinn's care, his gunshot wound and rib had healed. He still had some pain when he moved, but day by day he noticed an easement and hoped to be back to his former self soon. He'd been lucky.

Madison was recovering from his wound as well, so now stayed in the jail. Although the sheriff remained on the lookout for Nate Bartholomew, he didn't have much hope of catching the man. George didn't think they ever would, but he doubted the scum would show his face in this town again. Madison had admitted under questioning he'd been responsible for Dr. Stuart's carriage going off the road that fateful night. So, even if his indiscretion against Miss Wellingham couldn't be proven, he'd be held in custody for the doctor's murder as well as his assault on George and the Stuarts.

At a flower stand outside the hotel, George purchased an assortment of mixed blooms to present to Cassidy. Although he'd informally proposed, he intended to do so again today in formal fashion. He'd not allow the lady to slip his grasp again.

Ascending the steps to the porch, he glanced at the house. As a boy, he'd dreamed of living in a place like this. He'd spent as much time here with Josh as he could. Going home to the shack he shared with his father shamed and depressed him, but he also had real fear of what his old man might do if he displeased him.

Sarah greeted him at the door. She wore a wrapper, her hair hidden beneath a cloth cap. "Come right in, George." She motioned him to beyond the foyer. "Cassie's waiting for you in the parlor."

He removed his hat and swallowed hard. He'd rehearsed what he planned to say to her, but all of the flowery words fled his mind. She wouldn't turn him down after all they'd been through, but nagging doubt held him back.

Sarah turned, frowning. "Well, c'mon George. What are you waiting for?"

He smiled and moved past Sarah to the entrance of the parlor. The door stood ajar. Glancing inside, he caught sight of Cassidy. An open book lay on her lap; a frown marred her beautiful features. When he stepped inside, she glanced up.

"I hope I'm not disturbing you, Cassie."

"Oh, no." She closed the book, placing it on the side table. A medical text, he noted.

"You still have all summer before you go off to Philadelphia."

She beamed, patting the chair beside her. "Sit down. I want to talk to you before dinner's ready."

"All right." He settled in the chair and handed her the bouquet. She cradled the flowers, smiling. Her dark hair and bewitching green eyes sent his pulse racing. He longed to take her in his arms, kiss her thoroughly, then propose, but fear of rejection paralyzed him.

"George..." Cassidy frowned. "What is it?"

"I—I don't quite know how to put this."

She leaned over and patted his arm, placing the flowers on the table. "Is something wrong? Tell me what's on your mind."

"Cassie..." He cleared his throat. "Damn, this is just as hard as the first time." He stared at his hands in his lap.

She stroked the back of his hand, sending delicious tingles coursing through his body. He sought her gaze.

"I know you're going off to Philadelphia in a few months, and I have no quarrel with that. In fact, I'm mighty proud of you for being accepted as a medical student."

Her face flushed. "I'm so glad."

"But the thing is, I would like you to consider marrying me."

Her gaze dropped and his heart sank. He'd hoped when she'd learned he worked as a Pinkerton detective, instead of earning his keep as a professional gambler, she'd be eager to accept his proposal, but as a lawman he'd offer her a life of uncertainty. What had he been thinking?

"I'm sorry, Cassie. I'll be taking my leave now." He rose and turned to go.

"George." She stood and stepped to block his way. "Where are you going?"

"I love you, Cassie, but I've never been good enough for you, and now I've chosen a profession that'll put us both in danger. I can't ask you to do that. You go off to the city and find a man who'll do you proud."

She reached for both his hands. "You do me proud, George Masters. And I will *not* allow you to take your marriage proposal back again."

"Are you saying...?" Hope rose as he studied her face.

"I'm going to marry you, mister, whether you like it or not." She dropped his hands and fisted hers on her hips.

"Well..." His arms circled her waist. "I'll just have to hold you to it." He lowered his mouth to hers and tasted heaven. She laid her head against his chest, her warmth and sweetness threatening to send him beyond propriety.

He eased her away. "I think that will have to be enough for now. We have to be presentable to go in to dinner."

She smiled and cupped his face in her hands for a chaste kiss. "This will hold you until later, I reckon."

"Indeed it will."

****

Friday evening, Cassidy announced their engagement at dinner. Her family was thrilled with the news. She still planned to attend school in the fall but didn't want to wait until she completed her studies to marry George. She'd waited much too long already.

He took his leave only to return later in the evening with another announcement. Drawing him into the parlor, Cassidy motioned him to sit.

"What is it?" She studied his face, searching for clues. "Don't dare keep me in suspense."

"I've obtained a position as a deputy here in town. Two businessmen are planning an expansion, including shops, banks and a hospital right here in Burkeville, hoping to draw newcomers. The sheriff wants to be prepared for more people and bring in trained help now. After you finish school, we'll settle here in town."

She looked away, biting her lip.

"If that's what you want." He reached for her hand. "I should have asked you first, if you wanted to live here."

Cassidy turned to him and kissed his hand. "You've just made me a very happy woman, George Masters. Although it will be fun staying in a big city for a while, my heart is here...in this town and with you."

He grinned. "Then I reckon we should start planning a wedding."

****

Eight days later, Cassidy fidgeted in her room trying to adjust her wedding veil. Sarah and her mother had helped her pick the material and construct the gown. Sewing wasn't Cassidy's forte, except when she used her skill to stitch up a patient.

George settled in as a deputy and looked to purchase a home here in town. He promised to keep the house up with the help of her mother, while she was away.

After the wedding, Sarah, Wesley, and their new baby would be heading home to York. And Quinn would keep up the practice, once Cassidy went off to medical school. After all, he'd be the only doctor in town and now courted Miss Baker. Cassidy hoped another wedding would be announced soon.

"Cassie, aren't you ready yet?" Sarah hissed. "You're keeping the men waiting."

After one last glance in the full-length mirror, she nodded. "I'm as ready as I'll ever be."

Her stomach fluttered as she followed her mother and Sarah down the staircase and into the parlor where the men of the family, along with the minister, gathered.

Quinn stepped to the open doorway and took her arm to lead her to her future husband. George's dark eyes widened as he eyed her new gown.

"You look beautiful," he whispered. Her brother placed her hand in his.

As the minister read the marriage ceremony and she and George recited their vows, Cassidy couldn't help but wonder what would have happened if George hadn't stepped back into her life.

At the close of the ceremony, family and friends surrounded the couple. With the man of her dreams at her side, nothing or no one could ruin her elation.

"I now pronounce you man and wife," the minister intoned. He smiled and nodded at George. "You may now kiss your bride."

She turned to her husband. He cradled her face in his hands and kissed her. Her thoughts scattered, and she realized after so long, they at last were married.

At the reception afterward, she sat with her sister, mother and friends, watching the men as they congregated.

Cassidy couldn't take her gaze off her new husband. Her thoughts drifted back to when they were children and he'd teased her. She never would've thought that boy and the roguish young man he'd grown into would turn out to be the perfect man for her.

Sarah gazed at Wesley and beamed. "How handsome they all are!"

Her mother sighed. "That they are."

Cassidy smiled as she noted her mother's gaze set on her two sons, dressed in their best suits.

"I'd best go check on Johnny," Sarah said.

"I'll get him," her mother volunteered. With a swish of her skirts, she left the room.

Sarah turned to Cassidy. "I'm so glad you've finally found happiness. You deserve this, after all you've been through."

"Thank you, Sarah." She leaned forward to kiss her sister's cheek. "But of all the men..." Her face heated as she gazed at George.

Sarah smirked. "You two were meant for each other, I reckon. And I'm sure your future life will be very exciting."

Cassidy shook her head. "I've had enough excitement to last a lifetime. All I want now is a family and a small practice where I can use my skills to ease suffering. And hopefully, gain respect for my profession."

"You will, Cassie." Sarah glanced up as her mother eased into the room, little Johnny snuggled in her arms.

"I think he wants his mother." Ma settled the baby in Sarah's lap.

She laughed. "I think it's time for this little man to be fed." She stood. "If you'll excuse me."

"Bring him back when you're both through," Cassidy said. "I haven't seen enough of him with all the distractions."

Nodding, Sarah left the room.

Later, George and Cassidy left by carriage to spend the night in his hotel room. He promised the house he'd purchased would be ready for them the next day.

He undressed her with reverence, then laid her on the bed. She ached to undress him too, but he wouldn't allow her.

"I want to gaze at your beautiful body while I undress. Then you'll have your chance at me." He grinned.

He slipped out of his clothing. When finished, he lay beside her and stroked her cheek.

"Do you remember the first time we spent in this bed?"

She nodded. He moved closer, pressing the length of his heated body against her. His lips covered hers, and she drifted to heaven. Then his mouth roved down her throat to her breasts. Heat shot to her core as his tongue laved her nipples.

Now she knew what to expect, she had no fear or trepidation. She wanted this more than anything in her entire life.

As he eased himself into her, a thrill like no other threatened to shatter her. Will it always be this wonderful? Each time proved more exciting than before.

Once she lay nestled in her husband's arms, she knew the war that had brought them together and torn them apart was over. But the war to be a respected female physician was just beginning.

A word about the author...

Susan Macatee sets her stories of romance during and just after the American Civil War. Her passion for this period in American history also extends to the paranormal. You'll find time travelers, ghosts, and vampires in the mix.

Her interest in the period stems from her years spent as a civilian Civil War reenactor, alongside her husband, who did the military side, with the 28th Pennsylvania Volunteer Regiment for about ten years.

Her other love is science fiction, which she reads voraciously and hopes to incorporate into future romance plots.

She lives with her husband and sons, and the family dog, a boxer mix named Chase. She spends her free time cheering on her local baseball team, the Philadelphia Phillies, spending time with Chase and her husband, watching favorite old movies, and inhaling books.

Thank you for purchasing
this Wild Rose Press publication.
For other wonderful stories of romance,
please visit our on-line bookstore at
www.thewildrosepress.com.

For questions or more information
contact us at
info@thewildrosepress.com.

The Wild Rose Press
www.TheWildRosePress.com

To visit with authors of The Wild Rose Press
join our yahoo loop at
http://groups.yahoo.com/group/thewildrosepress/